BRANCHING OUT

Also by Kerstin March

FAMILY TREES

Published by Kensington Publishing Corp.

BRANCHING OUT

KERSTIN MARCH

KENSINGTON BOOKS
www.kensingtonbooks.com

KENSINGTON BOOKS are published by

Kensington Publishing Corp.
119 West 40th Street
New York, NY 10018

All Kensington titles, imprints, and distributed lines are available at special quantity discounts for bulk purchases for sales promotion, premiums, fundraising, educational, or institutional use.

Special book excerpts or customized printings can also be created to fit specific needs. For details, write or phone the office of the Kensington Sales Manager: Kensington Publishing Corp., 119 West 40th Street, New York, NY 10018. Attn. Sales Department. Phone: 1-800-221-2647.

Kensington and the K logo Reg. U.S. Pat. & TM Off.

eISBN-13: 978-1-61773-527-1
eISBN-10: 1-61773-527-2
First Kensington Electronic Edition: December 2015

ISBN-13: 978-1-61773-526-4
ISBN-10: 1-61773-526-4
First Kensington Trade Paperback Printing: December 2015

10 9 8 7 6 5 4 3 2 1

Printed in the United States of America

In loving memory of Lily

I have to be gone for a season or so.
My business awhile is with different trees,
Less carefully nourished, less fruitful than these,
And such as is done to their wood with an axe—
Maples and birches and tamaracks.
I wish I could promise to lie in the night
And think of an orchard's arboreal plight
When slowly (and nobody comes with a light)
Its heart sinks lower under the sod.
But something has to be left to God.

—"Good-bye and Keep Cold," Robert Frost

CHAPTER 1

DARK CORNERS

Shelby Meyers's ivory dress brushed along the barn floor and collected a powdering of dust along its delicate hem. She leaned against the wide, open doorway and peered out upon her grandparents' orchard. An intimate gathering of friends and family were finding their seats amidst the rows of white garden chairs on the lawn that faced an arbor and acres of blooming apple trees. Blush-white petals fell like snowflakes in the breeze and scattered on the grass and softened the palpable tension that existed between the two families.

Shelby felt the gentle touch of her grandmother's hand upon her shoulder, nudging her away from the doorway. "Come on now. Haven't I told you it's bad luck to see the groom before your wedding?"

"You know that's just an old superstition, don't you?" Shelby said. Nonetheless, she stepped back and absentmindedly began rubbing the thumb of her right hand over the delicate band of her engagement ring, which held a brilliant round center stone that was surrounded by a halo of smaller diamonds.

"The wedding hasn't even started and already this day is more beautiful than anything I could have imagined," Ginny Meyers said. "I'm so happy for you, sweetheart. Don't forget to slow down, breathe. Take it all in. This will be a moment to remember for the rest of your life."

Shelby smiled at her grandmother, proud to have such a strong, lovely woman at her side. Thanks to the generosity of her fiancé, Ryan Chambers, her grandmother was wearing pearls and a Parisian dress made of silver-gray raw silk that had been perfectly tailored to fit her petite frame. But then, Shelby had always considered her an elegant lady, even with pastry flour on her cheek and striped socks peeking out from beneath the cuffs of her jeans.

"I just can't get over it. This old barn cleans up pretty well," Ginny said. "Everything looks incredible. Lord knows that Charlotte went over the top, but I'll be the first to admit that you and Ryan deserve it all, sweetheart."

"Thanks, Gran. I can't believe today's the day." she said, overjoyed to be marrying Ryan in the place she loved most.

Her family's orchard, which sat atop the bluffs of Bayfield, Wisconsin, had been transformed into something magical. Ryan's mother, Charlotte, had orchestrated most of the wedding planning from her high-rise apartment in Chicago. While some brides may have felt that Charlotte was overstepping her bounds, Shelby was relieved to surrender the details to her. Since moving to Chicago the previous summer, she had been immersed in setting up her first apartment, returning to college to complete her degree, acclimating to Ryan's public lifestyle, and then graduating one week before the wedding. The last thing she wanted to take on was planning an elaborate wedding. In fact, Shelby would have been happy with a church basement wedding and a backyard barbeque. So when Charlotte offered to help, Shelby readily agreed and had very few requests—mainly, that they marry at Meyers Orchard.

Charlotte's creation was magical. She had planned a dazzling reception that was the perfect blend of uptown elegance and hometown charm. The barn, a weathered building that had neither the stature nor the sophistication to host an elegant reception, was now "dressed" for the occasion. Its faded exterior had been sanded and freshly painted red, the farming equipment and empty apple crates had been neatly stowed away, and the cobwebbed corners and dusty surfaces had been swept away. With the transformation complete, the barn looked dazzling with suspended chandeliers, strands of white lights, and oversized jars of flowers placed on tables dressed in linens.

"I didn't see Ryan outside. Have you seen him?" Shelby asked her grandmother.

"Of course."

"How is he? Does he seem nervous?"

"Not in the least. I'd say the only thing that man cares about right now is hearing you say, 'I do.'"

In addition to orchestrating the reception, Ryan and his family had been careful to keep this day from becoming a media spectacle. For now, it appeared they had been successful. Shelby offered a silent prayer that everything would go as planned.

Ginny adjusted a delicate spray of blossoms that were tucked into the tumble of loose braids and curls swept back at the nape of Shelby's neck. "As I was saying, I've never seen a more handsome groom."

Her grandmother appeared so calm. It was as if she knew something that Shelby didn't. Shelby had always believed that her grandparents were her greatest joy—her solid foundation—and after her grandfather passed away, Shelby didn't know how their family would move forward. But they had. The farm was doing well. Her mother, Jackie, although still outrageously inappropriate and slow to accomplish anything resembling *real* work, was at least trying to make up for lost time. And Shelby had found the strength to leave the security of her hometown for a chance at love.

On her wedding day, Shelby realized that her greatest gift wasn't family. It was having the courage to walk away from what was safe in order for her heart to grow. Loving Ryan, and accepting his proposal to share a life, freed her from her inner worries and opened up a new world. With newfound confidence, Shelby felt the strength to overcome the insecurities and fears that had been holding her back.

Although Shelby wasn't one to seek the center of attention, this time she welcomed the opportunity to express her love for this man to all those who were gathered on the lawn. She knew she wouldn't falter.

"Are you ready?" Ginny asked.

"You know me," Shelby said, looking up at the array of lights that draped down from the rafters. "This is all so beautiful, but I would have been just as happy to marry Ryan out here in the barn, without all of the fanfare. Something simple, with just you and his parents."

"And Jackie . . . of course you'd include Jackie."

Shelby's twisted smile said it all. After years of being a negligent parent, Jackie had been making an effort to repair their relationship since Olen's death. She had also proven to be somewhat helpful to Ginny since moving back to the farm, which Shelby appreciated.

"Speaking of—shouldn't she be here by now?" Shelby asked. The sound of low chatter on the lawn was replaced by the serene music of a string quartet. The wedding would start shortly, and she hadn't seen her mother since the women were getting dressed inside the house. In fact, she hadn't seen her maid of honor, either. "I've lost track of Nic, too."

"I'm sure they'll come along soon. . . ." Ginny pressed her eyebrows together with concern as she looked over Shelby's shoulder.

Just as Shelby was about to suggest they send someone to check the house, she heard sounds coming from the far end of the barn.

Shelby looked up to see Nic, with her usually rumpled pixie-cut platinum hair combed sleek and adorned with a sprig of flowers tucked behind one ear. She held the skirt of her bridesmaid dress in her hands and raised the hem above her shoes as she rushed into the barn. The high-heeled sandals, which Nic despised but wore out of loyalty, were an obvious encumbrance as she ran awkwardly toward the two women. Shelby would have laughed at the sight of her best friend dressed like a lady and running in a lopsided trot if it weren't for the distinct look of concern on her face.

"Just in time!" Shelby called out.

Shelby had missed Nic while living in Chicago. After growing up together and sharing everything, they both eventually decided to move away. First, Shelby left Bayfield to join Ryan in Chicago. Not long afterward, Nicole "Nic" Simone had married Hank Palmer and celebrated in a church basement potluck reception before moving to the Twin Cities. Although the two did their best to stay in touch, Shelby still wondered if she'd ever know Mrs. Palmer as well as she'd known the feisty Miss Simone.

"Is she here?" Nic asked Ginny.

Ginny shook her head.

"Everything's good," Nic forced a smile for Shelby's benefit and then hurried across to the opposite side of the barn, calling over her shoulder, "Don't start the wedding without me—this will just take a minute!"

"What's going on?" Shelby asked.

"Everything is fine," Ginny said, patting Shelby's back. "It's all under control."

"The look on your face says otherwise. Come on, what is it?" Shelby insisted.

Ginny hesitated with a heavy sigh, then answered outright, "Jackie's missing."

"What do you mean, *missing?* She was in the house less than an hour ago."

"We seemed to have lost track of her. Nic's probably heading back to the house; I think Hank is checking outside."

"Why am I not surprised?"

Ginny kept her voice calm and reassuring. "Don't give it another thought. She's bound to turn up sooner or later—you and I both know she's not about to miss out on her opportunity to put on a show."

Shelby's mother had been a college student living in California and pursuing a so-called better life than what she imagined on the family's small-town farm on Lake Superior's South Shore. Jackie didn't have the time or interest in raising a child who was the result of one reckless summer night.

"Look at the two of us. These dresses really were much too expensive; Ryan shouldn't have," Ginny said, admiring the intricately beaded bodice of Shelby's gown and smoothing out the ethereal layers of its skirt. They both knew the dress didn't need adjusting. Ginny was killing time. "But I don't think I've ever seen a lovelier bride."

As Shelby looked into her grandmother's eyes, the things Shelby had intended to say to her on this wedding day, the words that had been running through her head when she tried to sleep over the past several days, the expressions that never seemed equal to the gratefulness she felt in her heart—the words, all disappeared. Ginny gently ran her thumb across Shelby's clasped hand, a gesture that always soothed her worries while growing up, causing her emotions to build. All of the words . . . the thoughts, memories, and gratitude tumbled out in a few simple words.

"I love you, Gran."

Ginny grasped Shelby's hands tighter and raised them to her lips, kissing them and holding them close to her, as if they were joined together in prayer. "I love you, too, and I've never been prouder of you than I am today."

Shelby let go of her grandmother's hands and pulled her small but strong frame into a hug. "Thanks for walking down the aisle with me. There's no one else I'd rather have by my side."

"I wouldn't have missed it for the world," Ginny said with a catch in her voice. "Your grandfather would have loved to see this day."

"I miss him."

"Me too, honey." Ginny raised her fingers to the corners of her eyes to snub out any tears. "Me too." After a moment, she took a deep breath and stepped out of their embrace, stood tall, and gave a quick pat to her cheeks. "Now, after you get married, don't forget what I told you—whenever you miss him. . . ."

"Look for the signs." Shelby nodded. She had noticed them many times since his death—discovering fishing bobbers in places where she'd never expect them, and a lone seagull that occasionally landed atop the barn's roof and slowly walked around the copper weathervane while calling out to her below.

"Come on, now, if we start crying you're going to make me smudge all of this makeup. And considering I only put on lipstick for weddings and funerals, I'd like to keep it on for more than an hour. Now, speaking of your grandfather, I have something for you." Ginny discretely reached down the front of her dress and pulled a white tissue from the confines of her brassiere.

Shelby threw up her hands. "Thanks, but I don't need *that*."

"Don't be ridiculous." Ginny carefully unwrapped the tissue and withdrew a turquoise pendant that dangled from the end of a delicate silver chain.

Something blue. It had been a gift from Shelby's grandfather, given to her when she was young. Even though he was no longer with them, in some small way he would still be a part of her wedding. It was the very thing she needed to put one foot in front of the next and walk into the next phase of her life. It was her time. She was branching out.

"You've worn this necklace every day for more years than I can count," Ginny said. Shelby lifted her hair off of her shoulders as Ginny clasped the necklace around her neck. "So I thought it best that you wear it on your wedding day as well." Her grandmother then wrapped her arms around Shelby and, just as she was about to kiss her on her cheek, Ginny flinched.

"For the love of Pete," Ginny uttered under her breath.

Seeing Ginny's eyes narrow and her lips press firmly together, Shelby pulled back. "What is it?" she asked, turning to look at whatever had grabbed her grandmother's attention.

The mother of the bride was walking out of a horse stall in the darkened back corner of the barn, adjusting the skirt of her smoky lavender dress with one hand and smoothing out her disheveled hairdo with the other.

"Stay here, Shel," Ginny said through clenched teeth. "I'm going to have a little chat with your mother, to let her know that the service is about to begin."

Not one to be deterred, Shelby lifted the hem of her dress above her shoes and followed her grandmother's lead. "I'm right behind you!"

Once they reached Jackie, Ginny took a firm hold of her elbow. As if an afterthought, she looked around to make sure they were alone, and then returned her attention to her daughter.

"What on earth is going on here?" Ginny said between clenched teeth. "Where have you been?"

Jackie jerked her arm out of Ginny's grasp. "I'm not sure I know what you mean, Mother."

"Have you seen yourself? Your skin is blotchy, your hair is a mess, and . . ." Ginny leaned in for a better inspection. "Would you mind telling me how you managed to get lipstick on your *ear?*" She licked her thumb and reached up to clean the lipstick smudge as if she were removing smeared chocolate from a child's face. Jackie brushed away Ginny's hand and rubbed the makeup off herself.

"Where is he?" Shelby asked the obvious. She was a fool to think that today, for once in Shelby's life, Jackie would behave like a mother. Although Jackie didn't have the time or interest in raising Shelby, Ginny and Olen assumed parental roles without hesitation and with full hearts.

"The music's playing out on the lawn—isn't that our cue?" Jackie said, bypassing Ginny and Shelby as she took steps toward the open barn doors. But she wasn't fast enough. Shelby heard a something move within the horse stall. Like a rat venturing out of its hole in the wall, a strange man emerged from the stall. Shelby didn't recognize him, and judging from the look on Ginny's face, she hadn't, either. He had a ruddy complexion, a short crop of hair around a bald crown, and a spotty beard that covered the soft contour of his jawline. He was dressed in a summer suit and a spring green tie, which would have been fitting for the wedding if it weren't for the inch of shirt material that stuck out of his half-zipped trousers like a chick peeking out of its nest.

"You're incredible," Shelby said, shaking her head at her mother, who had stopped and turned when she heard the

man's footsteps. Shelby couldn't decide who had more audac-
ity, the stranger who walked straight up to them with a smile
and an outstretched hand or Jackie for bringing him in the first
place.

Before anyone said a word, Nic raced in through the open
doors and didn't stop until she reached the group.

"So," Nic said, catching her breath. "I see you found your
mom."

"Hello, Mrs. Meyers, good to see you again," the man said
to Ginny, who refused to shake his extended hand and instead
stared at him with skepticism.

"Again?" Ginny asked.

"Again?!" Nic echoed.

Shelby gave her friend a subtle nudge and Nic dropped her
hands from Shelby's and Ginny's shoulders.

"Mother, you remember Chad . . ." Jackie said.

"Covington," he said, finishing her introduction. "Chad
Covington. We met years ago. I went to Ashland High
School?"

"He was a year ahead of me," Jackie added.

"I don't remember," Ginny replied flatly.

"Actually, we used to call him Stubbie," Jackie said. "Don't
you remember? He played football for Ashland and he and his
friends used to hang out with my group once in a while?"

Ginny shook her head while Shelby looked on.

"Chad's the one who helped Dad fix the flat on his truck
that one summer, down at the marina, the year he had a broken arm," Jackie continued. "I'm sure you remember that."

Chad turned his ruddy face toward Shelby, bared his
smoke-stained teeth in a debonair smile, and said simply,
"Good to finally meet you, Shelby. I'm your father."

"Holy crap . . ." Nic's typically booming voice, coming
from just behind Shelby's ear, was barely a whisper.

"Jacqueline!" Ginny gasped, raising her hand to cover her mouth.

Shelby's heart pounded against the confining bodice of her wedding dress. It wasn't just the way her mother was going to humiliate her, again, and on her wedding day. It was knowing that, with Jackie as an inept role model—Shelby felt the guilt of not being honest with Ryan during their discussions about their future. About starting a family. Nothing her mother could do to harm her would ever create as much pain for Shelby as the fear that, one day, she might bring similar emotional pain to her own child. While Ryan became elated at the thought of raising a family with Shelby, she was reserved and apprehensive.

I should have been honest with him. My God, why wasn't I honest with him? Shelby closed her eyes, breathed deeply, and listened for sounds that could calm her mind. The creak of the barn door as it gently swung inward when caught by a light breeze. The flutter of wings in a nest tucked in the rafters overhead. *Maybe I'll feel differently once we're married. Maybe I will be a good mother. I won't be like her. I'm different.*

Shelby opened her eyes and looked squarely into the cool blue eyes of her mother's conquest and said, "Mr. Covington, if you're my mother's guest, you are welcome to stay. But as for this absurd—and, let's be honest, incredibly insensitive—suggestion that we are somehow related I will have you know that the only father figure in my life was my grandparent and no one will ever replace him, let alone some man who thinks it appropriate to have sex with my mother in some dark corner of this barn just moments before I walk down the aisle."

"Shelby!" Jackie burst out, setting her hand firmly on Chad's coat sleeve and turning to speak to him. "Chad, I'm so sorry, I don't know what's gotten into . . ."

"And as for you, Mother," Shelby said, turning her attention to Jackie, "please find a mirror, put yourself together, and take a seat in the yard. Gran and I are about to walk down the aisle, with or without you. Don't bother with the processional."

With that, she turned and walked away with her grandmother at her side, clutching her chest and shaking her head in exasperation, and Nic trailing behind awkwardly in her uncomfortable shoes.

The only sound in the barn was that of the women's footsteps, the distant lure of violins playing on the lawn, and the faint *swish* of Shelby's dress as she walked purposefully toward the open doorway.

CHAPTER 2

UNSPOKEN WORDS

The sun was low in the sky when William Ryan Chambers Jr. took his place at the altar, beneath an arbor of flowering branches and twisted vines. The early-evening light cast a golden glow upon the grounds and the white blooms that flocked the apple trees. A sparkle of light glinted from the top of the barn and caught Ryan's eye. He looked up to the cupola to see the copper weather vane that he had admired the first time he visited the Meyerses' property. Shaped in the image of a horse galloping into the wind, it caught the day's final rays of light on its ribboned tail.

Ryan set his hand upon his breast pocket. Feeling the shape of his bride's wedding ring through his tailored summer suit, he thought back to the proposal. He didn't plan anything elaborate. It wasn't her style. It was to be a quiet day away from the city crowds, out on the water where he knew she would feel at peace. Lake Michigan wasn't Superior, but it was the next best thing.

On a hazy morning in late August, they set out from the

Chicago Yacht Club on Ryan's sailboat, the *Horizon,* for a weekend trip along Michigan's northwest shore.

The first time Shelby sailed with him on the *Horizon,* she had immediately recognized the Darfur as the same model he had chartered out of Bayfield when the two of them sailed to Devil's Island on Lake Superior. So much had happened between them since that October weekend when he returned to Bayfield and their lives connected. He had checked the forecast before they left port, pleased that the weather was ideal for an easy sail across the bay and up along the Michigan shoreline. After anchoring in Sutton's Bay inlet harbor, he would propose over dinner on the boat and a bottle of wine.

But that didn't happen.

They weren't more than ninety minutes outside of the harbor when the wind disappeared and the *Horizon* went from a steady clip down to a lazy drift. The needle on the speed gauge barely moved. Ryan frantically worked to tighten the jib, reset the mainsail, change tack, trying anything he could to catch the wind. But it was useless. The boat would sit still in the water until the wind picked up again.

He had been so focused on reaching their destination that he had failed to notice how happy Shelby was, reclining on the cushioned bench in the cockpit with her legs sprawled out before her and her head tipped back to catch the sun.

"Isn't it perfect?" She sighed.

No! It's all wrong! he had thought to himself. "No, I wanted to reach Sutton's Bay today, but at this rate, we'll be lucky to make it make it across the bay before dusk, let alone all the way up to the harbor."

"Shh," she whispered. "Listen."

All he could hear was the listless ruffle of a windless sail, hanging slack against the mast, and the gentle lapping of water against the hull. While she lolled in the sunlight, he moved about the boat, trying to catch the meager wind in their sails.

"I'll just have to start up the motor," he finally said, dejected and casting his frustration at the sails.

"Ryan, stop. Come here." She extended her hand to him, encouraging him to sit down beside her. He let out a sigh, dropped the slack line in his hand, and moved across the cockpit to join her.

"Listen," she said.

"I can't hear anything."

"Exactly." She look up at him. "It's gone."

He placed his hand over hers and asked, "What's gone?"

"*Everything.* The street noises, the taxi horns, all of the people talking on their phones. Talking and talking. Out here, it's just the two of us."

He knew that the past year had been difficult for her—not only leaving home and finishing her studies, but facing a degree of public scrutiny that went along with his family's life. And yet, she never complained. Not a single word. When he saw her face, out on Lake Michigan that morning, it hit him. This was the face of the woman he had fallen in love with in Bayfield. In the few short months she had been in Chicago, Shelby had developed lines above her brow, and a tightening in her jaw whenever she was confronted in the city. Out on the water, the physical signs of stress were gone. This was the Shelby he knew best.

"I love you, Shelby." He raised his hand to his chest, feeling the ring that was hidden deep within his inner jacket pocket. Several months earlier, when she surprised him at his debut photography exhibit, *Family Trees—A Bayfield Story* in Chicago's River North district, Shelby took his breath away. It was incredible to find her there, standing before a large framed portrait of herself sitting on the Madeline Island cliffs over Lake Superior. Until that moment, he doubted he would ever see her again. But there she was. When they left the exhibit on that warm July evening, he held her hand, knowing he'd never want to let it go.

"I love you, too." After a moment, when he didn't respond, Shelby sat up. "Ryan, what is it?" She placed her hand on his shoulder. "Are you all right?"

"I don't know how you do it," he began. "You're taking risks and adjusting to so many changes. School. Moving. Staying connected with your family, and business on the orchard."

"And yet, somehow I'm still finding time to sneak out onto the lake with you."

"That's best thing about your coming to Chicago," Ryan said, and meant it. "But seriously, you did all of that for yourself while being thrown into the public eye."

Shelby groaned and leaned back, her face lifted to the sun. "I don't want to think about that right now. Let's just enjoy floating out here, alone, without any distractions or anywhere to go."

When she first arrived in Chicago and began to attend functions with Ryan, the media seemed to adored her. They called her fresh. A natural beauty. She wasn't as enamored with them as they were of her, however, and it wasn't long before Shelby was being photographed entering a room with her eyes cast down, her head turned, or her body positioned out of view behind Ryan's broader frame.

Often, whenever she went out—to get coffee, running to class, or meeting up with a friend—they were there, trying to stir a reaction out of her. The more aggressive they became, and the more negative the coverage, the more Shelby retreated into herself.

She declined interviews and rarely acknowledged photographers who called out her name from the street as she rushed toward a car, out of a restaurant, or into Ryan's apartment.

The process was heartbreaking to witness and made Ryan want to lash out at the paparazzi and protect her, but he knew better.

"You're only going to make it worse," his mother, Charlotte, would say. "Don't worry. It's bound to blow over. She'll either find her way, or the media will lose interest. You know it's all very cyclical, Ryan. These stories don't last forever. Soon they'll be on to someone else and you two will be free to live in peace."

His father had other words. "Seriously, Ryan, you have to talk to her. Ask her to give those vultures at least a *hint* of a smile now and again. Get them off of her tail. The PR people at the office are having a hell of a time trying to clean up the publicity messes you two are stirring up. I never would have said this to you before, but perhaps you two should take a little time. Head back to Bayfield. Let things cool down."

Before long, the press grew tired of the one-sided relationship and the novelty of the rural Wisconsinite wore off. They began to call her aloof. Shallow. And a particular favorite was comparing Shelby's demeanor to her beloved Lake Superior: icy cold.

On the boat, Ryan felt a breeze lift off of Lake Michigan and blow across the cockpit. The sails gave a gentle rustle and the halyard sounded like a bell as it clanged against the mast. "Shel, do you remember the night you came to see me at the gallery opening?"

"Of course I do," she said with lazy contentment. "My God, I was so nervous. And out of place. All of those people, and your work—it was amazing to see it displayed throughout the gallery. I'll never forget it."

"You were so beautiful that night."

"I'm not so sure," she recalled. "I was a wreck. I could barely walk in those shoes."

He smiled at the memory; he considered her careful footing in high heels endearing.

"Do you remember what I said to you?"

"Tell me again."

"I said that if you'd let me, I'd spend the rest of my life loving you."

"I remember."

"It's truer now than ever before."

"I love you, too," she said, then paused. "Are you sure everything is all right? You seem a little, I don't know—distracted."

"No." *Nervous. Anxious. Heart exploding with anticipation. Hands trembling. Exhilarated by the prospect that you could answer yes to a question they haven't discussed.* He took in a deep breath to steady his nerves and then went down on one knee. "Shelby?"

When she opened her eyes and sat up again, the look of surprise came over her face the moment she realized his distraction.

"I mean it. I know you're still settling in here, and so much is changing right now, but here's the thing . . . I don't believe in chance meetings or destiny, and I've never believed in love at first sight. But I also know what I felt the first time I saw you on the lake. And I remember how much when I thought I'd never see you again. I know how it feels to fall in love, and be in love, because of you."

"Ryan, I—"

"Please, before you say anything . . ." He reached into his jacket pocket and withdrew a delicate ring that he knew was perfect the moment he saw it during a private appointment with a Michigan Avenue jeweler. Elegant and lovely, without being ostentatious, it was a brilliant cushion diamond encircled by a double row of bead-set diamonds that continued around the band. While the ring felt small in his hands, it held the weight of his future.

"I want to spend my life cheering you on when you succeed, and comforting you when you fall. I want to be there for everything. The good. The bad. I want to dream with you. Live, laugh, and cry with you," he said, holding out the ring, which sparkled as brightly as the sun's gleam off the water. "If you'll let me, I want to be at your side to experience it all with you."

She knelt down to the cockpit floor to face Ryan and hold his free hand as he asked, "Shelby Julia Meyers . . . will you marry me?"

Showing more interest in Ryan than the ring, Shelby kissed his lips between each word in her reply, saying with tenderness, "Nothing. Would. Make me. Happier."

Members of the string quartet sat in a cluster of teak lawn chairs; the viola player dressed neatly in a seersucker suit, while the cellist and two brunette violinists wore dresses in complementing shades of linen. They lifted their bows, the cellist gave a nod, and the foursome began to play the wedding party's processional. The piece was "Just like Heaven," by The Cure, a selection Ryan and Shelby had chosen as a harmless act of rebellion against Charlotte's formality. Ryan laughed to himself, knowing that Shelby was in earshot of the music and must be smiling, too, as she awaited her walk down the aisle.

Ryan glanced over at his parents, who sat together in the front row of garden chairs, clearly unaware of the song choice.

His father, William Chambers Sr., was the president and CEO of Chambers Media, a media conglomerate headquartered in Chicago. He sat with a straight back and legs crossed, dressed impeccably in a worsted wool summer suit. And Ryan's mother looked elegant in a belted, powder-blue dress and pearls. "It's haute couture," she had said with pride when he first saw her at the wedding, though the significance was lost on Ryan. Outwardly, they were the picture of proud parents. Ryan knew, however, that they had their doubts. Even today, as he and Shelby were prepared to make their vows.

No one would have suspected how far Ryan and Shelby had come in improving—although not yet solidifying—their relationships with their respective families. It had taken Ryan's parents time to accept his relationship with Shelby, and to relinquish their hope that he would someday marry into an equally prominent family. But Shelby's charm quickly melted their resolve as she found her way into the guarded place in their hearts. Ryan noticed his mother reach over to take his father's hand, and the moment their hands clasped, the chiseled intensity of his father's face softened. His father smiled and patted the top of her hand, then leaned over to kiss her cheek.

As the quartet played on, Ryan looked at the others gathered on the lawn. His friend Pete Whitfield sat with his wife, Meredith. Brad Thorson stood beside him as the best man, while his wife, Holly, smiled at them from the fifth row with their young daughter fidgeting in her lap. Ryan's sister, Martha, had traveled from South Carolina with her husband, Joe, and their two young children. Shelby's closest friends sat together with Nic's husband, Hank. And, although Ryan wasn't overjoyed to see him sitting near the back, Shelby's childhood friend John Karlsson was also there.

Ryan and the wedding guests looked up in their seats when they heard voices coming from the barn and saw the swag of sheer curtain beside the open doorway flutter. Instead of the wedding party emerging, Jackie and a man Ryan didn't recognize scurried out of the barn. The heels of Jackie's shoes appeared to be digging into the ground, causing her run across the lawn in a dramatic manner that resembled a panicked pink flamingo racing across the beach. Jackie stopped suddenly and grabbed on to her companion's shoulder for balance while kicking off her offending shoes. When the musicians noticed the commotion, their bows slid to a stop on their strings with as much grace as cars screeching to a halt on an icy road.

The mother-of-the-bride picked up her shoes in one hand, looked straight ahead, and led her gentleman friend to their seats. No one muttered a word or dared to clear their throat. They wore bewildered expressions and even the children sat silently with their mouths agape.

Then, during that moment of uncomfortable silence, just as Jackie and her escort were about to take their seats in the front row, a low-flying seagull passed overhead. It flew alone. Its white wings were fanned out wide, and its head was held high. It didn't make a sound until it approached the wedding in a descending glide, swooped down low, and opened its beak to let out a piercing screech. Jackie looked up. In that instant, the gull released an airborne glob of white excrement. Before Jackie could duck, it landed squarely between her brows and dripped down the bridge of her powdered nose while she shrieked in a high pitch that matched that of the triumphant, departing gull.

An audible gasp rippled across the lawn, which triggered muffled chuckles by some and uncontrolled giggles by others. Jackie threw her shoes into the grass and ran barefoot, past Ryan at the altar, and all the way to the Meyerses' farmhouse, with her companion chasing after her.

Ryan turned away from the spectacle and looked toward the barn once again. This time, he caught a glimpse of Ginny and Shelby pulling back the curtain and standing just within the barn doors. As the musicians in the string quartet picked up their bows once again, his bride and her grandmother fell into each other's arms, unable to contain their laughter.

CHAPTER 3

TRUTH AND VOWS

Afooter the front door of the Meyerses' home slammed shut behind Jackie and her companion, Ryan was still looking curiously in their direction when the musicians cued their instruments again and he felt Brad give him a sideways nudge.

"Wow, Ryan," Brad whispered. "She looks *stunning*."

Ryan looked up as his bride and her grandmother walked out of the barn arm in arm. They made their way down the grassy aisle, causing a shuffle on the lawn as everyone in attendance stood and turned to welcome the bride. Without seeing the guests' faces, Ryan knew they were as transfixed by Shelby as he was. Her grace and beauty left him breathless.

When Shelby's eyes fixed on Ryan's, the world seemed to drop away. Everyone and everything seemed to disappear—their guests, their surroundings, the sound of string instruments—it all faded away.

Emotion took him by surprise. He didn't think it would, but there he was, his eyes welling and a powerful wave of pride and love rolling through him. There were no words. She was radiant and lovelier than ever. She was the woman with whom he would grow old, start a family, make a life. In Shelby, his image of wife and life partner was right there, walking toward him. She had said yes.

They embraced at the altar and Ginny whispered into Shelby's ear, which brought a smile to her face. Then Ginny touched Shelby's cheek, gave Ryan an approving nod, and walked to her seat beside the empty chair where Jackie would have been.

Shelby accepted Ryan's outstretched hand and everything felt right. They vowed to live well and with open hearts, forgive each other's failures, and strive to find joy amidst the hardships. And with an exchange of rings, they promised to love each other for a lifetime.

He looked into her eyes, brimming with adoration and full of wonder. Ryan wrapped his arms gently around her waist and held her close, for she had chosen him; they were family. The enormity of their commitment filled him with over-whelming pride and love.

With his lips a whisper away from hers, he waited for the pastor's final words: "You may kiss the bride."

She was his wife. *My wife!* With a mischievous grin and one graceful move, Ryan turned Shelby in his arms and dipped her ever so slightly. She piqued all of his senses. The sight of her. The floral hint of her perfume. The feel of lace and tulle in his hands and bouquet petals against the back of his neck as her arms wrapped around his shoulders. And the taste of her lips. He was whole with her and lost in her. He barely heard the pastor announce, "It is my honor to present to you, Mr. and Mrs. Chambers," to the applause of their guests.

Without warning, a flash of a tragic memory cut through the moment like a knife plunging into a wedding cake and Ryan's heart skipped a beat in his chest. He eased Shelby out of the dip and then stepped back to loosen his tie and fumble with the top button of his dress shirt. His fingers were weak, trembling. He forced a smile—*everything's wonderful*—while inside, he was terrified.

"Ryan?" Shelby whispered with concern.

He knew everyone was waiting for him to escort Shelby back down the aisle and into the reception, but he couldn't move. His mind flashed back to the ice. The snowstorm. The hard, frozen surface breaking suddenly and knocking him off his feet. Shelby's grandfather, Olen Meyers, clinging to a jagged shard of ice.

"Ryan!" Olen had called out on that terrifying day on the ice, not so long ago. "Throw me that line!" The frayed end of a nylon rope was no more than eight feet from Ryan's grasp. "Ryan!" Olen had called out again. And again once more. While Ryan remained still, useless, and frozen in fear.

As much as Ryan had tried to forget what had happened that day, the memory was rising to the surface again. After Olen's death and Ryan's rescue from the ice and storm, many had called him heroic. Brave. But the truth? The truth had been swept away in snow and ice that day. The truth was— Ryan's cowardice had cost Olen his life. Nothing, not the memorial fund that Ryan had created in Olen's name, not the financial support he offered Ginny to run the orchard, and not even a vow to love and respect Olen's granddaughter for the remainder of his life—nothing could rid him of the guilt.

"Ryan?" This time the voice in his head wasn't Olen's but Shelby's, bringing him back to the present.

He reached for the comfort of her hand, closed his fingers tightly around hers, and took in a calming breath. He pushed away his trepidation to return to the moment. A reassuring smile. Another tender kiss. The groom was ready to escort his new bride back down the aisle.

"Shall we?" he asked, with a wink and a nod toward the barn.

As they walked down the grassy aisle, passing their guests who stood to recognize the newly married couple with applause, he swallowed hard. In marrying Olen's beloved granddaughter on the Meyers family land, Ryan knew he didn't have the blessing of Olen's spirit. And more importantly, if Shelby knew the truth about Ryan's role in her grandfather's death, Ryan knew she would never have agreed to marry him.

CHAPTER 4

FLOWER GIRL

Walking through the barn's curtained doorway was like walking through C. S. Lewis's wardrobe to Narnia. The barn was an aging structure with a high, cavernous ceiling, ribbed concrete flooring, and dusty stalls that contained farm equipment, supplies, and apple crates. On this day, however, it had been entirely transformed. And like Narnia, the barn's interior was now a dazzling spectacle as white as mystical snow.

Endless strands of miniature lights draped down from the rafters like arcs of evening stars. Temporary chandeliers made of painted iron and antique lights hung from overhead beams to illuminate long rows of dinner tables, set with white cloths, elegant table settings, flowers in vases of varying heights and widths, and candles. Everywhere there were candles. They burned brightly in hurricane flutes and Ginny's glass Mason jars that were tied up in ribbons.

After the cocktail reception, and once everyone was seated at the dining tables, Ryan stood at the head table with a glass of champagne raised in his hand. The room quieted and Ryan turned to his bride, focusing his sole attention on her—just as he had nearly two years earlier, in the same barn on a warm night such as this, when their relationship was just beginning.

"I won't say too much, because I know how you like to keep your private life private, but we're among family and friends," Ryan continued. "Excluding Brad, of course."

"Of course," she concurred, reaching over to pat Brad's hand.

"When I first arrived in Bayfield two summers ago, I was looking for an escape. I said it was just a kayaking trip with the guys; a trip to see a part of the Midwest that I had read so much about, but have never seen. But it wasn't just a vacation. I was running. I had no direction or purpose. I never expected to meet anyone. Somehow, from that very moment I saw Shelby, I realized I needed a change." Ryan paused before continuing. "From that moment forward, the direction of my life altered for the better.

"People have said that I've led a blessed life. A privileged life. I am grateful for the opportunities I've had, and I don't take those advantages lightly. But honestly, none of that comes close to the *true* blessing in my life—falling in love with a woman who encourages me to embrace all that life has to offer.

"So, please join me in a toast to my *wife,* Shelby Chambers," Ryan said with absolute pride as the room joined him in "Cheers!" and a chorus of clinking glasses.

He took Shelby's hands in his and leaned down to kiss her. "I love you, Shel," he said, loud enough for only her to hear.

"I love you, too," she whispered back, her eyes gleaming.

A short while later, Shelby heard the delicate *ting* of a knife tapping against a crystal wineglass to draw everyone's attention. This time, it was her grandmother who rose to her feet.

"Those of you who know me best know that I'm a talker.

But, oddly enough, I'm a terrible public speaker. Nonetheless, I'm the head of the Meyers family now and you're all guests in my home, so I'd like to say a few words tonight—but only a few, I promise you." Shelby could hear equal amounts of pride and nervousness in her grandmother's voice.

"Shelby, you are—and always have been—our angel. You're like the sparkle that dances on the lake. So lovely and full of life, always there to lift my spirits, and yet far too special to keep to myself. You have places to go. I am immensely proud to be your guardian for life." Then, turning to Ryan, Ginny continued, "And Ryan, let's cut to the chase, shall we? You're going to have your hands full. Your wife is as determined as she is beautiful, and as spirited as she is bright. There's no telling where your life will lead with Shelby at your side, but I do know it's going to be one heck of a journey."

Ryan raised his glass with a nod to Ginny and gently rubbed Shelby's back, knowing that the most difficult aspect of living in Chicago was being apart from her grandmother.

"Now, there's just one more thing. If my husband, Olen, were with us today, he would—" Ginny paused when her voice broke, and she was unable to continue. She cast her eyes down and patted her flushed cheeks, something Shelby had seen her do countless times in the past to calm her nerves. After a quiet moment, Ginny looked up again, took a deep breath, and continued. "If Olen were here tonight, I know he wouldn't have gotten caught up in the wedding plans and small details. He would have left that to the rest of us. My husband would, however, insist on two things. First, he would offer a toast to Shelby and Ryan and give you two his heartfelt blessing."

Shelby turned to Ryan and mouthed, "He loved you like a son." She interpreted the pained look in Ryan's eyes as missing her grandfather as much as she did. But then, he didn't say anything to her in return.

"And second," Ginny said, "Olen would have asked Shelby to dance."

The guests joined Ginny in raising their glasses with "Cheers!" Ginny then set down her glass, pointed an arm in Shelby's direction, broke out in a mischievous smile, and nodded toward the open dance floor. "So, whad'ya say, kid? Should we show 'em how it's done?"

The cocktails were flowing, spirits were high, and there were so many people now on the makeshift dance floor that Shelby wondered if the old barn would survive the night. The vibrations of sound and celebration alone were enough to take down the structure. While decorated beautifully like a veteran performer at a late-night cabaret, signs of the building's age became more apparent as the evening wore on. Cobwebs still shrouded dark corners and the musty aroma of old apples and cider permeated the woodwork. And from the highest peaks of the barn's vaulted ceiling, specs of dust floated downward through the canopy of miniature lights with every shake of the rafters.

Shelby was standing in a small clutch of Chambers family friends, holding Ryan's hand and talking amicably to people she had only just met. It was something she was learning to perfect, attending events with Ryan and feigning interest in the opinions and stories of strangers when in fact all she really wanted to do was dash back to the security of her own home. No matter how hard she tried to fit in, she always felt more of an observer than a participant. *I'm sure that will change now that we're married,* she thought.

The voices of those around her buzzed while she smiled and waited for an opportunity to break away. At the moment, Mrs. Edith Forsyth, a jaunty woman with rouged cheeks and plum-colored lipstick that stained the perimeter of her lips but was smudged off in the center, was discussing her newly improved golf swing.

Shelby glanced over Mrs. Forsyth's shoulder and spotted a child who was sitting with Mr. Carlson, a friend of her grandparents. She remembered that the Carlsons were bringing their visiting granddaughter to the wedding. She watched Mr. Carlson head toward a refreshment table while the girl stayed seated beside a cascading flowerpot that sat atop a wooden barrel.

Shelby noticed how the girl seemed transfixed by a pair of children who were holding hands and spinning on the dance floor. The girls were dressed impeccably in periwinkle dresses made of organza with taffeta sashes and tulle-ruffled slips. It was a look that Shelby knew well. She used to be that child.

Shelby turned her attention back to the adults just as Mrs. Forsyth was rousing some interest in a foursome to play nine holes in the morning. Giving Ryan's hand a squeeze, Shelby said, "Thank you again for coming; I hope you'll stay and dance. Now if you'll excuse me, I'll leave you to your planning while I check up on someone."

Shelby walked toward the young girl, stopping at the head table just long enough to retrieve her bridal bouquet and admire the dancing girls as she crossed the dance floor. Once Shelby reached Mr. Carlson's granddaughter, she lifted the full skirt of her dress and crouched down to meet her at eye level.

Shelby began with a simple hello. "I'm Shelby."

The girl nodded and looked at Shelby with round, beautiful brown eyes.

"You're here with your grandparents, right? The Carlsons?"

The girl nodded, and her shiny brunette hair, pulled

loosely into a thick side braid, fell over her shoulder. Her hands fidgeted with the folds in her skirt.

"They're friends of *my* grandparents. Did you know that?"

A slight shake of the head, no.

"I've known them for years," Shelby continued with a gentle voice. "Let me guess. You're spending the weekend with them?"

"Uh-huh." The girl's voice was tender and light.

"What is your name?"

A pause. She turned to look over her shoulder, in the direction of her grandfather, who caught her eye and waved reassurance as a bartender poured two glasses of lemonade. "Kate."

"Well, Kate, when I saw you standing here, I just had to come over and introduce myself because you are, by far, one of the prettiest girls I have ever seen," Shelby said, and she meant it. "Your dress is gorgeous, too."

A blush as rosy and pure as the girl's dress warmed her cheeks.

"But, hmm . . ." Shelby continued, tapping her finger to her lips in consideration. "I wonder if there's missing something."

Kate's expression changed to curiosity as she watched Shelby pull a pale-pink rose from her bouquet.

"May I?" Shelby asked, holding the rose out toward the child's side-swept braid.

Kate nodded, her eyes on the flower in Shelby's hand.

Shelby proceeded to break away the excess stem from the flower and tuck the rose into Kate's braided hair.

"Maybe a few more?" Shelby suggested.

"Okay . . ." Kate's face lit up in a smile.

"There," Shelby said, standing up to admire her work. Kate

had a nosegay of bridal flowers tucked all along her braid, and a wide, gap-toothed smile that was even lovelier. "It's perfect."

"Bapa!" Kate burst out joyfully when they were joined by Mr. Carlson.

"Well, Kate, don't *you* look like a princess?" her grandfather said, and handed her a glass of lemonade. "As do *you,* Shelby. Congratulations. We couldn't be happier for you and your husband."

"Thank you, Mr. Carlson," Shelby replied, standing up and adjusting her dress. "I'm so glad you were able to bring Kate. She's welcome here anytime."

Shelby was happier seeing Kate's newfound smile than she had been speaking with all of the Mrs. Forsyths in the room.

"So, young lady, how 'bout you and I cool off with these drinks and then get back out there on the dance floor?" Mr. Carlson asked his granddaughter, before congratulating Shelby again and then walking away with Kate's hand held in his.

Shelby smiled to herself, remembering the similar moments she had shared in this same barn with her own grandfather. She found herself looking toward the open barn doors, imaging that at any moment, he would enter the reception and ask her to dance.

As the evening wore on, the dancers grew tired and one by one guests began to say good night and taper off. Those who remained in the later hours were still laughing, raising glasses, and whirling about the dance floor.

Ryan's parents continued to circulate among the guests, seeming to enjoy themselves. Ginny held center court in a clutch of her closest friends, talking animatedly with her hands while one of the women uncorked another bottle of wine to share. And after the fiasco that took place just before the ceremony, Jackie and her male friend had been polite and drew very little attention to themselves.

Ryan and Shelby embraced each other on a quiet corner of the dance floor as they swayed to the music. The music seemed to fade away. Voices hushed. In Ryan's arms, Shelby imagined it was just the two of them. One of his hands rested on the small of her back while the other clasped her right hand and held it close to his heart. Feeling the warmth of his cheek against hers, she closed her eyes and breathed deeply. Ryan lowered his head, kissed her lightly, and whispered, "Thank you for saying 'yes.' "

"Thank you for asking."

"So, *Mrs.* Chambers . . ."

"I like the sound of that," Shelby said, running her fingers slowly across his jawline until she touched his lips. "Say it again."

"Mrs. Chambers—I have something for you."

"You do?"

He released her from his arms just long enough to slip his hand into the vest pocket of his suit coat and withdraw a thin, blue satin ribbon.

"What is it?" she asked, smiling in anticipation.

When Ryan extended his hand, there was a solitary key dangling back and forth from the end of the ribbon that was entwined around his fingers.

She tilted her head to the side and looked from the key to his eyes. "A key?"

Ryan slipped the ribbon from his fingers to hers.

"Is it a room key? Are we staying somewhere in town?"

"Think bigger," he said, clearly amused.

"It's not a boat key. . . ."

"Why don't I just show you? That is, if you're ready to sneak out of here," Ryan whispered in her ear.

"I thought you'd never ask."

Even though they knew the right thing to do would be to walk through the reception one more time to say their good-byes, they looked at each other like a pair of teenagers conspiring to sneak out of class. He took her hand and, without needing to say another word, led her out of the barn and into their new life.

CHAPTER 5

EYES SHUT

"Eyes still closed?" Ryan asked while pulling the car off of the moonlit main road and turning onto an unmarked, narrow dirt road that wound through a thick grove of trees.

"Still closed," Shelby said, grinning underneath the hands that she held over her eyes. "We're on gravel now, aren't we?"

"We are," he said. "Just a bit farther."

He continued to drive carefully through the woods. The overhead canopy of trees blocked out the moon and left only the car's headlights to cast light across the road. The car traveled slowly over the gravel, bumping on occasion as it rolled over ruts and ridges in the road, until it reached their destination. Once the car came to a stop, Ryan put it in Park and removed the keys from the ignition. He was glad to see a warm amber light coming from the living room windows of the cottage that stood before them. Earlier in the evening, his instructions to Nic and Hank had been simple. Ryan was grateful that they had agreed to break away from the wedding reception just early enough to help pull this off. Looking over at Shelby, who was still covering her eyes, he was sure she never noticed when he gave them a nod across the room while he was holding her on the dance floor.

"We've stopped," she said, turning toward him. "The suspense is killing me, you know."

"Go ahead, Shel. You can open your eyes." He watched as Shelby dropped her hands to her lap. Her eyes fluttered open and adjusted to the new surroundings.

"The cottage?" she asked, leaning forward to get a better look out the windshield. She turned to him, a smile lighting up her face. "You rented the cottage again? For tonight? It's perfect."

He exited the car and walked around to the passenger side, opened her door, and offered his hand to help her out.

"Huh—I'm not quite sure how to maneuver out of the car in this dress," she admitted, nodding toward the cumbersome folds of her wedding gown. "Maybe if you grab this part of the skirt . . . ?"

"I can do better than that," he replied, reaching into the car to gather her in his arms and easily lift her out of the vehicle. As he carried his bride down the stone-lined footpath, her arms were wrapped tightly around his neck and the billowy fabric of her dress floated about them. "Let's take a look around. It's been a while."

"The lights are on. Is someone here?" she asked, looking into the windows of the lakeside cottage that he had rented during his time in Bayfield, the year they had first fallen in love.

"I'm not sure." He set her down gently at the front door. "Go ahead inside," he said, grinning.

"Wait! I think I left the key in the car."

"Try opening it. You might not need the key—maybe it's unlocked."

Shelby reached out and turned the doorknob tentatively and upon hearing the *click* of the latch gave him a curious glance.

She was about to take a step tentatively into the cottage when Ryan reached for her again, saying, "Hold on—let's do this right."

Before she could say a word, he swooped her up once more in an armful of lace and tulle and carried her gallantly over the threshold.

The room was quiet, aside from the snapping crackle of the fire in the hearth and the soft rustle of Shelby's dress as she walked through the cottage's modest living room. Her gown reflected the firelight and made her look even lovelier. Ryan shut the door behind him, turned the lock, and stood in the entryway, watching as she moved about the room. He couldn't have pulled it off without the help of Ginny and some of their friends.

It was a warm atmosphere, infused with the subtle perfume of flowers and the homey scent of wood fire and candles burning in hurricane flutes. She took it all in and was left speechless. The same variety of flowers from her bridal bouquet were arranged in antique vases and placed throughout the cottage. There were also photographs of the two of them, along with their family and close friends, hanging on the wall.

Ryan enjoyed watching as she discovered the special touches made just for her, knowing that she didn't fully comprehend the cottage's transformation since the last time they were on the property.

As Shelby ran her hands over the new furniture, appreciating the curved lines and the array of plush pillows in varying shades of blue, Ryan walked over to the stereo in the living room. He selected an album, slid a vinyl record out of its cover, and set it on the turntable. The melodic strumming of a guitar filled the room.

"When did you take an interest in old records?" she asked, amused by his choice in music.

"Ginny's idea," he admitted. "She said it would add a touch of nostalgia to this place."

"I should have guessed. My grandparents have a pretty impressive record collection at home. I love Van Morrison—is this album one of theirs?"

"She gave us a few, but this is one I picked up in Chicago." He never fully appreciated Morrison's lyrics about a woman being as sweet as Tupelo honey until he saw the way the firelight shone upon his lovely bride.

Shelby retrieved a silver frame from the mantel and looked over at Ryan. "Is this Gran's, too?" He crossed the room to join her. In her hands, she held a simple silver frame. Stretched taut behind the glass was a cross-stitching of a flowering tree.

"She's a talented lady," he said, setting his hand lightly upon Shelby's shoulder. He looked down at the handcrafted art, which Ginny had shown him just the day before. She had carefully hand-stitched leaves and blossoms on the tree and placed a crimson heart in the center of the tree trunk. On one of the branches, Ginny had included a pair of tiny birds. With painstakingly careful stitching, Ginny had also carefully entwined the names of their immediate family members among the lower branches and leaves. Charlotte. William. Martha. Jacqueline. Ginny. Olen. As well as Ryan's grandparents, Norman, Elizabeth, Charles, and Claire. Near the top, Ginny had stitched in Ryan's and Shelby's names. Ryan had noticed there was room at the very top of the tree to add in the names of Ginny's future grandchildren. She had confided in him that she was eager to see the family grow.

"'Branching Out,'" Shelby said softly, running her finger over Ginny's words stitched beneath the tree. "I absolutely love it. How did she—how did you two . . . ?"

"Ginny and I were talking about how much you love your family's land and what it took for you to leave it," Ryan explained as he began to run his fingers gently up and down her back, admiring the way her bare shoulders glowed in the firelight. "I hope you don't mind, but I told her what you said—about the orchard reminding you of a community, with so many different family trees. She wanted you to have your own family tree, wherever you decided to live."

"It's perfect," she said, replacing the frame on the mantel and then turning into his embrace. "Someone did a lot of work here."

"It took a bit of work," he admitted. "And a lot of help."

"Gran did this, too?"

"She did, among others," he said. "Turns out, she's a great coconspirator. And contractor."

"Contractor?" Shelby said with a surprised laugh.

"Just wait until you see this place in the daylight," he said. "We made a few improvements to the property, as well."

"A few improvements," she said, shaking her head. "I mean, I just can't believe this—if I could create a place of my very own, I don't think I would have been able to make it as perfect as this one."

He drew her closer. "That's good to hear, considering . . ." Ryan reached up his hand and tenderly brushed aside a tendril of hair that had fallen from her updo and kissed the soft curve of her neck.

"Considering what?" she said under her breath, closing her

eyes as his hand traveled slowly down the nape of her neck until it reached the delicate buttons that ran down the arch of her back like a string of pearls. He moved his other hand from her waist, to her back, and, one by one, he slowly unbuttoned her bridal gown. He felt the softness of her cheek pressed against his and felt the quickening of her breath.

"This is yours, Shelby," he whispered in her ear, his hands traveling farther down her back with the release of each satin button. The warmth of her skin being released from the binds of her wedding gown caused him to feel even more impatient. And yet, he took his time. Moving slowly, deliberately. Heightening the anticipation. He wanted this to be a night they would both remember.

"I fell in love with you here—and as soon as you agreed to marry me, I knew I had to find a way to buy this cottage and prepare it just for you."

"For us."

"But mainly for you. You're giving up so much to be with me—to enter my life and everything that comes with being in the Chambers family." He felt her kiss that soft spot on his neck, just below his ears, and the sensual distraction caused him to falter.

"I want you to have a place to come home to whenever you need it. When you need a break. It won't always be easy, being a bit more in the public eye," he continued. Her kisses moved across his jaw. "A vacation. Time with your grandmother." Shelby raised her hand to his face and, with gentle pressure, pulled him to her waiting lips.

"I don't know what to say," she said with a catch in her breath.

He felt his control disappearing.

"If you ever need time away from Chicago," he said, his

lips a breath away from hers. She was sensual. Intoxicating. Her fingers now moving down the front of his shirt, doing a far better job than he had at undoing buttons. "Whenever you need to get away, I hope you'll come here. It's yours," he repeated.

"*Ours*," she said, looking from his eyes to his lips. She ran a hand beneath his unbuttoned shirt and caressed his chest. He felt a rush of passion and was about to give in to her but took in a calming breath instead. Ryan wouldn't rush their wedding night. He steadied his breathing and concentrated solely on her. He kissed her deeply, passionately, and then stepped back.

"Slowly," he whispered.

He moved to stand behind her, set his hands on the smooth skin of her bare shoulders, and let them travel down the open space on her back that was exposed beneath an unbuttoned bodice. With confidence and steady hands, he took his time unbuttoning the last of the tiny buttons and then gently eased the dress away from her body and let it fall into a cloud at her feet. He removed his own shirt and settled in behind her, feeling the warmth of her soft skin against his.

Later, he would take her hand and they would explore the rest of the cottage. She would find a bottle of champagne chilling in the kitchen and her favorite chocolates set beside a bouquet on the dining table. The next day, in the morning light, she would discover her favorite books had been lined up neatly in a bookcase along with an old childhood diary, the one with a red leather cover and pages with faded gold gilded edges. And later, when she was ready to get dressed, she would open the bedroom closet to discover a special memory box with trinkets from her youth and a cherished red Badger cap from her alma mater in Madison. Finally, within the drawer of her bedside table, Shelby would find an envelope containing two first-class tickets to Zurich, Switzerland.

But for now, the only thing on Ryan's mind was his bride. He would love her as their wedding night rolled into the early morning hours and the beginning of their married life together.

CHAPTER 6

WAKE-UP CALL

Shelby should have been sleeping peacefully beside her husband the morning after the wedding, but she was awake before the sun rose. Images from the day before had been racing through her head. Rather than the happy remembrances of an extraordinary day, her thoughts kept flashing back to Jackie and her uninvited guest. And the fact that he had the nerve to call himself Shelby's father.

She looked across the bed to her slumbering husband and, not wanting to wake him, peeled back the bedcovers and quietly walked out of the room. She winced when the door latch clicked loudly behind her, but still Ryan did not wake. She padded her way across the kitchen, where she found her purse on the counter, retrieved her cell phone, and pulled up Jenna's number.

Shelby walked to the kitchen window as the phone rang and she looked out toward the Lake Superior view, which was just beginning to waken in the light of dusk. After numerous rings, Shelby was about to hang up when her friend answered.

"Shelby?"

"Sorry. Did I wake you?"

"Yeah, you could say that. God, what time is it?" came Jenna's groggy voice through the phone. "What are you doing, calling me this morning? You're supposed to be on your honeymoon!"

"Sorry. We're driving to the airport in a few hours and I wanted to catch you before we leave."

"Perfect. Call me back in a few hours then."

"No, wait—just give me a minute," Shelby said quickly. "I need to ask a favor."

"All right, but hey—where's Ryan? I didn't think you'd come out from that bedroom for days. . . ."

Shelby looked over her shoulder from where she stood and, seeing the bedroom door was still closed, felt safe to continue talking quietly. "He's sleeping."

"I'll bet he is," Jenna said. She muttered something inaudible and then whispered, "So, what's going on?"

"Hey . . ." Shelby could hear something in the background.

"What?"

"What's that noise?" Shelby asked. "Are you alone?"

Jenna muffled a laugh.

"You're not, are you?" Shelby asked, shaking her head to herself in the darkened kitchen. "You're unbelievable. You've only been in town for what, less than forty-eight hours?" She thought back to the night before, trying to guess who the "lucky" guy could be.

"You know what they say about weddings . . ." Jenna teased.

"Who is it?"

"You don't want to know."

"You're right; I don't. I need to ask you a favor," Shelby said. She thought for a moment before changing her mind. "Wait, yes, I do—who is it?"

"Hold on," Jenna said. Shelby could hear more muffled

sounds and then she heard a door squeak open and then close. "Okay. I closed the door so we can talk."

"So?" Shelby asked.

"You won't get mad?"

"Why would I get mad?"

"John."

There was a stretch of awkward silence on Shelby's end of the line. "Are you really?"

"Yes."

"*My* John?" Shelby laid her hand firmly on the window ledge, trying to grasp what Jenna was telling her.

"Yours?"

Is he mine? No, of course not, she thought, moving to take a seat at the kitchen table. John Karlsson was Shelby's childhood friend. He loved her and she had had the chance to be with him. She simply didn't have the same feelings for him and in her college years had chosen Jeff over him. And then, years later, she had left John in their hometown in order to be with Ryan. John had always been her constant, her trusted friend, her sure thing. She never really imagined him being with another woman. *What kind of friend am I, who never really knew anything about any of the women he dated?* And why did she feel a sick ache in her stomach now, as if she had just been hit in the stomach, at the thought of him having sex with her Chicago friend? Was it a sense of disrespect? Betrayal? Or was it a pang of jealousy?

My God, how can I possibly feel jealous after spending the most romantic night of my life? "Of course he's not mine, in that sense; I'm just surprised that you two . . . found each other," Shelby said, regretting that she had asked in the first place. "I didn't even see you two talking last night."

"You were pretty busy yourself, Mrs. Chambers," Jenna said. "Besides, I'm just messin' with you. This guy's name is Jake."

"Wait, you aren't with John?" Shelby leaned back in her chair, relieved. "Then . . . who's Jake?"

"The bartender."

"Seriously?" Shelby burst out a bit louder than planned. Then she dropped her voice back down to a hush. "The bartender."

"Shaken. Not stirred."

Shelby held her hand over her mouth to hold back a laugh so as not to wake Ryan.

"So, I don't think you called me at this hour to talk about the hunky bartender who's sprawled out naked in the next room. Did you?"

Shelby met Jenna shortly after moving to Chicago. She had taken a leap of faith when relocating from northern Wisconsin to the city, but it wasn't as much of a risk as Ryan had taken when he moved to Bayfield the previous year, which was based on little more than an inspired whim. After everything they had gone through together, it was her turn to take a chance on love.

But inwardly, she knew it was more than that. Her childhood home had become more than a comfort to her—it was her safe haven. It was the one place where she didn't have to take chances. Where life could be easy and predictable. Her move to Chicago was as much about Ryan as it was about breaking free from her hometown ties, because the longer she stayed in one place, the less confident she was in pursuing her dreams.

Ryan had offered to help her financially, but she was determined that if she was going to break away from her hometown, she would do it in her own way—with money saved from working at Meyers Orchard, her grandmother's blessing, and grandfather's gumption.

One of the first things she did in Chicago was find a way to finish her bachelor's degree. It was something she had put on hold for several years after her boyfriend, Jeff, died in a drowning accident during the summer before their senior year at the University of Wisconsin-Madison. After being readmitted through the university's distant learning program, she gained access to the John Crerar Library at the University of Chicago, which turned out to be a convenient and private place to study and research, not to mention, it was a short walk away from her first apartment.

What the modest property lacked in size and amenities it made up for in its proximity to U Chicago, a neighborhood that offered small-town charm. The apartment had a pair of French doors that made Shelby feel as if she were living in a Paris flat instead of a one-bedroom studio. The doors opened up to a balcony with ornate cast-iron railings. It offered just enough space for a potted geranium and a single patio chair and was the perfect place to enjoy a cup of coffee and an obstructed view of Washington Park.

It wasn't an easy transition returning to school after an extended break, but it gave Shelby purpose as she adjusted to the changes in her life—as well as a distraction from the attention she was garnering from the press solely because of her relationship with Ryan.

The university was well into its fall semester when Shelby first met Jenna Taylor. It was a blustery day in late November and Shelby was studying over lunch at Pudge's Sandwich Shop, a family-owned business that was less than two blocks from her apartment. Sitting at a window-side counter near to the entrance, Shelby looked up from her work when the wind picked up outside and a sudden onslaught of sleet pelted the window.

The front door flung open and startled several patrons

seated nearby. Shelby bristled against the offensive cold air and pulled her heavy cardigan tighter across her chest. She glanced at the entryway just as a young woman burst through the door, shaking wet clumps of snow off of her bluntly cut black hair.

"Damn it!" Jenna cursed when she looked down at her suede boots that were spotted with watermarks and sidewalk salt. Shelby turned back to her half-eaten BLT sandwich and the task of editing her essay for Professor Neilson's environmental journalism class.

Shelby was distracted again when Jenna dropped her bag next to Shelby's open book, the weight of which caused Shelby's plate to bounce up from the counter and rattle back down. Slightly annoyed that Jenna couldn't have chosen one of the many other open tables and chairs instead of the spot directly next to her, Shelby shrugged over her work and tried to ignore the interruption.

"Is that any good?" Jenna asked as she uncinched the belt on her trench coat.

"Excuse me?"

"Your sandwich," she said, nodding toward Shelby's plate. "I'm famished—do you recommend the BLT?"

"Sure. It's my favorite."

"Perfect—watch my stuff, will you?"

"What?"

Instead of responding, Jenna cast off her coat onto the barstool beside Shelby and headed off to order a bacon-lettuce-tomato from among the twenty or sandwiches listed on an overhead chalkboard.

Shelby shifted in her seat so she was angled toward the door, with her back to Jenna's chosen seat. It was the subtle, universal message that said: *I would prefer to keep to myself, thank you very much.* She picked up her pen and refocused on her work.

When Jenna returned, she peered over Shelby's shoulder to see what she was working on. "You go to U Chicago?"

"No." Shelby turned just enough to be heard. "Sorry, I don't mean to be rude, but I'm on a deadline."

"So why are you here instead of the library or somewhere private? Why come to a place where people can talk to you?"

Shelby let her pen drop onto her notebook. "Excuse me?"

"People who study in public places—coffee shops, sandwich joints, and so on—are doing it under the guise of working, but really they're bored out of their mind and want to get their stuff done but also enjoy being out. Whether it's people watching, eavesdropping on other conversations, getting out of work or school. If you really wanted to finish your essay in a timely manner, you definitely picked the wrong place to work."

"I don't know where you get the idea that—"

"Hi. I'm Jenna," she said, without extending her hand, as if it were a statement that would be the gateway to opening Shelby up for further conversation. "Jenna Taylor."

"Hi."

"And you are?"

"*Really* trying to get this work done."

"Do you need a refill on your iced tea?" Jenna asked.

Without responding, Shelby picked up her pen and tried once more to refocus on her assignment.

"Looks like my sandwich is ready, so I can easily get'cha a refill while I'm up there." Jenna leaned into Shelby slightly as she reached across to grab her glass, which was nearly empty aside from a tea-stained lemon wedge and some half-melted ice cubes.

Then Jenna was gone again, leaving behind her bags, her coat, and the trace of jasmine-scented perfume.

Shelby considered packing up her belongings and leaving. But there wasn't enough time to trek all the way back to her apartment to finish her work before her one o'clock class. And she didn't have time to go to the library to work after class because it was Friday—the kind of wonderful Friday that feels like a blessing after a particularly demanding week—and she had promised to meet Ryan at his apartment. He was cooking, which she loved. Puttanesca. She'd be bringing the wine and small box of cherry-topped rum babas that she purchased earlier that morning at Amelia's Italian Pastry Shop, just down the street from her apartment.

A refilled glass of iced tea appeared before her as Jenna set down her plate and a Coke. "So, what are you writing about?"

"Environmentalism."

"Specifically . . . ?"

"*Specifically,* a story about prescription drugs that are contaminating Lake Michigan."

"The sewage outfalls coming out of Milwaukee?"

"Um, yes."

"Yeah, I covered that a year ago. New research suggests that the lake is not diluting the compounds as most scientists expected. The ability of the drugs to travel and remain at relatively high concentrations means that fish and other aquatic life are exposed, so there could be some serious near-shore impacts, according to my source. In addition, Milwaukee draws its drinking water from Lake Michigan, although no pharmaceuticals have been detected in the city's water. The researchers reported that fourteen of the chemicals 'were found to be of medium or high ecological risk' and that the concentrations 'indicate a significant threat to the health of the Great Lakes.' Nevertheless, it is not clear what, if any, effects the drugs are having on fish and other creatures in Lake Michigan. Have you checked with the university?"

Shelby stared at this strange, intrusive woman in utter disbelief. "No, I haven't."

"And this is for what publication?"

"It's not. I'm a student."

"Ah. Journalism class."

"Something like that.

"I don't want to put a damper on that research paper of yours, but are you sure journalism is the way you want to go? Not public relations or marketing? Maybe teaching?" Jenna asked. "With every Tom, Dick, and Harry publishing their own so-called 'news' with blogs and Twitter feeds, and paper publications falling by the wayside to online news with shared sourcing and downsizing . . . it's not the career it used to be."

"I'm not sure I agree."

"People will do just about anything to write that break-through article, you know—it can get pretty desperate out there."

"So, I'm going to get back to it," Shelby said before shifting in her seat, setting her elbow on the counter and leaning into it, trying to create a wall between them and return to her work.

"I would have gone to U Chicago myself, except that I couldn't afford it," Jenna continued on, as if the conversation were two-sided. "I went to a small liberal arts school instead. I'm a reporter now, though. Have you heard of *The Daily?*"

Of course she's a reporter. Ryan's dad was right—maybe I am too naïve to handle the press. I can't even recognize a reporter when she comes right up and sits right down next to me.

Without another word to Jenna, Shelby hopped down off of the stool and gathered her belongings, preferring to trudge through the inclement weather to finish at the university library than to spend one more minute sitting next to an intrusive reporter.

"Hey, wait," Jenna said, setting her hand on Shelby's elbow. Shelby jerked her arm away from the reporter's grasp and took a step back. "Excuse me! I don't know what your intentions are, but we are done."

"This isn't what you think," Jenna said.

Shelby offered no response, quickly closing her book bag and reaching for her coat.

"Have you wondered if photos of you are showing up online?"

Why can't they just leave me alone?

"Walking across campus. Riding your bike through Washington Park? Leaving Ryan's apartment early in the morning?"

"You really have some nerve, you know that?" Shelby spat at Jenna, despising the hostility in her voice, but fed up with the brazen tactics photographers had used to get photographs of her lately. She was sure Jenna was another wolf in the pack.

"The photographers are getting tip-offs," Jenna said without urgency, as if she knew Shelby would be interested enough to sit back down. "Tips from Chambers Media."

Shelby stopped zipping her coat and looked at Jenna directly. "What did you say?"

"It's true. Someone inside of your boyfriend's family business is passing along information about your schedule, your routine—your dating life." Jenna took a hearty bite of her sandwich. She stopped chewing long enough to add, "And I think it's bullshit."

As Jenna took a second bite, Shelby set her things back down, slid out of her coat, and returned to her seat. "I'm listening."

As the sleet continued to cover the road and sidewalk outside of Pudge's with a layer of slush, and cold droplets clung to the window and trailed down in a slow slide, the women talked. Jenna didn't waste any more time in getting to the truth. She had been working in Chambers Media's public relations department in an entry level position until recently, when she took a job as an entry level reporter for *The Daily,* an alternative Chicago weekly that mainly covered the arts and music scene.

"Truth is, I'm a grunt. Low woman on the proverbial totem pole. A peon in an ever-changing business. My articles get buried. In fact, my byline is barely noticeable between the weekly ad for discounted guitars at High Rock and the community service announcements on hearing aid recalls."

Shelby smiled, despite feeling betrayed—allegedly—by a few employees at Chambers Media.

Back in her honeymoon cottage in Bayfield, Shelby pulled her chair away from the dining table and moved to the kitchen window, watching as the first rays of morning shone upon the lake.

"So, what's going on, Shelby?" Jenna asked over the phone. "Why the urgency?"

Shelby placed her hand on the windowpane, transfixed by the lake she had known all of her life. *It feels so good to be home,* she thought.

"I need a favor," Shelby said, her voice distant.

"Anything—shoot."

"How long will you be in town?"

"Checkout's at noon, so I thought I'd grab something for lunch and then head back to Chicago. Unless . . ."

"Unless?"

"You know, unless something else—or *someone else*—piques my interest."

"Fine. Keep that to yourself." Shelby took a deep breath. "This is about my mother, and that . . . that guy she was with. Chad Covington."

"Oh my God, Shelby. I've been dying to talk to you about that! What the hell? Is he really your father?"

"Absolutely not," Shelby said firmly, catching herself from raising her voice and waking Ryan. "At least I don't think so. He can't be."

"What's his story?"

"I have no idea. Any chance you could do some digging for me?"

"Yeah, of course."

"There can't be any truth to his story," Shelby said. She glanced toward the bedroom, hearing the sounds of her husband rousing. "I want to nip it in the bud."

"I'm on it."

"And Jenna? You have to be discreet. The last thing Ryan and his family need right now is another distraction."

"This could be that big news break I need—"

"Don't even think about it. This isn't an opportunity. It's personal."

CHAPTER 7

LUNE DE MIEL

After a long day of travel from Wisconsin to Switzerland, Ryan and Shelby boarded the Matterhorn Gotthard Bahn train in the Swiss town of Visp. They were now seated together in a private compartment with the armrest between them folded up and Ryan had his arm wrapped snugly around her shoulders. They looked out of their window and marveled at the scenery while the burgundy-red train wound its way up and through the country's deepest cleft valley toward the idyllic village of Zermatt.

At some points along the narrow-gauge and cog railway, the train rounded harrowing curves and hugged the mountainside as it passed closely beneath craggy overhangs. The couple could look down the steep terrain and see the Vispa River running far below; and above them, they admired the steep peaks of the Täschhorn, Dom, and Weisshorn mountains.

Shelby turned away from the window just long enough to kiss Ryan fully on the lips. "Incredible! I've never seen anything so beautiful."

Ryan enjoyed her childlike wonder as she continued to peer out on to the landscape. She held one hand pressed flat against the windowpane while the other reached back to hold his, squeezing it whenever they skirted another bend or the mountain face dropped off in a steep pitch toward the river.

"We're almost there," Ryan told her, giving her hand a gentle squeeze in return. He looked over Shelby's shoulder and watched as beams of the setting sun shone through the valley and cast the mountain slopes in a brilliant array of rose-colored light and shadows.

"I don't know," Shelby said, more to herself than to him. "I think we've already arrived."

Their honeymoon destination had been a well-kept secret. It was a place Ryan had visited once during college, and he had immediately fallen for its charm. He knew it would be the perfect honeymoon. Or, as the Swiss woman who had helped him make the arrangements had called it, a romantic *lune de miel.* Tucked away in the protective valley of a colossal mountain peak, the private town was absent of automobiles, city lights, and crowds. Over the past several months, he had been anxiously anticipating Shelby's reaction to walking along Zermatt's cobblestone streets, where the only sounds came from pedestrian chatter, church bells, and the occasional passing of an electric taxi or horse-drawn carriage. He knew she would love breathing in the fresh mountain air as they strolled past boutiques, chocolatiers, and enticing bakeries that were nestled all along the Bahnhofstrasse, the narrow street that ran through the center of town.

Ryan shifted in his seat so he could share her view of the river running through the gorge below and the few chalet-style homes that were set off from the railway, each with colorful flower boxes that adorned lace-curtained windows.

While their wedding day had been something he would

never forget, he was inwardly relieved to finally be away from Bayfield. Ryan knew how much Shelby was compromising by marrying into his family in order for them to be together. She was willing to leave her hometown to build a life with him in Chicago. Inwardly, he knew he was falling short by comparison. How could he ever admit to her that on their wedding day he felt the presence of her grandfather more than ever before? And rather than giving Ryan a sense of comfort, the feeling of Olen's presence had raised the hairs on the back of his neck.

"What are you thinking about?" she asked, still watching the scenery pass by.

"The wedding," he said, tucking a wisp of fallen hair behind her ear.

"It was perfect, wasn't it?"

Nothing is ever entirely perfect, he thought to himself, wondering how long he should wait before he told her the truth. His fingers gently caressed the skin on her cheek, over her ear, and down to the nape of her neck.

"Except for my mother, that is," Shelby said, suddenly sitting up straight. "I keep trying to forget about her and that man—God, what do I call him? Her friend? Boyfriend . . . ?"

"I guess we should just call him Chad, until we know for sure."

"Chad," she repeated. "Right. I still can't believe they pulled that stunt on our wedding day. I mean, where did he come from? Who is he? I keep replaying it all in my head. It doesn't make sense."

"Come on, Shel, let's not let it spoil our trip. We'll have plenty of time to sort it out when we get back home."

As much as he wanted to cast thoughts out of his mind that if Shelby ever discovered his actions on that day with Olen—as a winter storm raged around the two men and ultimately took

Olen's life—were far worse than any of Jackie's wrongdoings. It was devastating enough that, if Shelby had known the truth, Ryan was certain she wouldn't be with him now.

"That's one of the things I love about you—you're always so sure that things will work out in the end," she said.

Ryan held Shelby close while her words hung in the air and the train continued its rhythmic trek up the mountain rails.

"We're all settled!" Ryan called from the front door of their private alpine chalet, letting the iron latch on the door click solidly behind him. "The porter just brought up our luggage and I know you're tired, so I went ahead and ordered dinner and wine to be delivered."

When she didn't reply, he assumed she was freshening up after their long travel day, so he picked up one of her travel bags and carried it to her. He made his way through the open living room, with its vibrant red Persian rugs and oversized leather furniture. Above him was a vaulted, exposed-beam ceiling that showcased a broad, A-frame portrait window with a sweeping view of the Matterhorn. He couldn't help but notice how, set against the backdrop of a lavender evening sky, the mountain's snowcapped peak resembled a crooked witch's hat.

"Shelby?" he called out again, quieter this time. Ryan proceeded to walk past the fire, which flickered and snapped quietly in a stone hearth, and continued down a wood-paneled corridor that led to the master bedroom.

"In here . . ." came her voice from the behind the partially opened bedroom door. "I picked up something for you in that little shop by the train station."

He gave the door a gentle push and it swung open slowly. Then, seeing his bride, he dropped the bag to the floor.

Inside the room, there was a tall, four-post bed covered

with a white down comforter that looked pillow soft. Upon it, Shelby lay on her side with her head set upon her hand and propped up on one elbow, wearing nothing at all. A flat gold box, tied with a white satin bow, balancing atop the smooth arc of her bare hip. The long ends of the ribbon draped over her hip and drew his eyes across the length of her body.

Ryan took a step toward her, as if he had no control over his movements. He was drawn to her.

"It's been such a long day," she said, taking her time while twirling the length of the ribbon around her finger and then letting it fall back down again. "I thought you might be in the mood for something sweet."

"How thoughtful," he said, smiling as he entered the room.

"I've heard that Swiss chocolate is the best in the world."

"It is." Once he reached the bed, he set his hands atop the comforter and looked at every sensual curve on his wife's body. He reached his hand out and set it on her calf, keeping his eyes intent on hers as his touch slowly traveled up her leg, toward the gold box. "But there's something I have to ask."

She let out her breath as he slowly untied the satin ribbon, let it fall softly across her waist, and opened the gift. He removed the gilded wrapper from within the chocolate box, picked one of the confections, and brought it to his mouth. He bit into it, tasting the dark chocolate melt against his tongue, before easing himself closer to her.

"What is it?" she whispered.

"Exactly when did you manage to lose all of your clothes, Mrs. Chambers?"

"The better question is, why are yours still on?"

His hand continued to caress her skin before he climbed onto the bed beside her, eased her back, and then kissed her down the length of her body. The sway of her back, the soft indent of her navel—each part of her body more irresistible than the next. He became lost in the sensual feel and taste of her, which lingered in his mouth with the sweetness of choco-late.

He paused just long enough to pull his shirt over his head, and that's when she stopped him. Shelby sat up and, with a firm but loving hand, eased him down onto the bed. It was her time to take control.

CHAPTER 8

MOUNTAIN PEAKS

Shelby and Ryan's honeymoon days were spent strolling through cobblestone streets and hiking cool mountain paths. Their evenings were spent alone in the intimacy of their chalet. On one of their last evenings together here, they sat at a round table tucked in the back corner of a candlelit restaurant. The entire dining room was made of wood, from the high-pitched ceiling with a crisscross of beamed rafters to the wood-planked walls and flooring. Everything in the room matched the hue of candlelight, except for the Swiss mountain chairs placed around each table. They were bleached white and had beautifully carved backs and seat cushions that were upholstered in varying patterns of red and gold.

"Is it a sin to be this happy?" Shelby asked as she took her time swirling a skewered cube of crusty bread into a shallow ceramic pot filled with fondue and suspended over a low, blue flame.

"Not at all," Ryan answered, putting a hunk of bread into his mouth before the cheese could drip down his chin.

"How about gluttony?" she said, licking a dab of cheese off of her lower lip.

"I suppose that's right," he said, playing along. "That is, if you think eating a dinner made entirely of cheese is gluttonous."

"Add in the wine?"

"You have a point," he agreed, plunging another fondue fork of peasant bread into the irresistible blend of aged Gruyère and Sauvignon Blanc.

"And making love?"

He loved the mischief he saw in her eyes. "There's certainly no sin in that," he said, leaning over to kiss her lips.

"I'm not ready to go home," she said. "Why don't we just stay here? Find a little farmhouse in the mountains. I could write and you would have your photography. We wouldn't have to think about everything we have to deal with in the city."

"And here I was thinking you were starting to actually like Chicago."

"Chicago is fine. It's just not . . ."

"Home?"

"No, it just doesn't feel like home," she admitted. "At least not *yet*."

"A little Swiss house. I like it. The only thing missing would be children—we'd have to have lots of children."

She skewered another bread chunk and drowned it in the vat of cheese.

When she stopped playing along, he leaned forward to look into her eyes. "Shelby?"

"Hmm . . ."

"You okay?"

"Yep. It's nothing," she said, tapping her fondue fork against the rim of the pot. "One step at a time, right? It's going to take

me a while just to get used to being your *wife,* let alone someone's mother."

"You're absolutely right," he said, setting their conversation
back on course. "In fact, we only have a few days left of this
honeymoon. I don't know about you, but I think we should
head back to the chalet for some more *adjustment time. . . .*"

"Ever the charmer," she said, and her smile returned.

On the last full day of their trip, Shelby and Ryan arose
early in the morning and took a gondola up to Trockener Steg
mountain station, a massive concrete structure that can with-
stand the harsh winds and temperatures during the coldest
days of winter. On this day, the weather was bright and mild as
the sun rose over the mountains and presented an exception-
ally close view of the Matterhorn. They trekked down a
marked trail and stopped at one point to look across the gorge
to watch a small group of climbers scale the Matterhorn's
Hörnligrat ridge.

Hours later, they arrived at Chalet Alpenrose, a humble
mountainside restaurant that offered a cheerful welcome after
an arduous hike; a cobalt blue entrance painted with spotted
cows and flowering vines, and inside, lively music and the hearty
whiff of cervelas sausages and ale coming from the kitchen.

Since it was warm enough to stay outdoors, Shelby and
Ryan found a table on the restaurant's back deck. Against the
sweeping backdrop of the mountains, they enjoyed two orders of
Käseschnitte, which consisted of a thick slice of toasted bread
soaked in wine and topped with broiled Emmental cheese and a
fried egg. As Ryan had joked earlier on in the trip, a honeymoon
wasn't the time to hold back. They enjoyed every decadent
morsel.

After their meal, Shelby leaned her head back in her chair
and closed her eyes to enjoy the midday sun, while Ryan

took the opportunity to remove his cell phone from his pants pocket for a quick check. It chirped as soon as he turned it on.

"Hey, you need to put the phone away—we'll be back in Chicago soon enough," Shelby said with one eye open and her hand reaching for his phone. "I get you all to myself, at least for another day."

"I know; you're right. This will just take a minute. I'm expecting something," he said. "Then I'll turn it off."

She closed her eyes and leaned back again. "Some kind of news?"

"I can't believe I can get a signal out here," he said, distracted.

She wasn't as impressed as Ryan, preferring the sun on her face over cellular coverage.

Then he saw it. A message from Cullie James, the videographer who had worked with Ryan on the Great Lakes feature. "This might be what I was waiting for," he told her. "We're waiting to hear back from our editorial review committee."

"They're going to love it."

Over the past year, Ryan had spent a considerable amount of time working on a film project that had stemmed from the Olen G. Meyers memorial fund that Ryan established shortly after Olen's death. Under Ryan's leadership, the film would serve as an extension of Chambers Media's community affairs efforts with proceeds helping to further Great Lakes conservation. Chambers Media planned to release Ryan's work at Chicago's annual film festival in mid-October.

Ryan had been transparent about his travel schedule and the hours spent at the office working through the logistics, research, and content for the project, but he had purposefully kept the story line hidden from Shelby. He wanted to wait until she could see it in its entirety, completed and perfect. In honoring her grandfather's name and spotlighting a part of the country that she loved most, he hoped to make her proud.

As Ryan scrolled his thumb over the phone screen to read Cullie's message, his jaw tightened while reading the news. He then powered off the device and set it facedown on the table.

"Ryan?"

Ryan leaned forward in his chair, his elbows resting on his knees, shaking his head. "I can't believe this," he said. His father must have known. Why wouldn't he have said something to Ryan when they saw each other at the wedding? He must have known.

"What is it?" she asked.

"They turned us down."

"Who did? What are you talking about?"

"Our editorial board." *What went wrong? Damn it! Why didn't anyone from the office say anything to us earlier?*

"What? You mean your Great Lakes project?"

He nodded.

"After all of the work you guys have put into it? All of those hours?"

He looked over his shoulder and caught the attention of their waiter, who was standing near the kitchen door smoking a cigarette. Ryan pointed to a nearby table, gesturing to the patrons' pints of beer, which was just enough information for the waiter to snuff out his cigarette with the heel of his boot and head inside to place an order at the bar.

"Did they cancel it entirely? Or is it an editing situation?" Shelby asked.

He appreciated her concern, but there were dynamics at his father's company that he didn't want to share with her just yet. Her friend Jenna already told her how a certain group of public relations staffers were responsible for many of the photographs that had been printed of Shelby and Ryan together, as well as of Shelby alone in the city. Shelby had been irate, considering it a blatant intrusion into her private life—which it was, clearly. In a convoluted way, it was also a calculated plan to generate public interest in Ryan's romantic life, with the hopes that a love story would also cast favorable light on Chambers Media.

This time, however, he didn't understand the company's intention. "Why would they do this now? With the debut roughly four months away? We have to either scrap the project entirely or go back and rework it, and God knows if we'd have enough time to get it right."

"Slow down," she said, pulling her chair closer to his and offering a consoling hand on his knee. "What did the e-mail say, exactly?"

The waiter interrupted with two pilsners poured into pint glasses. Ryan took several long sips of beer, staring blankly out on to the mountains before saying, "They love the photography and the premise, but they don't think there's enough emotional pull in the narrative. As it stands, the film is not good enough to meet the project objectives. It's lacking a—what did he call it?" Ryan rubbed the tension from the back of his neck while he recalled Cullie's message. "It's lacking a compelling theme to weave all of the stories together. At least that's the reason they're giving. It could be more. But that's just me, speculating."

"So you go back into editing and rework the script—can't you do that?"

"I wish it was that easy. We need better interviews, better writing. We'll need a talented editor who can help pull the new footage into what we've already shot, and—I don't know if it would even matter."

"You can't just go back to the original video and edit in new quotes?"

"The editor and I went over the B-roll thoroughly. I just

don't think it's going to be there," he said. "It's fine, Shel. I'm sure we can figure something out. Let's not worry about it now. As you said, right now we just need to focus on each other."

He set his hand over hers, but he was distracted; she wanted to help him find a solution.

"I just can't imagine that the film would lack an emotional connection. I mean, that's what prompted this entire project. Your personal connection to the lake and the people whom you've met there. And talking to people comes so easily to you."

"It's my fault, really. I should have done a better job with the interviews in the front end. The truth is, I don't think they really opened up to me. The people we spoke with didn't open up in a way that is compelling enough. It's missing that personal connection. That warmth," he said, thinking back to the time he spent on the road visiting small towns along the Lake Superior shoreline. "I recognized it at the time, and I was naïve to think we could cover it up in the final edits. And now the board is seeing through that."

"I still think you're being hard on yourself," she said. "But I know you have to do what you think is right. So, what's next?"

"I think the only thing we can do is go back and redo some of the interviews."

"Is there time?"

"Maybe, if we move quickly."

"When would you leave?"

"As soon as possible, I suppose. Early next week, if I can pull together the right people."

"So much for adjusting to married life. . . ."

"I know. This isn't at all what I had planned," he said. "It may take several weeks on the road. And then long hours editing in the studio."

"Take whatever time you need. You only get one shot at a debut—do whatever it takes to make it right."

When Ryan heard the *ding* on his phone's in-box, he opened up his e-mail and read a new message from his friend Brad.

From: Brad Thorson
To: Will Chambers
RE: media

Will—
I know you and Shelby are still traveling, and I don't want to disturb you. But if you happen to check your messages, I wanted to give you a heads-up that there's been a bit of news coverage building around your wedding. I know you anticipated that the news would get out eventually, and that it would be relatively light.

It's not light.

There's a bit of a shit storm brewing here. And your parents—especially your dad—are livid. It has something to do with Shelby's mom and that guy she was with at the wedding. And since you guys have been out of the country, these damn reporters say no one is corroborating the stories coming out of Bayfield—and it's sort of blown out of proportion.

So get ready to put out some fires when you get home. Or pray that something that's actually "news-worthy" happens soon and pulls these guys off of your story.

—Brad

"Do you have someone in mind to do the interviews?" Shelby asked, unaware of the second e-mail Ryan had just received. "You'd want someone who would come across easily to people—make them feel comfortable. Someone who would encourage them to open up, don't you think?"

"Yes," he replied, distracted by Brad's warning.

"What about that guy that I met in your office a while back, the one who worked on the Gateway Green project?"

"Jackson?"

"Right. Jackson," she said, nodding. "You told me that you loved his writing."

"He'd be perfect, except that he left the company for a job in New York back in April."

"So, get someone else to handle the interviews and script writing. Or postpone the shoot," she suggested. "It's not a timely piece. Would you ever consider releasing it next year instead?"

"I want to keep our commitment and debut it at the film festival. We rushed the final edits because of the wedding, and now we're up against this new deadline. If I don't deliver the film, corporate affairs will consider the project a failure and I'll have to find a new way to generate exposure for the fund."

"I wish there was something I could do."

They sat quietly, both of them looking out on to the mountainous landscape while deep in thought. After the wedding, he had hoped he wouldn't have to return soon to Lake Superior, where Olen's presence was distinctly felt on the farm and his ashes were now one with the lake. Ryan knew there would be occasional visits, holidays and long weekends at his and Shelby's cottage, but for the most part—if he was honest with himself—he had hoped she would feel free to visit often without him.

The dull ache of anxiety crept into his chest, building pressure that wrapped around to his shoulders. Pressing and squeezing. He rolled his shoulders and stretched out his back, to no avail. The only way to finish what he started, and to rid himself of guilt, was to face it head-on.

"What about me?" Shelby asked suddenly, breaking into his thoughts.

"Hmm?" he mumbled. "Sorry, Shel, what was that?"

"Let me help you," she said, her eyes lighting up.

He turned toward her with eyebrows raised, wondering if he had heard her correctly.

"It's the perfect solution. Why don't you let me do the interviews for you, which would free you up for production and editing. Just let me know which areas need to be redone. I know the area, and the background on your piece. We'd be the perfect team."

"I appreciate the offer, really," he said. "But I don't want you to have to traipse around with me. They'd be long days, a lot of running around. Very little sleep."

"Have you already forgotten that's where I grew up? I'm hardly a stranger to long days and hard work."

"No, I know that."

"Give me one good reason why this wouldn't work."

Because all I could think about during the shoot was your grandfather. Because the time that passes after his death only intensifies my feeling of responsibility, and if you knew, I know you'd never forgive me. He said nothing, instead holding back the truth.

"You don't think I'm good enough," she said. "Is that it?"

"No, of course not," he said quietly, looking away from her and back to the vast landscape that surrounded them.

"I get it."

He felt it immediately. That block of separation that forms between couples, which is felt but not seen, when one person lets down the other.

"I promise you, it has nothing to do with that. You're an exceptional writer, and I'd be lucky to have you on the team. In fact, you're right. You would be the ideal person to handle the new interviews. You know the area. You're incredible with people. I know you'd be able to bring out that warmth and personality that is seriously lacking."

"Then what is it?"

Because this piece has become less of a conservation story, and more about appeasing my own relentless guilt. Because the rewrite alone won't be enough to get this project back on track, and to pull you into the business side of this project would mean bringing you to the table with my father. Because the lines have blurred between professional and personal and I don't want you to see this side of me. Just not yet. And above all else, I want you to view it once it's perfect, so that maybe—God willing—I can find a glimmer of Olen's forgiveness through your eyes.

"Because I wanted to keep the final film a surprise for you. I really wanted to do this for you and your family. It's important to me because . . ." He paused.

"Because?"

"Your family has given me so much. This is something I can do in return."

"Well . . . keep it as a surprise, then."

"I knew you'd understand," he said, letting out a sigh of relief. "I'll make sure to arrange everything quickly. I don't want you to have to be in the city alone any longer than necessary."

"Actually, that's not what I was saying at all." Shelby shifted in her chair to face him. "I *am* coming with you. We're going to get those additional interviews, rework the narrative, and then—once we're back in Chicago—you can go off on your own to finish the piece with your editing team. In the meantime, I'll be happy to wait until you're ready to show it to me.

And, if we play our cards right, we'll finish everything in time for the film festival."

He saw the look of determination on her face and knew that, for her, the decision had been made. And, he had to admit, it made the most sense. Considering the time constraints of the project and the fact that she was right. She'd be the perfect person to do these final interviews, and he wouldn't have to worry about leaving her alone in Chicago to enter into her new life as a Chambers family member. He could protect her. It made sense. As long as he could also tell her about what really happened out on the ice that winter with Olen.

She would have to change her plans once more, putting Ryan's interests ahead of her own. On the one hand, he realized she would make the project better than anyone else could. They had interviews set up in towns that were like home to her, with people who loved the lake as much as she did. They would open up to her in ways he would never be able to achieve. On the other hand, he wasn't sure he'd be able to hide his feelings of cowardice and guilt that had hit him during the wedding—and that would surely be something to contend with on the road.

"So there have been a few setbacks," she said. "Your story will be wonderful. They're going to love it."

"You've made so many compromises to be with me already—more than your fair share. Are you sure you really want to do this?"

"Don't give it another thought," she said with a coy smile. "In fact, why don't we just think of it as an extended honeymoon."

His concern shifted to mischief. "Now I really can't take you along."

"What now?"

"You're going to be too much of a distraction. . . ."

CHAPTER 9

MOTHER MOON

While in Switzerland, after Ryan had agreed to Shelby's suggestion to join his video crew on the road, she made him promise that they wouldn't spend the last precious day of their honeymoon discussing the project. True to his word, Ryan kept his thoughts about copy edits and scene changes to himself during the remainder of their trip.

They spent most of their long flight home going over the Great Lakes project. Ryan described the overall story line to her, as well as highlights from the supporting interviews, but she kept thinking back to the company's feedback. The film lacked a narrative theme that could tie the stories together and spark a call to action for Great Lakes conservation. Ryan's interviews had gone well, but the story was lacking. *What's missing?*

"Excuse me, miss, would you care for a soda?" the stewardess asked as she arrived at Shelby and Ryan's row of seats on the airplane.

"No thank you," she answered. "But I'd love some water."

And that's when it hit her. The missing piece. The thing

she loved most about living on the south shore of Lake Superior. Water.

She turned to Ryan. "We need to include the lake in every interview. Whether we shoot an interview on a fishing dock, the beach, during a walk along the shore—even if it's just seen through a window, or off in the distance. I think the imagery of water is going to help you weave your interviews together."

A smile came over his face. "Remind me why I didn't bring you onto this project from the very beginning?"

By the time they dropped their bags in their apartment in Chicago, they had a plan. They bypassed the wedding gifts that were piled up for them in the dining room, quickly sorted through mail and phone messages, and barely took time to unpack. In a matter of days, Ryan had reviewed the original footage with their editor while Shelby reviewed the narrative and came up with a new angle for the additional interviews. Once they had their follow-up interviews set, they were ready to head up north with a small crew—just the two of them, a sound and lighting technician, and Ryan's original videographer. The newlyweds hadn't been in Chicago for more than a week before they were packing to leave again. Their Chicago life would be put on hold once more, and Shelby wasn't at all disappointed.

Thunder clouds were rolling out onto Lake Superior just as a black Chambers Media van passed a road sign that read, "Welcome to Tamarack, Wisconsin, Pop. 1,032." After making the long drive from Chicago, the vehicle turned onto Pine Street, which ran through the center of town. The van pulled up to the curb and parked in a residual stream of rain water that flowed down the street.

"Is this a good spot, Ryan, since you wanted to take a look around?" asked the driver, Cullie James, the burly cameraman who wore his dark hair long and flowing and his beard trimmed short across an angled jaw. He twisted in the driver's seat to speak with Shelby and Ryan, who sat together in the backseat. Shelby's eyes were fixed on the black-and-green serpent tattoo that lay coiled and seemed ready to attack from its perch on Cullie's right bicep.

"Don't you need help unloading?" Ryan asked.

"Nah, we can take care of it," insisted Tina Leighton, their sound and lighting technician, who sat in the front passenger seat.

Shelby had been surprised when she first met Tina in the Chambers Media parking lot as they loaded up the van. It hardly seemed possible that the petite woman with slight arms and legs would have the strength to handle the sound equipment, but she hoisted each box, boom, and crate with seemingly little effort. With her long blond braid, denim cutoffs, and fringed suede boots, Tina looked like she was heading to an indie folk concert rather than a photo assignment in northern Wisconsin.

"We'll meet you back here in. . . ." Cullie said, looking down at his watch and then up at Tina. "Let's say, what—an hour or so? Five o'clock?"

"Maybe closer to five thirty," Tina muttered under her breath to Cullie, then diverted her eyes and turned toward her window.

Pine Street was deserted, aside from an elderly couple dressed in raincoats and walking along the sidewalk with plastics bags stretched full of groceries dangling from their fisted hands. "Sure. Looks like there's a little pizza place about a block up." Shelby pointed in the direction of a rectangular red sign that extended over the doorway of a converted bank building. "We could meet there."

"Mama Pott's," Cullie said as he read the sign aloud. "Got it."

Shelby opened her car door and breathed in the cool Lake Superior air that reminded her of home. The lake breeze felt cool on her skin and was rich in the earthy scent of balsam, pine, and summer rain. She stretched out her legs, stiff from the long trip, took hold of her purse and notebook, and stepped out of the van.

Cullie and Tina gave Shelby and Ryan a hasty good-bye, giving them just enough time to step up onto the curb before they drove off down Pine, turned at the first corner, and disappeared.

"So, this is Tamarack," Ryan said, looking around to get his bearings in this, the first of several stops on their trip.

"I haven't been here for *years,* and even then, we just drove through."

"I'm glad you're here. I have a feeling people are going to talk to you a lot more freely than they did with me, during the first round of interviews."

"I hope so. But say—completely unrelated—did you know about those two before they signed on for this project?" she asked her husband.

"Cullie and Tina?"

Shelby nodded.

"Not in the slightest."

She peered down the street and could make out Lake Superior glistening in the near distance, just beyond the bend in the road where Pine Street curved north. "Such an unlikely couple."

"Some have said that about us," he teased.

"We're back on my turf now—let's try to forget about the media."

"Shelby, have you forgotten? Today, you *are* the media."

They laughed and rehashed some of the stories they had heard on the car ride—Tina's retelling of her days as a backup singer on a cruise ship that traversed the Bahamas, and Cullie's regaling them with colorful anecdotes about growing up in Las Vegas with his single father.

"Just when you think you know someone," Ryan said in a way that brought them to laughter, the sound seeming to carry down the otherwise quiet street.

Shelby noticed a bearded man with a sleeveless shirt, roomy jeans, and orange suspenders had paused at the entrance to a nearby bar and was giving them a curious look.

"Don't look now, but we're being watched," she whispered to Ryan with a nudge.

Ryan nodded toward the man, which was enough to cause him to break his stare and head up the street.

"I need to stretch my legs," Ryan said, taking a good look at the downtown area. "Are you up for a walk?"

"I'd love to, except that I'm wiped out—and a bit light-headed," she admitted, hoping she wasn't coming down with something. "I didn't eat much on the ride up—I'm sure that's it. Are you hungry?"

"No, but I'll sit with you. How about we go to that place we saw on the corner . . . what was it called?" He looked for the red sign. "Mama Pott's."

"You don't need to do that. I'll be fine." They were standing in front of a building that had a sign above its weathered door. It simply read: BAR. There was something about its simplicity that piqued her interest. *If nothing else, it might make for a good story later,* she thought.

"Why don't you take a walk, and I'll go grab a table inside this place. You can meet me back here when you're done."

"It's mid-afternoon and you're already hitting the bar?" he asked, shaking his head with a grin. "Well, that's *one* way to kick off this leg of the trip."

"Consider it research. You do know that one of the best

ways to get acquainted with a small town is to stop in the corner bar, don't you?"

"I'll have to take your word for it."

"I'll chalk that up as reason number three hundred why I am the perfect person to help you finish this job."

"You are." Ryan brushed the side of her cheek and then drew her in for a brief kiss. "Call me if you need anything. Do you have your phone?"

She searched through her purse until she came up with the cell phone he had given her shortly after moving to Chicago. She rarely used it, or kept it properly charged. Shelby wasn't interested in having an online presence or being dependent on a device, but she knew it was important for Ryan to stay connected.

Ryan walked down the street alone while Shelby slipped her phone back into her purse and approached the bar. When she pulled open the heavy door, Shelby was greeted by the pungent aroma of beer-stained wood, fryer grease, and stale smoke that still lingered in the thick folds of drapes that blacked out the sunlight. A Rolling Stones ballad crooned quietly from the wall speakers mounted in four corners of the space. As she approached the bar, Shelby noticed the impressive nautical motif carved into its edging. The floorboards creaked beneath each step, as if she were walking along the deck of an old fishing boat.

Aside from her and the bartender, there were no more than a handful of people in the place. Most of them sat together at the table closest to the television, watching a Brewers game.

"Hey," said the bartender from behind the tall bar.

"Hey," Shelby replied, looking over the bartender's shoulder at a message written on the chalkboard behind him. *Ask me about Crafts,* it read. "Okay, I'm game," she said to him. "What can you tell me about craft beers?"

He returned her smile with a knowing nod and replied,

"Well, to put it mildly, I'm pretty obsessed with Wisconsin craft beers. Minnesota brews, too, for that matter. I always have a couple of cold ones on hand for people to try. Always something different."

"I'm in."

"Excellent," he said, leaning down to open the fridge beneath the bar. "Let's see . . . today I have New Glarus Totally Naked, Hopalicious from Asylum, a couple of Lift Bridge Hop Dish out of Stillwater—and a Fatty Boombalatty."

While most people were drawn to the unique flavors of craft beers, it was the interesting names that Shelby enjoyed most. "I'll try that last one." Shelby set down her purse and peered over the bar to see what he would pull from the fridge.

"Boombalatty?"

"That's the one."

He set down a brown bottle with its denim blue and yellow label in front of her. After paying, she lifted the bottle and tipped it in his direction with a "thanks," grabbed her purse, and left to find an empty table.

Shelby felt more at ease in this nameless bar than she did in the upscale restaurants and clubs she visited in Chicago with Ryan. Those venues were beautiful and the food was incredible, but she had more appreciation for mismatched card stock coasters with embossed logos of local beers, dinner plates with simple food, and wood-planked walls covered in curious mementoes and old photographs—staples of the places she had known growing up.

After taking a few sips of the beer, Shelby slid her bottle aside and opened her notebook. She then removed the profile sheet that was tucked inside: *Mr. Helge Wilmer—Wilmer Fishery.* Their crew was set to meet Mr. Wilmer down at his boat dock precisely at five the next morning to join him and his grandson as they trolled for whitefish out on the lake. She reread

Ryan's notes on the profile sheet, which indicated that the Wilmer family had been fishing in the area since 1906. The family represented five generations—more than one hundred descendants born and raised in a single community—and today, four households remained in Tamarack. As the oldest living family member, Mr. Wilmer was as close as it comes to the town's living historian.

Shelby was reaching into her purse for a pen when a woman appeared, as if from out of nowhere, and pulled out the chair across from Shelby.

"This seat is taken," the woman asked, but it wasn't a question. She had a plump, weathered face that was the color of tea and milk, and her ash-gray hair was pulled back into a loose braid that roped down her spine. She suddenly burst into a smile that was as vibrant as her orange *Go Jump in the Lake* T-shirt.

"Actually, I'm waiting for my husband." Considering the way she met Nic at a Chicago sandwich shop nearly a year earlier, and the betrayal that followed, Shelby had learned her lesson. With narrowed eyes, her hands clenched, and with squared-off shoulders, Shelby set up her wall; she wouldn't be susceptible to another chance encounter. "The seat's taken."

Not taking the hint, the elderly woman pulled the chair away from the table with a loud scrape against the flooring and settled in. She then turned toward the bar, raised her arm, and snapped her fingers at the bartender. Once she had his attention, she pointed to the empty space on table in front of her. Without needing her order, he promptly brought her a basket of potato chips and what appeared to be a lowball of bourbon on ice.

"Name's Bernice," the woman told Shelby before popping a chip into her mouth and exposing boxy teeth that were cigarette stained and slightly gray beneath the enamel. "And you are . . . ?"

"My name is Shelby." She watched Bernice's eyes for any

sign of recognition. Growing up in Bayfield, she enjoyed getting to know people like Bernice. Social Midwesterners who enjoyed stories, making connections, and discovering "what makes someone tick." Since moving to Chicago, however, she had learned the importance of protecting her privacy—something she hadn't fully grasped until after meeting Jenna. Shelby looked toward the door, knowing that she ought to leave at the first sign that Bernice was probing into her married life.

"What kind of name is Shelby? You from around here?"

"I grew up just north of here."

"Porcupine Lake?"

She doesn't seem to know me, Shelby thought, relieved. "Bayfield."

"Ah, Bayfield," Bernice said, leaning back in her chair. "Then you know Red Cliff."

"Yes, of course." Red Cliff was a Native American community located on the lakeshore just north of Bayfield.

The ice shifted in the bourbon and clinked against the glass as Bernice took her first long sip. Setting the glass down beside the chip bowl, she tried unsuccessfully to muffle a belch within the pouches of her sagging cheeks. She cracked a smile that offered no apology.

"I have a niece who works at the new casino up there. At least I think she does. Haven't seen her in a while. . . ." Bernice said. "That's her son over there, behind the bar. Nelson."

Shelby nodded, looking in his direction.

"Everybody just *loves* Nelson," Bernice added before taking another drink and nestling her fingers back into the chip bowl. "It's those brown eyes. Real trustworthy kid, that one."

Shelby looked in the direction of the young man drying a beer glass with a striped bar towel. He must have noticed because, when he looked up and their eyes met, he smiled.

"Of course, my husband, Emmit, had blue eyes. Blue eyes that were so big and bright, it was almost like he had two little robin's eggs nestled in his head. A bit strange, really. But he was a keeper."

Shelby lifted her beer to her lips, but then decided against it. A slight wave of nausea came over her. She set the bottle back down and pushed it aside. Perhaps it was the beer or smell of wet potato chips on Bernice's breath. *Long day,* she thought to herself, willing herself not to get sick during the trip. "It was nice to meet you, Bernice, but I have to get going."

As Shelby pushed her chair back, Bernice asked, "Before you leave, would you like to talk about your children?"

"I'm sorry. I think you're mistaking me for someone else." Shelby slipped the interview sheet back into her notebook and slung her purse over her shoulder. "I don't have any children."

"Oh, there's no mistake," Bernice said with assurance. "I have a keen sense about the strength of family trees, and I sense the foundation you're creating with your husband is strong. Being married to a man who lives in the public eye and puts you on a pedestal, it makes me wonder why you're sitting here having a drink with an old woman."

Family trees?

Shelby wasn't sure if she heard Bernice correctly. There was something about her expression as she mentioned family trees—as if she knew, somehow, that Shelby had always considered her grandparents' apple orchard a metaphor for family. Her intuition told her to look past her experiences in Chicago—where photographers cross boundaries, and aspects of her private life are made public—and trust in the inherent good nature of people. For that's how she was raised.

Shelby set her things back on the table and sat down.

"So you say you're from Bayfield?" Bernice continued.

Shelby nodded, reaching for her beer bottle—not to drink, but to keep her hands occupied.

"Mmm," Bernice said, and nodded. "But you don't live there now."

"I'm married," Shelby said simply. "We drove up from Illinois."

"Yes. You're part of that film crew, aren't you?"

Shelby nodded again. "You're mistaken about children, you know. Not all women are meant to be parents."

"That's true. That's very true," Bernice said. "But you are."

"I don't have a child."

"Just because he isn't in your arms doesn't mean he isn't here."

Shelby sighed. *This is crazy.*

"Have you been down to the water yet?" Bernice asked, mercifully changing the subject.

"Not yet."

"Hmm. That surprises me. You don't feel drawn to it?"

"Of course. Isn't everyone?"

Bernice said nothing.

"Actually, we're going out on a boat tomorrow morning."

"Ah." Bernice picked up her glass and swirled the ice around in it, listening as it bounced along the inside of the lowball glass like chimes clinking in a breeze. "Have you ever heard of a woman named Louisa May Alcott?" Bernice asked before raising the drink to her lips.

So many questions! Shelby realized how Bernice had so cleverly changed the tables on her. She was the one who was in town to conduct the interviews, and yet she was the one providing all of the answers. *Louisa May Alcott?* Bernice waited patiently for an answer.

"Does she live here in town?" Shelby asked.

"Nope."

It took a moment before recognition set in. Junior high school. The shelf in her childhood bedroom that was laden with books. "The author?" Shelby remembered reading Alcott's *Little Women* when she was thirteen or fourteen years old. It had been her grandmother's recommendation. In a flash of memory,

Shelby pictured her younger self sitting on the couch beside her grandmother and reading aloud the March girls' story. They took turns reading, passing the book back and forth after every few pages or so. When her grandmother read, Shelby sat close beside her and listened to the story while watching a fire flicker and glow in the fireplace. Shelby missed that time when it was just the three of them, herself and her grandparents, and life was simpler.

"Yes, the author. She also wrote poetry."

"I didn't know that," Shelby wondered where this was all going. She glanced over her shoulder to the door. Still no sign of Ryan.

"'As the tranquil evening moon looks on that restless sea, / So a mother's gentle face, / Little child, is watching thee,'" Bernice recited with gentle inflection, all the while looking into Shelby's eyes.

"That's lovely, but I'm not sure what that has to do with—" Shelby began before being interrupted by Bernice.

"Those words were written over a century ago, and yet they are perfect for you today. On this very day, in fact. They are perfect for *you.*"

"I don't understand."

"You are drawn to the lake like a child to her mother. Your Mother Moon is always there for you. She shines down upon you and Lake Superior's waters. She takes care of those you love, while you live your life grieving. While you live your life afraid."

"Excuse me?" Shelby chuckled and shook her hand as if to wave off the suggestion. "I'm not afraid."

"And she will be there for you when your first child is born. When you need her, she'll be waiting for you at the lake. When you need answers, go to her," Bernice said before easing her chair away from the table and standing up. She walked over to Shelby and, tipping her head slightly to the side and giving a knowing nod, set a gentle hand upon Shelby's shoulder. "Come on; you look like you've seen a ghost. Don't you go worrying or thinking I'm some crazy old soothsayer. I was just messin' with you, honey."

Without saying another word, Bernice dropped her hand from Shelby's shoulder and swung it to the rhythm of her steps as she sauntered across the bar, called out, "Be good, Nelson!" to the bartender, and continued toward door.

Shelby was left alone in the corner with the sudsy remains of her Boombalatty, dumbfounded by her encounter with an oddly endearing woman, and the notion that a nineteenth-century poem about her "Mother Moon" could possibly reflect her life. Looking across the table, Shelby saw that Bernice had left a folded copy of the town's weekly beside her empty glass. The partial headline read: "Chambers to Visit . . ." So that was it, Shelby thought. Their stop in Tamarack had made the news and Bernice saw an opportunity to have a little fun with her.

Ryan entered the bar just as Bernice reached the door. Coming face-to-face with him, Bernice paused, then looked over her shoulder and gave Shelby a knowing nod.

CHAPTER 10

FOG AND WAVES

Several days into their trip, Shelby, Ryan, Tina, and Cullie had established a rhythm. Grab coffee and a quick breakfast at a diner—every town on their route had one—and then head to the interview location that they had scouted out the evening before. Cullie and Tina would handle the equipment and Ryan would set the shot while Shelby went through her notes, making any last-minute changes before their interviewee arrived.

On this morning, they parked the van at Hamilton Beach and waited for Beth Dillard to arrive for her interview. No one seemed concerned that the lake view was completely hidden beneath a heavy shroud of morning fog. In fact, since they were early, Ryan disappeared into the fog as he walked down to the beach while the others remained in the van.

"I checked the footage last night and we have some pretty good stuff," Cullie said before grabbing his foil-wrapped egg sandwich and taking a messy, yolk-and-mayo-dripping bite.

"Gross," Tina grumbled, offering him a paper napkin. She sat slouched down low in front passenger seat with her long, slender legs stretched out and her bare feet propped up on the console. Tina held a paper cup of coffee in her hand and stared out at the fog that enveloped their van. Shelby had learned early on that Tina would be in this state of morning irritation until the caffeine kicked in and her personality warmed to tepid.

"My favorite interview so far was Wilmer, the fisherman from Tamarack. You'd never know it from looking at him, but *damn,* he was like a walking textbook on the lake," Cullie said.

"He was," Shelby replied as she sat in the back, pulling off pieces of her cranberry muffin and popping them into her mouth. There was something about the fog. She couldn't stop staring at it through the car window. She could imagine Bernice walking out of the mist, her hair braided down her back, reciting poetry about a mother moon who can "chase all your clouds away." Shelby hadn't told Ryan about her encounter with Bernice. How could she, when she hardly understood it herself?

"I felt like I was right back in school. In fact, that guy should be a professor or something," Cullie said with admiration.

"He's like . . . eighty years old," Tina grumbled from the front seat.

"Well, he doesn't act like it," Cullie replied. "All that knowledge about ecological changes in the lake. The impact on the fishing industry here in this area. Jesus. I had no idea."

Helge Wilmer's accounts about the impact climate change was having on Lake Superior and the Great Lakes as a whole hadn't been a surprise to Shelby. She had been hearing about it for years from her grandfather and his fishing companions. But it was heartbreaking nonetheless. During Mr. Wilmer's interview, he explained how environmental changes were adding stress to the lakes by altering water temperature to levels that were more suitable for invasive species, drying the coastal wetlands that served as pollution filters, and increasing the occurrence of violent storms. It affected the fisheries and Mr. Wilmer's livelihood.

The fog continued to hover around the van without showing signs of rising. The vehicle seemed warm, too warm. The air felt stagnant and reeked of eggs and Cullie's "lucky" socks—which she found out the night before he only washes at the end of the video shoots as part of a strange superstition.

"Hey, Tina, would you mind calling Beth? Tell her that we're going to postpone the shoot for another hour or so, until the fog lifts? I'm sure she'll understand," Shelby said as she opened the van door.

"Fine," Tina huffed, making it clear that she did not want to initiate a conversation so early in the morning.

"Where ya headed?" Cullie asked. Nothing remained of his sandwich but a smear of yolk on his chin.

"A little fresh air—and I'll see if I can find Ryan," Shelby said. "I'll just be a minute."

Shelby couldn't see the shoreline through the fog, but she could hear the waves breaking on the sand. She walked toward the sound, enjoying the feel of the cool mist on her skin. It helped to clear her head.

She made her way across the narrow strip of beach to the water's edge. The only part of the expansive lake that was within view was the frothy wash of waves that rolled over the pebbled shoreline. Out on the water, she couldn't see much farther than a stone's throw distance before the fog shrouded the view. Looking over her shoulder, she couldn't see the van, and there were no signs of Ryan. She didn't call out his name, for she wanted some time alone.

She sat down on the beach and dragged her fingers through the fine grains of sand, making patterns and swirls around her crossed legs. She realized it was the first time she had been alone in weeks.

It wasn't long before the sun warmed the morning air enough to begin lifting the fog off of the water. Shelby picked up a handful of the sand and let the grains fall through the cracks between her fingers. A new idea was becoming clear. There was more to the Great Lakes story. She stood up from her spot on the beach and brushed the sand from her clothes as she started back toward the van, knowing how they would turn the project around in a way that would really honor her grandfather. Unlike so-called journalists like Jenna, Shelby knew she could do better. The written word, when based on truth, would always have the ability to make a positive impact.

CHAPTER 11

SAVE YOURSELF

Several weeks after finishing the video tour and returning home to Chicago, Ryan and Shelby's newlywed life felt more exciting and real now that their travels were over and they were settled in his apartment. In *their* apartment.

Ryan had been up early and was now reentering the dimly lit bedroom, expecting Shelby to be awake. "Good news, Shelby, we're all set! I just got off the phone with Cullie. He's logged all of the footage—from Tamarack to Grand Marais—and today we're all set to—"

"Stop," she interrupted. "Stay over there. You don't want to kiss me this morning." Shelby moaned, rolling onto her side and pulling the quilt up tighter beneath her chin. "I think I have the flu."

"Is that so?" He walked to her side of the bed, carrying a glass of ginger ale. "Big day today. We need to head over to the studio, remember? That actor we hired is recording voice-overs today—voice-overs for the script that *you* wrote. I know you wouldn't want to miss it."

"I mean it. I feel awful." She turned away from him and rolled onto her other side. "Keep your distance."

He set the ginger ale on her bedside table and sat down next to her on the bed. "I'll take my chances."

She pulled a blanket over her head and groaned from beneath it. "Go. Away. Save yourself."

He rubbed her back through the bedding. "You don't have the flu, Shel."

She groaned.

"Or food poisoning," he added.

"I'm pretty sure I'm contagious. Go on without me."

He pulled down a corner of the blanket, just far enough that he could see her head pushed deep into her pillow. "You're pregnant."

With that, her eyes opened wide, she threw the covers off of her body and darted into the bathroom. Ryan shook his head as he heard his wife suffering from nausea again, as she had for the past several mornings. He knew she would rebound within the hour, be tired throughout the day, and continue with her new aversion to poultry.

The pregnancy had been his mother's observation, not his own. Charlotte had stopped by a week ago, saying she was "in the area" when clearly she hadn't been. His mother had been making notes on their apartment and its slow transition from a bachelor pad into a family home. He wasn't in a rush and Shelby hadn't expressed interest, so Charlotte seemed to feel it was her responsibility to "help" by having a new rug delivered, or bringing over a vase that she came upon at her favorite Michigan Avenue boutique. If Ryan or Shelby gave her even the slightest encouragement, Charlotte would have her interior designer knocking at their door within hours.

"It's in her complexion as clear as day, William. I'm as certain that Shelby is pregnant as I am that the sun will come up again in the morning," his mother had told him in the foyer after Shelby had said good-bye and gone into the bedroom to lie down.

"Pregnant?" Ryan whispered, completely taken aback.

"From the look on your face, I take it this wasn't planned?"

"Well, no. I mean we always . . . but no, not really." He ran his hands through his hair and thought back on the past several weeks. Had he noticed the symptoms? Had she? Shelby never mentioned her period being late or anything else that would have been a clear sign. In fact, whenever he brought up the subject of their future family she scoffed at the idea. It surprised him that a woman with such natural abilities to care for others and connect with children wouldn't want to think about raising her own someday.

"Mmm-hmm," Charlotte said knowingly. She set her purse down on the entryway table and proceeded directly to Ryan and Shelby's kitchen. With him walking behind her, a dazed yet delighted look on his face, Charlotte proceeded to rummage about the kitchen until she found two cans of ginger ale and a box of water crackers. "Bring this to her. Make sure she eats slowly before stepping foot out of her bed each morning. Believe me, it will help. Before long, the nausea will wear off and she'll feel back to her old self. When that time comes, be prepared to provide her with anything and everything she wants to nourish herself and the baby. When I was pregnant with you, I couldn't eat enough banana flapjacks."

Ryan took the ginger ale and crackers but didn't move. "Banana flapjacks?"

"Come on, now," his mother said, and swooshed him out of the kitchen with a wave of her arms. "I'll help myself out. You're going to be a father—now go take care of your family!"

Shelby padded slowly back from the bathroom, looking miserable.

"Feel better?" Ryan asked.

"I'm *not* pregnant."

"But hasn't it been a while since you had you last . . . *you know* . . . ?"

"When did you become such an expert?" She swung back into bed and punched her pillow before setting down her head. "Sorry. Didn't mean to snap."

"Well . . . is it possible?"

She groaned and stared blankly at the bedroom wall, seemingly doing the math in her head and putting the pieces together. Finally, she rolled over onto her back and looked up at Ryan, who was sitting down on the edge of the bed beside her. She suggested a possible date with a sigh.

"But that's, what—" he wondered aloud, counting out the weeks in his head.

"About nine weeks. Give or take," she said before he reached the same conclusion.

"Shelby, that's wonderful!" He leaned down to kiss her full on the lips, unable to contain his excitement.

"Is it?"

"What?"

"Nothing," she said, and smiled, reflecting his happiness.

He set his hand tenderly on her abdomen. "A baby!" he said in wonder, cracking open a can of the ginger ale and extending it to Shelby.

"A baby," she repeated quietly.

"A baby!" Ginny shrieked into the phone when Shelby called her later that day to share the news. "I can't believe it. So soon! I mean, not *too* soon, of course, but it's just that—my goodness, I'm going to be a grandmother!"

"Actually, Gran, technically you'd be—"

"Oh, hush. I'm much too young to be a *great*-grandmother, Shelby. Don't you dare teach that baby of yours to call me Great-Grandma. No, no. We'll definitely have to come up with something better than that. Oh, Shelby, isn't this wonderful!" her grandmother gushed.

"It is," Shelby said, unable to deny her grandmother's joy.

"How far along are you? I have to put these dates in my calendar right away. Do you have a physician picked out yet? I'm sure Ryan's family can recommend the best care."

"Slow down, Gran." Shelby laughed. "This is all new for us. I'm sure we'll have plenty of time to figure all of that out."

Shelby had been speaking with her grandmother regularly since moving to Chicago and always looked forward to their calls. Although at times Ginny's stories were redundant, as time had a way of making her more forgetful, the routine and ease of their conversations helped Shelby get through some of the difficulties she had encountered while living in the city.

After their talk of the baby, Ginny carefully switched topics.

"I read the story that your friend Jenna wrote for *The Daily*—although, frankly, we can't really call her a friend now, can we?"

"No." Shelby leaned her head against the plush back of the armchair and ran her fingers across the smooth fabric on its armrest. Shortly after their return from Switzerland, she and Ryan read the article Jenna had written for a regional magazine. Its coverage was limited, but through social media the story had traveled well beyond the Midwest. It had been a betrayal of trust unlike anything that Shelby had ever experienced. It made her mother's harsh words seem mild in comparison.

"Why didn't you tell me earlier? When you first read the article?"

"I didn't see the point of it, Gran. It would have only upset you. And Mom," Shelby said. "Maybe I just hoped it would go away."

"Little did Ryan Chambers know when he married Wisconsin native Shelby Meyers in an idyllic June wedding in the Bayfield countryside that he was entering into a family of wolves" was how Jenna had started her article. She went on to dismantle all of the qualities that made Shelby proud of her family—things that she had confided in Jenna during a time when she needed a friend to trust in her new surroundings.

Shelby had unknowingly given Jenna the story she had been waiting for when she asked for her help in tracking down Chad Covington.

> The shiny façade of the Chambers Media legacy wasn't just scratched on that fateful wedding day; it was shattered. Imagine William Chambers Sr.'s astonishment when he discovered that his new daughter-in-law was in fact the illegitimate child of a man who, for roughly 25 years, had abandoned his parental responsibilities. Although, considering the list of men who could have fathered William Chambers Jr.'s bride, perhaps it simply took that long to identify him as the rightful male.

"I have the mind to call up the editor of that filthy publication myself and give them something real to talk about!" Ginny said.

"No, I don't want to make it worse."

"I don't know how you do it."

I'm not doing it, Shelby thought, but wouldn't admit it to her grandmother. The truth would only cause her more concern and worry about something that she had no control over. That was the last thing Shelby wanted.

"How is Mom taking this?" she asked.

"She's pretty tight-lipped about it all," Ginny said, and then paused before continuing. "I've said it before, but I've honestly seen a noticeable change in her since she moved back to the farm. And as for Chad, he really isn't as bad as everyone's making him out to be. Truly, Shelby, he's become a big help around here."

"I believe you."

> *Dear Shelby,*
>
> *I haven't heard from you in a while, but I know you've been busy with everything. I feel like we need to talk about what happened on your wedding day with Chad, and everything. We're not really ones to talk over the phone, so maybe we can find some time to talk during your next visit home. There are some things that you just don't understand, and you and I know that what they're writing in the press is pure bullshit.*
>
> *Anyway. Gran seems to be doing well. I think we'll have a strong harvest this year. Hard not to think about Dad at this time of year, but you know that better than anyone. Congratulations again on the baby. You must be getting very excited. We all are.*
>
> *Love, Mom*

CHAPTER 12

SILVER REFLECTIONS

Shelby had always been a light sleeper, and pregnancy made it even worse. Even though her baby's kicks and jabs were gentle at this time in her pregnancy, she was like the princess and the pea—she was unable to sleep if she felt even the smallest discomfort. When Shelby was awake, Ryan often woke up with her and tried to do what he could to soothe her back to sleep. The trouble was, even when he could coax Shelby back to sleep, he couldn't do the same for himself.

That was how Ryan had given up on sleep by five o'clock on this autumn morning and was already in the kitchen quietly brewing a pot of coffee while Shelby remained in the bedroom curled up in a cocoon of blankets.

In bare feet and wearing pajama pants tied loosely at the hip, a freshly brewed mug of coffee in hand, Ryan entered the living room without turning on the lights and sat down in an oversized chair by the window. While tired, he appreciated the quiet.

Gazing out the window, Ryan watched the sun make its slow rise over the lake. He regretted how the past several months seemed to have passed by quickly in a series of deadlines and tasks. While he had become consumed with work that was un-expectedly rewarding, he also knew that the consequence was being away from his wife during her first year in the Chambers family. She was an adventurous soul, and he loved that about her. He knew that she would no sooner hole away in this apartment than an eagle would stay confined in its nest.

But the venturing out, naïve to her new environment, had been detrimental to her spirit. Shelby enjoyed the people she met in the city. It was the media she abhorred. And they had been ruthless in catching her in all of her awkward moments, skewing the truth and portraying her as cold, all for the sake of a "good" story.

"Say what they like," she often said. "No one really cares about where I go, or what I wear. God knows there is much more pressing news in the world than what's happening in my life."

He set down his coffee on the end table by his side and stood up and stretched his back against the light of an autumn sunrise that shone through the windows.

Not wanting to wake Shelby, Ryan didn't even take time to shower. He simply threw on a pullover and jeans, grabbed his leather jacket and a gray knit hat, and, in a last-minute de-cision, slung his camera over his shoulder. Heading down the elevator before anyone else in his building seemed to stir, he was eager to walk freely through Millennium Park as he had countless times during his bachelor days.

Ryan walked unnoticed across the grassy park lawns, with no particular plan or destination in mind. Simply being out-doors, alone with his thoughts and free from his obligations, was enough.

He had quickly scribbled a note for Shelby and left it on the kitchen counter where she was sure to find it once she eventually woke for the day. He knew, without having to ask, that she would have encouraged the long morning walk.

"I love you too much to watch you put your interests on hold. You need to get outside. Take photographs. I hardly ever see you pick up your camera anymore. You're much too talented to put it aside." What she didn't know—what he hadn't confessed to her—was that he had tried to take photographs many times over the past several months but that his work left him unsatisfied. He wasn't sure if it was the city, the people he came upon, or a lapse in his own creativity, but none of his recent photographs gave him as much pleasure as those from Bayfield and his first Chicago exhibit, *Family Trees*.

The other part of the reason, which he wouldn't let on to Shelby during her pregnancy, was that the increase in media attention that spiraled after their wedding and the disruption caused by her mother and Chad Covington made it nearly impossible for Ryan to do the work he loved. Now he and Shelby were drawing more attention than ever before. What he loved most about his photographic work was being able to capture portraits that offered a glimpse into a person's personality, not merely a moment in their life. And the only way he was able to do that successfully was to be unnoticed, to activate his camera's shutter without being seen.

He would never blame his wife for affecting his work in this way—she wanted the attention even less than he did—but life had changed dramatically for both of them since their return from Switzerland.

Following a trail of windswept fall leaves along a walking path, he continued until he reached the *Cloud Gate*. It was a sculpture by Anish Kapoor that was the centerpiece of the park's central plaza and usually attracted a large gathering of onlookers. Referred to by many as "The Bean" because of its shape, the piece was made of 168 stainless-steel plates that were welded together and highly polished. The exterior had no visible seams and appeared like an organic mirror with a surface that reflected and distorted the city's skyline.

He stopped to sit down at a vacant bench near *Cloud Gate* to rest a moment, realizing it was getting late and he should begin to think about heading back to the apartment soon. Shelby was certainly awake by now, and they had a full afternoon planned. It was then that he saw a small child dart out from behind the sculpture. Ryan looked around the empty plaza. The child appeared to be alone, although Ryan assumed that was only temporary. The young boy had probably run ahead of whoever was caring for him.

The child wore blue jeans, a light-blue sweatshirt with the hood tucked out of the back of a zipped jacket that was the same red as his sneakers. Ryan watched as the boy ran in circles with his arms spread out like airplane wings, spinning and gliding over concrete pavers and crisp leaves. He seemed filled with boundless energy, delighted and free to run with the leaves, seemingly unstoppable until he noticed his reflection in "The Bean" and stopped abruptly.

Ryan reached for his camera, removed the lens cap and placed it in his jacket pocket, and then raised the camera to his eye. He looked through the viewfinder eyepiece and he carefully adjusted the focus until the boy was clearly in view.

From this angle, seated on the bench on the perimeter of the plaza, unnoticed by the child, Ryan smiled as the boy considered his reflection in the sculpture's shiny surface. His head tilted to one side and then the other. Then the boy stuck out his tongue and Ryan took his first shot.

Click.

Then the boy wiggled his body, slightly at first and then in a wild dance of arms and legs twisting and kicking in a manic dance of childhood zeal. Ryan chuckled to himself.

Click.

The boy then stopped dancing and walked toward the

sculpture with his hand extended toward it. As he moved closer, his reflection reached back. Considering the sky that was also reflected in the piece, the overall image through Ryan's camera lens left him with the impression of a boy on earth reaching out to another child in the clouds. Ryan zoomed in closer, narrowing in on the shot, and wasn't able to pinpoint exactly what it was about the scene that made his heart ache. A child reaching out. A heavenly boy unable to leave the clouds and dance with his reflection on the cement pavers and scattered leaves. A young life yearning for more.

Click.

The moment ended as quickly as it began, with the boy's parents rushing out from behind the sculpture with frantic words. His father grabbed him firmly by the crux of his elbow and they continued off to another area of the park. Ryan was glad that no one had noticed him, as he now realized it could have been awkward to have to explain himself—a man sitting alone on a park bench taking photos of children. *Wouldn't the tabloids love to twist that story into something contemptible?*

When he stood up to replace his lens cap on his camera and begin his walk back home, he felt his cell phone vibrate in his pocket. He slung the camera back over his shoulder and withdrew the phone as he walked.

MISSED CALL (2): SHELBY

"Shit," he muttered, wondering how he had managed to miss her twice. She had even left a message.

"Hey, it's me. I know you're on a walk. Don't rush home," came the sound of her voice, livelier than he had heard for a while. Quite a while, actually, and the sound of it made him smile. *God, I missed this side of her,* he thought. He hadn't realized how much of her spirit had slipped away until he listened to her brief message. How had he not noticed it before? "I just wanted to let you know that we have a surprise weekend guest. She just showed up unannounced—to join us at the Film Festival tonight! You'll just have to come home and see for yourself!" Shelby had hung up in the midst of laughter. That sweet, giddy laughter of the optimistic woman he had married. At this point, as he picked up his speed to walk back to their apartment, he didn't care who was visiting. Whoever it was could stay for the weekend. Hell, he wouldn't mind if it was the entire week or more. There was only one thing he cared about.

Shelby sounded happy.

The surprise guest turned out to be Nic Palmer, Shelby's best friend and Ryan's good fortune. If anyone could help draw out the lighter side of Shelby's personality, it was Nic. The two had called one another regularly since the wedding, often talking long into the evening. When Shelby moved into another room of their apartment, Nic cornered Ryan in the kitchen.

"So, is it as bad as I think it is?"

"You mean Shelby?" he asked.

"Over the phone, she isn't telling me stories anymore. It's almost as if she's telling me what she thinks I want to hear—proving to me that everything is *normal*. You and I both know it's a crock."

Later that evening, Ryan dressed in a dark-charcoal suit and a crisp white, open-collared dress shirt to attend the long-awaited film release. When a black chauffeured town car arrived to take them to the Whitney Theatre, Ryan proudly stepped out of their apartment with his wife, who was dressed beautifully in an ethereal empire-waist navy-blue dress with a beaded bodice and airy skirt that fell softly over her pregnant silhouette.

"You're going to be the most beautiful woman there," he told her as he took her hand and helped her into the backseat of the car. She touched his cheek and smiled before gathering the fabric of her skirt and settling into the seat.

"Hey, what about me?" came the distinctive voice behind him. "What am I? Chopped liver?" Nic quipped, as she followed the couple to the car.

"Of course not." He laughed. "No one is going to outshine you tonight, Nic. You look incredible."

"Now that's what I like to hear," she said, moving past Ryan to open the front passenger side door. "I paid good money for this dress."

"Nic, there's room for you to sit with us."

"What? And miss getting a front-row view of downtown Chicago at night?" she said, looking at him as if his idea were absurd. "No thank you." Nic slid into the front seat next to the driver without giving Ryan a chance to assist. He wondered to himself how she had managed so well in heels, considering how vocal she had been about her disdain for the shoes she wore at their wedding. The answer became apparent once she pulled her legs into the car and he saw a pair of sequined sneakers peeking out from beneath the hem of her dress.

She caught him looking at her legs and swatted him away from the car door, teasing him with her best Scarlett O'Hara impression, "Sir, you are no gentleman."

Nic was exactly what Shelby needed to bring lift to her spirits, which Ryan appreciated more than he could express—especially on the night of his film debut. Despite the banter between him and Nic and her untraditional approach, her kindness toward Shelby had absolutely proven that she was indeed a lady.

CHAPTER 13

LAKE VIEWS

Sitting in a plush seat at the magnificent Whitney Theatre, Shelby felt tremendous pride as the first images of Ryan's film appeared before the Chicago Film Festival audience. The screen was set upon a magnificent, historic stage that was adorned on either side with heavy, red velvet curtains. For the first time, she heard the words she had scripted, saw Lake Superior's shoreline communities through her husband's eyes, and marveled at the beauty of the lake she loved. Ryan was seated on the aisle, just beside her, while Nic was on her right. Ryan reached for her hand at the beginning of the film and held it tenderly as each scene transitioned smoothly into the next. From start to finish, *Lake Views* was a heartfelt film that deserved the exuberant applause it received once the credits rolled down the length of the screen.

Ryan wrapped his arm around her shoulder and leaned in to kiss her cheek. "What did you think?" he asked with eagerness and affection. He wanted her to love the film, and she did.

"Amazing," she said, kissing him on the lips. "You were

right. It was so much fun for me to wait, and see it in its entirety. So, so good!"

"You have no idea how good it makes me feel to hear you say that," Ryan said.

"Gran is going to go crazy for this film; she already can't contain her excitement. And Grandpa—well, he would have been so proud of you. Just like I am."

She knew those were the words Ryan wanted to hear, and she was relieved that they were true. It was a stunning film. There was no question about that.

As the audience's applause grew louder around them, and those seated in their vicinity began offering their congratulatory remarks to Ryan and his team, Shelby sat back in her upholstered seat, grateful that the house lights were still dim. Although she tried to deny it, Shelby had felt something else while watching *Lake Views*. It may have been homesickness. Or simply fatigue. But when she viewed the film and saw the people and places that reminded her so strongly of home, she felt better than she had in months. Ryan's film, his viewpoint, and the story line portrayed her beloved lake in breathtaking light. So much so that she felt she could walk into the screen and dip her feet in the cold, clear water. She could almost feel the wind lift off the waves and smell the familiar scent of pine and hemlock.

Ryan's distinct eye for still photography transferred incredibly well to cinematography. She was impressed and truly proud of his accomplishments. On the screen, visions of home were larger than life.

That all disappeared once the credits rolled and she returned to her Chicago reality, dressed beautifully in an elegant theater—accustomed to neither. She felt lost. The house lights turned up until they shone brightly. The dream was over.

"Holy crap, that was good," Nic said, slapping her knee and turning to face Shelby. "Who knew Ryan could pull that off? I mean, he practically made Bayfield look like Bali! I had no idea the shoreline was so frickin' awesome; did you?"

"He did an incredible job," Shelby agreed, feeling tremendously glad once again that her friend was visiting.

"And didn't you say you did all of the writing?"

"Some of the rewrites, but not much."

"Well, I'm not sure exactly which parts were your words, but let's just say yours were the best."

"What would I do without you?" Shelby smiled.

"Don't look now, but here come the 'rents," Nic nudged her in the arm with a nod in the direction of Ryan's parents, who were walking up the aisle toward them. "Ten o'clock."

"Oh, Shelby! William! You two did an outstanding job!" Charlotte said, setting one hand on her son's shoulder and reaching out her other hand toward Shelby. "I just knew you had it in you. So much *talent* in one family!"

"Nice work, William," his father added, shaking Ryan's hand as he stood up from his seat and joined them in the aisle.

"Thanks, Charlotte." Shelby smiled, remaining in her seat until she was obligated to "mingle and network," as Chambers family members did.

Nic peered out from behind Shelby and did nothing to conceal the noise as she cleared her throat.

"Oh, is this a friend of yours?" Charlotte asked, looking from Nic to Shelby, and then to her son with raised eyebrows.

"This is my friend Nicole Palmer," Shelby said, leaning back in her chair as Nic rose from her seat and extended a hand toward Charlotte and William.

"You remember Nic—from the wedding?" Ryan offered.

"Of course," Ryan's father replied, nodding toward his wife. "Shelby's maid of honor."

"Why of course," Charlotte echoed, leaning forward to accept Nic's hand. "So nice to see you again."

"Ready?" Ryan asked Shelby, taking her hand to help her

up. She placed her other hand firmly on the armrests and pushed herself out of the seat as gracefully as she could manage wearing high heels—particularly when her ever-changing body threw off her balance. She would have liked to stretch out her back and legs by going for a walk, but she knew better. There would be a reception. Followed by a dinner that would last well into the evening. It would be hours until she would be back in the comfort of her own home, wearing pajamas and a pair of wooly socks.

"So, is there a party or something after this?" Nic asked.

"Nic—"

"What?" She shrugged her shoulders. "I mean, we're all dressed up—no need to call it a night, right?"

"Right."

The aisle leading up to the theater exit was crowded with well-wishers and people whom Ryan and his parents seemed to know intimately but to Shelby were merely strangers. Of course she smiled and nodded, shaking hands and turning her body so as not to belly bump into the beautifully dressed attendees.

And there, with Shelby stuck in the center of a narrow theater aisle, it struck her. Her feelings were not only about her undeniable yearning to return home. It now occurred to her that to anyone, however generous or thoughtful, who watched the film or contributed toward the conservation cause the lake area was just a place. A pretty destination. But to her the lake was at the core of her life. Not on the peripheries. Being away from it for an extended time felt like being a migratory bird whose wing was clipped and who kept on circling back to center when all she wanted to do was fly north to home.

CHAPTER 14

DON'T GO

R yan checked his watch, realizing he had become so ener-
gized and involved in speaking with patrons of the film
festival—potential financial backers of the conservation fund—
that he had lost track of time. And he had lost sight of Shelby,
who he knew must be absolutely exhausted by now.

He excused himself from a small group of some of Chicago's
more generous benefactors and weaved through the crowd
quickly, trying to find her. Instead, he came face-to-face with his
mother.

"Hey, have you seen Shelby? Or Nic?" he stopped to ask
Charlotte.

"Yes, about twenty minutes ago," she said with a knowing
smile, standing elegantly with a champagne flute in hand. "In the
ladies' lounge."

"Twenty minutes ago?" He looked over his mother's shoulder to peruse the room again. "Have you seen her since?"

"No, I haven't."

"So, you don't know where she is?"

"I do, but that's an entirely different question."

"Mother, please. I'm not in the mood for games. I promised her that we wouldn't stay long, but I got caught up in some conversations over there and—never mind, it's not important. Where is she?"

"I sent her home."

"What do you mean 'sent her home'?"

"Well, I suppose I didn't *insist* that she return to the apartment with her friend. It was her decision." Charlotte lifted her glass and sipped the effervescent wine. "I merely suggested it."

"I'm leaving."

Just as he turned to leave, his mother reached for his arm. "Don't go," she insisted.

"Why?" he asked, looking down with surprise at the grasp she had on him. "What happened?"

"Nothing." She released him and gave a subtle glance around the lobby, smiling to appear delighted to anyone who might look their way. "As I said, I went into the lounge, only to discover Nic sitting beside Shelby on the chaise, consoling her."

"She was upset?" He reached into his pocket to withdraw his phone. "I need to call her. Head back to the apartment."

"You don't need to do that, Will. Everything is fine. She will be fine," Charlotte said. "Put your phone away for a moment. It would be best if you let me fill you in before you call her."

He reluctantly lowered his hand and placed the phone back into his pocket. But only for a moment. "All right. Here, let's move over there where we'll have a bit more privacy," he said, nodding toward a less crowded spot beside one of the caterer's cocktail bars. Once there, he asked, "Now, can you tell me what happened?"

"I went to her right away, of course. As it turns out, a reporter from *Signature* magazine was here tonight and found his way to your wife. She struck up a conversation with him, unaware he worked for the press—particularly *that* dreadful magazine. Anyway, one thing led to another, and before she knew

it the man became a bit aggressive—I think that's the word that
Shelby used. I won't tell you what Nic called him. Anyway, the
conversation turned sour—something about her mother's lover,
the baby, I'm not sure what else. It proved to be too much for her."

"She's been through too much, and I don't know what I
can do."

"I encouraged Nic to take her home."

"Good. That was the right thing to do. I just wish you had
come to me. I would have taken them home."

"Ryan. You can't be serious. This is your night. Your debut.
Shelby understands that, perhaps more than you do yourself. You
need to stay here. Nothing more will happen to her tonight.
You'll have all day tomorrow to make it up to her. And besides,
she isn't alone. Nic is with her."

"No, it doesn't feel right. I'm needed at home."

"I'm as concerned about her as you are, dear," Charlotte
said. "But can we be honest? She looks absolutely miserable,
William—not just tonight, but for a while now."

He knew Charlotte was right, but it wasn't the time or
place to discuss it.

"You see it, don't you?" she continued. "Pregnancies can be
challenging—believe me I do know that much—but I think
there's more to it than that. Wouldn't you agree?"

"I'm leaving now," he said, setting down his cocktail glass
on the bar.

Charlotte took his arm and stopped him from leaving.
"She needs to learn how to handle herself, you know," she insisted, taking on the lecturing tone he knew so well from his
adolescence. "I realize this isn't the environment that she grew up
in, but she made the conscious decision to join our family and
she needs to figure out how to navigate. This is her life now."

"It doesn't have to be. Hell, it doesn't even have to be mine,"
he realized with astounding clarity. What a fool he had been.
They were both so much happier during the time he lived in

Bayfield, away from all of this. "This is your lifestyle, Mother. And you're wrong. She doesn't have to adapt. I do."

"So young." Charlotte smiled, shaking her head. "So many ideas of how things ought to be. I understand. I was in your shoes once."

"With all due respect, I don't think you'll ever know what she's been through. Or how much of an adjustment this is for her."

"Mmm. Perhaps. But, then again, you may not know everything about your father's and my early years. But that's for another day."

He reached for his mother's waist and leaned in to give her a kiss on the cheek before leaving. "Thanks for being there for Shelby tonight. I appreciate it."

Before his mother could answer and just as Ryan was pulling out his phone again to call Shelby and head outside to find a car, they were interrupted by two college-aged women.

"Excuse me, Mr. Chambers," the taller of the two women interrupted. "I usually don't do this, but, um, may I have your autograph? I mean—can *we?*"

"Sure. Of course," he said, accepting her event program and ballpoint pen. "What's your name?"

"Emma Covington."

"Covington?" He signed his name quickly and returned the program to her. "I know a Covington."

"You do?" she asked, blushing and grabbing her friend's forearm to steady her enthusiasm. "Wow. I mean, cool."

"Where are you from?"

"We go to the University of Iowa, but we're staying with my roommate's parents this weekend," she said, eager to strike up a conversation.

"In Evanston," her friend added.

"Yeah, they're in Evanston," the taller gal said.

"So you don't know the Ashland Covingtons?" Ryan asked. He knew it was a long shot, and he was eager to leave, but if there was a slight chance he could get some information . . .

"Um, no, but my grandma does. How did you know?"

"What's this about, William?" He had nearly forgotten that his mother was standing at his side.

"By any chance, are you related to a Chad Covington?"

"Yes," the young woman said, clearly delighted. "He's my uncle, but I haven't seen him in, like, *forever*. How did you know?"

"Just a hunch," he said, glancing at the time on his phone. Shelby was with Nic. She would be all right. A few more minutes weren't going to hurt. "Do you have a minute? Can we talk privately?"

The college students looked at each other as if they had just been given backstage passes at a rock concert. He knew their answer would be "yes" before they replied.

CHAPTER 15

REMINDERS OF HOME

In late October, Shelby and Ryan were sitting in their sunlit kitchen, enjoying a quiet Sunday with several morning papers sprawled out on the table beside coffee cups and empty plates peppered with crumbs.

The reviews for *Lake Views* were in and, for the most part, favorable. There were some naysayers, which was to be expected. "Self-serving documentary filled with superfluous shots of Lake Superior's indisputable beauty, but lacking in any groundbreaking editorial content" was one review comment that stayed with Shelby.

The cool manner in which Ryan flipped through the reviews was incredible to her. She wouldn't know from the look on his face whether the words were supportive or not of the documentary. He smiled either way.

"It's visibility, Shel. The minute this review came out, more people heard our story. Of those, maybe a handful will offer support. And that's more support than we had yesterday."

"But this reporter just called you self-righteous! Can he

get away with that?" she blurted out one morning while reading an online review.

"Of course. It's one man's opinion. Even if I don't agree with him, he's certainly entitled to it."

"But based on what he's saying here, about sustainable fishing and Native American treaty rights, Ryan, this reviewer didn't even see the film! We did nothing at all to disparage any of the fisheries or fishermen on the lake!"

"It's not worth the fight, Shel," he said calmly. "Like you and the press here. They painted a portrait of you that was completely untrue and what did we do?"

"I tried to ignore it. And then they said I was aloof. Cold and self-absorbed."

"Yes." He laughed, not because of how difficult that time had been, but because of her dour expression. "And then—?"

"And then, they grew tired of that story and moved on."

"We'll keep the good reviews. Promote them. And we'll try to ignore the rest. Focus on the positive—just like we did with you."

"I don't know that I'll ever be equipped for this," she said, leaning back in her chair.

"Shel, we're going to be late!" Shelby heard Ryan call out from the entryway of their apartment. After a leisurely morning at home, she was now in the kitchen, throwing the last of the ice into an over-the-shoulder cooler that was just big enough for two. They were heading out for a day at the Art on the Lake event in the Park District, and she wanted plenty of water.

"Go ahead and get the elevator; I'll be right there!" she called back.

She heard his footsteps move swiftly across the foyer until he was standing beside her at the kitchen counter, helping her zip the cooler. "Don't tell me you were planning to carry this yourself?" he asked, tilting his head with raised eyebrows.

"Yes?"

"You know what your doctor said—from now on, you need to let me do the heavy lifting."

"I wanted to bring some extra water," she said.

"That's great, but no lifting," he insisted, slinging the cooler pack over his shoulder with ease and leading her out of the kitchen. "I know you're more than capable of taking care of yourself. But right now, your job is to take care of the baby, and allow me to take care of you."

Before opening the front door, he kissed her on the cheek until she relented and returned his smile.

"Okay," she lamented. "But just because I'm pregnant does *not* mean I'm weak or dependent on you. Besides, you weren't going to bring a cooler. I *am* taking care of myself, and the baby."

"No. I would have just bought some drinks for us," he said.

"When we have perfectly good water here, right out of the tap."

"Come on, let's get out of here."

Just as they were leaving, Shelby stopped again. "Wait! My phone—"

"I have it," he said, setting his hand on the small of her back to usher her out of the apartment, locking the door behind them.

"Jacket!"

"You left it in the car."

"I still can't believe you roped me into doing this event," he said, rocking back and forth on his heels while they waited for the elevator doors to open.

"It'll be good for you. And besides, you'll be helping Adrien."

When the elevator arrived Ryan swung his arm in to hold

the door for Shelby. She took a step into the elevator and then stopped short. "The ice! I think I left the door to the freezer open!"

"No, no—it's okay," he said, taking her hand and walking her back into the elevator, pushing the button to the lobby. "I took care of it. We're all set."

"I feel so scattered," she said, casting her eyes away from her reflection in the mirror. "Maybe we should cancel."

"Cancel?" He laughed. "What's going on with you today?"

The elevator doors closed with a quiet *shush* as Shelby leaned into the brass railing that ran across the three mirrored compartment walls. Glancing sideways at the wall, she could see the reflection of her round belly stretching across the cotton fabric of her white T-shirt. The physical reminder of the changes happening, both in her body and in her life. Nothing was as it used to be. And she wondered to herself how long it would take before she accepted those changes.

"I'm sure we'll have a great time," he tried to assure her. "Remember, this was your idea."

Poor guy, Shelby thought. She knew this wasn't his idea of a "great time." Lugging some of his framed prints down to the park to join Adrien Bouchard, a French-Canadian artist who shared Ryan's interest in Great Lakes photography, in his booth down at the popular art event. Ryan was doing it for her. And for her hometown, which he now loved nearly as much as she did. She knew that much was true. That was the easy sell when she first had the idea to partner with Bouchard and raise additional funds for Olen's memorial fund. The harder sell was convincing Ryan that it was okay to be a "celebrity guest" to help draw in patrons. It was just for a day. How bad could it be, really?

Shelby sat comfortably in the back of the black sedan, enjoying the soft leather seating and the warm stream from air from the heating vent as it blew over her shoulders. She looked over at Ryan, who held her hand but kept his eyes on the view out his passenger door window as they drove down North Lake Shore Drive.

"Is something wrong?" she asked. There had been a slight shift in his mood the moment they left the apartment, barely noticeable. But it was there.

"Nothing at all," he answered, turning long enough to offer a weak smile before looking back out the window.

"Is it the art fair? I'm sure they'd understand if we didn't—"

"It's okay, Shel," he insisted. "Really. It's nothing."

She looked down at their clasped hands, knowing that he was noticing the change in their lives, just as she was. But, unlike her, he wasn't talking about it with her. He was careful to keep everything upbeat. "It's all for the sake of the baby," he would say—and he'd mean it. She admired that in her husband. He would do anything for the sake of her and their unborn child.

All of her life, Shelby thought of cars as nothing more than a mode of transportation. It didn't matter what make or model, how old, what color or condition the vehicle was in as long as it moved her from point A to point B. She never dreamed that one day she would be living in a cosmopolitan city, in a spacious apartment overlooking Lake Michigan, with a driver available whenever she needed to travel about the city.

Contrary to her upbringing, Ryan grew up in the back of a chauffeured car beginning with his first trip home from the hospital after his birth. His parents owned their own cars, of course, but Ryan told her that they, on the one hand, always preferred the convenience of a driver. He, on the other hand, was eager to drive at sixteen—purchasing a used Jeep Wrangler, much to his parents' chagrin, so he could feel "normal" while driving with his school friends to see a movie or grab a slice at a neighborhood pizzeria. Later, as a young man on his own, Ryan preferred walking, biking, and taking the metro over driving. It never occurred to him to hire a driver. Ryan wouldn't think of it.

Until now, when he had a family to protect.

"Do you remember the first time we met, down at the park in Bayfield?" Shelby asked as the car pulled up to a stoplight at an intersection, trying to pull him out of his thoughts as he stared at pedestrians and bicyclists moving freely along the path that lined Lake Michigan's shore.

"Of course, but technically, that's not where we met."

"No, no, I don't mean when we *actually* met—I mean our first date."

He turned back to her now with a warm smile. Shelby was happy to see she had his attention. "Was it a date? I've never been quite sure."

"What?" She laughed. "Of course it was a date."

"I don't know. The way I remember it, I invited you to go out for drinks, but the only reason you joined me was because you were getting so much pressure that night from Ginny and Olen," he teased. "In fact, I'll bet if it wasn't for them, you never would have shown up."

"No, I would have," she said, smiling back at him. "I think."

"Uh-huh," he said, and then paused, looking into her eyes. "Have you ever thought of what would have happened? You know. If you hadn't shown up that night?"

Her mind flashed to a dark thought that perhaps it had been a mistake. If they hadn't met, perhaps he would have married someone else. Someone who was better suited for his lifestyle.

"Olen and Ginny had matchmaking instincts that day—I will be eternally grateful that they shoved you out the door that night." He laughed and then lifted her hand to his lips and kissed it. "But to answer your question, yes, of course I remember that night."

It had been a beautiful night, and a frightening one. The moon shone on the water. Long talks on a warm summer evening. Music coming off of the rooftop bar of The Inn. And then the terrified screams of a woman whose son had fallen into the dark water in the marina. Without hesitation, Ryan had run to the marina and instinctively dove into the water to save the child. It was the moment that had broken the ice between Shelby and Ryan that night. His protective nature was the first thing that truly drew her to his character, so it was not surprising that it would still be evident today.

Reaching the event site, their car continued to drive slowly through barricaded streets, past food trucks, fair stands, and visitors on the streets and sidewalks.

"I had no idea this place would be so crowded!" Ryan said, leaning forward to peer out the windshield. He spoke with their driver, who assured Ryan he could drive them down to a reserved parking area by the shore that was close to their outdoor gallery space.

"This is crazy," Shelby agreed. "I heard this event was busy, but this . . . this makes Applefest in Bayfield look like a regular Sunday afternoon in the park. There must be thousands of people here." She looked at her husband, doubting once more whether this was a good idea. The little bit of publicity the fair organizers had done must have carried far and wide, because this was an incredible turnout. And based on her observations of Ryan and his family, it was going to go one of two ways. The crowd would either respect Ryan and be polite and gracious—which she fully expected of Midwesterners—or become overly excited and she would regret ever getting him involved.

Once the car was parked, Ryan grabbed her cooler and an

over-the-shoulder satchel that held his laptop and extended his hand into the car to help her out.

"Ready?" he asked.

"Absolutely."

The steady stream of people flowing in and out of Ryan and Adrien's tent had been supportive and gracious. Perhaps it was because Ryan had agreed to participate without publicity or fanfare—just two photographers selling their work for a good cause. Or perhaps it was the event's friendly, Midwestern vibe. But Shelby felt more relaxed, and more herself, beneath the tarp of the pop-up art tent than at any gilded theater reception or crowded evenings with champagne glasses raised and superficial conversations with people whose names she could never recall. There were simply too many new people in her life to keep it all straight. Too many strangers. While Ryan seemed to glide effortlessly through those evenings, she felt like a child hanging on to her father's hand, unsure of where to go or whom to meet with next.

As the months passed, she wasn't gaining a sense of belonging in her new environment, something Shelby realized she had loved while living in Bayfield. Now her self-confidence was shifting as quickly as the inner changes of her pregnant body. She realized that in this unstoppable metamorphosis she was becoming someone she barely recognized. She was retreating further beneath Ryan's social and professional shadow.

"You're in your element today," Ryan said warmly, coming up behind her and reaching his arms around her waist. There was a brief lull in the crowd and this was the first time they could talk uninterrupted since arriving at the fair.

"Isn't this an incredible turnout?" She wrapped her arms over his. "People really seem to love your work."

"Honestly, I'm more excited about people's reaction to

hearing about our fund-raising work. There's a real interest here. I've been thinking—we may even want to expand it to cover Lake Michigan, or even the Great Lakes in their entirety."

"I know you can make that happen."

"We. *We* can make it happen," he insisted. "You're as much a part of this as anyone."

Am I, really? she wondered.

"Seeing everyone here today, down by the lake, it reminds me a bit of home."

"I hope that's a good thing."

"It is," she said, turning in his arms to face him. "And it also makes me miss that easygoing way of life. You remember, don't you? How you could have a productive day, but without the pressure that comes along with crowds and traffic and the attention? It's just you, your work, and the outdoors?"

"There's no question about it. Bayfield is a unique place. I miss it, too."

"We should go back next weekend. Or early this week. We could surprise Gran. Just you and me, a road trip. The cottage is all ready. The fall colors must be gorgeous right now." She grinned broadly, her enthusiasm radiating from her smile as she quickly put a plan together. "It's just what I need right now. Let's just go!"

He pulled away. "We'll go back someday. The holidays are coming up; we could visit then—"

"The holidays?" She was taken aback but tried to maintain her enthusiasm. "But that's still a ways off. Think about how nice it would be go get away for a while!"

"But that's just it, Shel. I don't feel the need to get away right now. In fact, it would be a terrible time for me to leave. It isn't the best time."

She dropped her smile just as Adrien, his timing impeccable, approached them.

"Hey, you two, what a turnout!" he said, placing his hands

squarely on each of their shoulders. "Looks like the crowds are settling down. If you want to head out, I can hold the fort."

"Maybe now is a good time for us to pack it up," Ryan said, looking at Shelby.

"Before you do, Ryan, would you mind heading down toward the water for a minute? I have an old colleague, an art curator from Miami, who has set up shop down at the edge of the park," Adrien said before turning to address Shelby. "That is, of course, if it's okay with you, Shelby."

"Go ahead," she said flatly. She was frustrated with her husband and, to be honest, she would rather stay at the art fair than go back to the quiet of an empty apartment. "I don't mind at all." And she meant it.

It was also good for Ryan to make contacts on his own, without using his family ties. Besides, Adrien had been good enough to bring two interns from his gallery to help with the art booth, so there wasn't much for her to do but talk to people and enjoy the community festival that reminded her of home.

"I won't be long," Ryan promised her. "And I'll give it some more thought—your idea about going to Bayfield. Maybe I can rearrange some meetings, work remotely. I'll see what I can do." He gave her a light kiss on the lips and then, just as quickly, disappeared into a group of passing fairgoers who moved in a throng of backpacks, strollers, and bags.

The two men hadn't been away for more than ten minutes when Shelby heard the sound of her name come from behind, followed by a gentle tap on her shoulder.

"Shelby Meyers?" the woman's voice repeated.

Shelby turned and recognized her immediately. The woman still had a wild mane of brown hair that she always had tried to tame by pulling it back tightly away from her face. The olive-colored skin that was always perfect, even back in their high school days when everyone was fighting off offending blemishes with creams, scrubs, and toning lotions. And the widest, brightest smile of anyone she had ever known.

"Lizzie!" Shelby exclaimed, immediately moving to hug the woman but stopping short, when she realized her old high school friend wasn't alone. "Oh my goodness, I'm so sorry! I didn't see you." She looked from Lizzie Clark's face down to a child who was the spitting image of his mother.

"Shelby, this is my son, Ethan," said her friend. "Ethan, this is an old friend of mine. Mrs. Chambers."

"How 'bout you just call me Shelby?" she said, crouching down on one knee to greet the boy and shake his small hand. "I'm happy to meet you. Are you having fun with your mom today?" He smiled with that same big, broad smile. For a fleeting moment, Shelby wondered which features of hers and Ryan's would be passed on to her own son. She tried to imagine people seeing them as a family, comparing their features and seeing that they belonged together. She tried to imagine it, but nothing clear came to mind.

Shelby then stood back up and embraced Lizzie. They caught up quickly in halting sentences and outbursts of laughter, the way old friends do. Shelby learned that Lizzie Clark was now Lizzie Farrington and that she and Ethan lived in Oconomowoc with her husband, Ty. She worked as an aide in Ethan's preschool while her husband taught eighth-grade math. They lived a quiet but good life, Lizzie said, in a home that was "small, but just big enough" on Lac La Belle.

"Where is he?" Shelby asked about Ty, looking over Lizzie's shoulder, thinking he would be nearby. "I'd love to meet him."

"He's with his cousin, Tony. Do you know Tony Dodd? He was a few years older than us."

"Sure I do."

"We're visiting the Dodds for a few days. Tony works at a special events company doing some of the AV work—the company that runs this art show. Anyway, Tony called Ty about twenty minutes ago, saying that they were having problems with some of the speakers. My husband is one of those guys who would much rather help tinker with electronics than walk around an art fair, so that's where he is right now. Ethan and I are on our own for a bit, aren't we, E.?" she said, ruffling the hair on the back of her son's head as he looked up at her.

"Small world," Shelby said, looking again at Ethan's perfect face.

"How 'bout you?"

"Hmm?" Shelby asked, her mind elsewhere.

"You're quite the talk around Bayfield," Lizzie said. "It's all Mom wants to chat about whenever I call—all of the updates about you, the wedding, which I heard was beautiful, your move to Chicago. It all sounds so *glamorous* compared to what I have going on down in Oconomowoc."

"Believe me," Shelby said, nodding toward Lizzie's son, "you have something much better than anything in my life. Really, Lizzie, I'm so happy for you."

"Well, he makes it easy, don't you, Ethan?" she replied, bending down to kiss her son on the cheek. "But it looks like you're going to experience the same thing before long."

"What?"

"Motherhood?" Lizzie said, nodding in the direction of Shelby's pregnant middle.

"Oh. Yes," Shelby replied, her voice drifting off. "I suppose I will."

As they continued to talk, fewer people passed by and Shelby noticed some of the neighboring vendors beginning to pack up their wares. The interns working Adrien's booth did the same, insisting that they could manage without her help. It was an entirely different experience for her, being there for support but without having a real job to do, unlike those many years when she helped her grandparents work the farm.

"Is Ryan here? I'd love to meet him," Lizzie said.

A swift breeze blew through the park, causing tent flaps to rustle and loose artist brochures and leaflets to fly off of display tables. Shelby felt a sudden drop in air temperature. "That's strange; I didn't think we were going to have any bad weather this afternoon. . . ." Shelby commented as the two women looked to the sky. Shelby knew enough from living on Lake Superior to realize that storms on the Great Lakes had a way of blowing in quickly and causing unexpected chaos. "Sorry, Lizzie, I have to help these guys close up the tent. We're definitely going to get some rain."

"Let me help." Ethan was still in tow as the women moved to help the others in the tent load Adrien's and Ryan's work into secure boxes.

"So, you were asking about Ryan," Shelby said as she and Lizzie worked side by side. "We were thinking of leaving, but then he decided to go meet an art curator with Adrien. I think he was feeling a bit cooped up in this tent—he's much happier moving about."

"I have to confess—I might just faint. I've never met a *real* celebrity."

"He'd be the first to tell you he's nothing close to being a celebrity." Shelby laughed. "In fact, he's probably more down-to-earth and normal than I am."

She was interrupted by one of the young interns. "Mrs. Chambers, we're ready to start bringing these to the truck. John went to get it—he just pulled around behind the tent."

"Perfect, thanks, Molly."

"He should be back any minute."

Another gust blew across the park, this time forcing one end of the exhibit tent across the way from them to pull out of the ground and then collapse into the grass. Ethan drew closer to his mother and wrapped an arm around her leg for protection. Lizzie picked him up, settling him on her hip as she looked to the sky. "Shelby. We need to get out of here."

Shelby stepped out of the tent and craned her neck just long enough to see a thundercloud moving in swiftly. In an instant the cloud blew across the sun and cast an ominous shadow over the park.

"Is everything on the truck?" Shelby called out to Molly and the others. They confirmed that all was secure. "You all head out in the truck; my friend and I are heading out in a minute," Shelby said with urgency as others rushed past her to seek shelter before the cloud opened up.

"I just need to secure these clasps, Lizzie; then you and Ethan can come with me—we have a car waiting. It's not far from here." As the two women worked quickly to secure the tent, the wind picked up strength, howling against the flimsy canvas walls. *Where is Ryan?* Shelby wondered nervously, looking at Ethan's frightened face and knowing they didn't have much time. She needed to make sure the child would be safe when the storm hit.

"I want Daddy!" Ethan cried out to his mother. Lizzie held him protectively while he wrapped his arms around her neck.

"Okay, let's run for the car," Shelby announced just as a violent rapping sound bounced off of the tent roof and while people hurried off for cover.

"Shelby!" Ryan ran up beside her. While Lizzie was able to run swiftly, even with a child in her arms, Shelby was more comfortable with a swift jog, holding her hand firmly against her round middle—the bulk of which pressed up and down against her insides, making her breathless and slightly nauseous. "Wait up!" Shelby and Lizzie slowed their jog down to a swift walk until Ryan caught up with them.

"I had hoped you had already made it to the car," he said, catching his breath and placing his hand on the small of her back to help her along. *I can hurry to the car on my own,* she thought, more upset that he had delayed his return than disdainful over being thought of as dependent. *I'm pregnant, not weak.*

"I wanted to make sure your art was secure."

"Screw the photographs, Shel. You're the one who has to be kept safe."

She shook off her irritation by changing the subject as they continued quickly to the car. "Ryan, this is Lizzie and Ethan. From Bayfield."

"Nice to meet you," he said, distracted as a pattering of rain hit the tents and splattered about them.

"I'm happy to—" Lizzie started to reply. But they were running out of breath and time. The sky opened up in an instant, turning the light rain into a full-blown downpour.

"Here, let me help. I can carry him," Ryan said of Ethan. "We'll be able to move faster."

There was no time for further introductions. Lizzie nodded as the four of them continued toward the car, rainwater streaming down their faces, their hair lying slick against their heads, and their clothes hanging wet and heavy over their bodies. Although Shelby should have felt distraught, she was exhilarated. Like the white vendor tents, the scent of popcorn in the air, the park crowds, and the lake nearby, an unexpected, bold thunderstorm capped off her nostalgic day, reminded her of who she was. Reminded her of her hometown roots.

CHAPTER 16

BABY DATES

In Chicago, winter snow and holiday lights had replaced the autumn leaves. Since Ryan and Shelby never had enough time to make the trip up to Bayfield in the fall, she was anxious to go back home for Christmas. Now in her eighth month, Shelby's pregnancy was progressing normally. At least that's what her obstetrician kept assuring her. But for Shelby, the growing presence inside her seemed anything but normal. As her body continued to grow, so did her anxiety over the new life inside of her and her ability to be a good mother.

Her restless nights continued. She spent her evenings either shifting positions in bed and adjusting her pillow to get comfortable, or she was to getting up to walk around the apartment until the baby's movements settled down. Ryan would offer to rub his hand over the baby's elbow jabs and kicks to try to coax him back to sleep, something that worked well enough on most nights; but usually, she was too upset to be touched.

On this day, Ryan had already left for Chambers Media by the time Shelby was awake on this morning. She now sat by the picture window in their den, staring out at the expanse of Lake Michigan and the ice that had formed along its edges to seal off the water for the winter. The screen on her laptop was open to an online news site and her thoughts were distracted by the sudden movements in her womb. She looked past the screen to the book that remained untouched, waiting for her, in the low bookshelf at her side. The book with its flowery pink spine. The one written by a renowned obstetrician. The one that would tell her all of the secrets of what was happening, month by month, inside her womb. The book that would tell her what she should be doing to care for her unborn child. But could it tell her how to feel, even a little bit, the way an expectant mother ought to feel?

She reached for the book, feeling its smooth cover. Ryan had given it to her months ago, as much for her as for his own anticipation. She reviewed each chapter dutifully, like a gardener reading the *Farmers' Almanac,* trying to forecast what was in store for the months and year ahead.

As she walked slowly to a leather chair in the adjacent room she felt a tug along her side. It shot pain across the underside of her protruding belly like a warning—*take this seriously, lady, because I'm coming one way or another!*

Massaging the cramp in her side, she sat down and opened to Chapter 12: "Your Eighth Month." She scanned the first few pages quickly, looking for advice on how to get some relief. Movements are distinct . . . baby's kicks, elbows, and jabs . . . stronger and more frequent . . . moving approximately thirty times each hour.

Tell me something I don't know, Shelby thought to herself. She ran her finger over the page, skimming for something—anything—to give her hope. She flipped through the pages until she reached the chapter's end. She laid the open book upon her protruding belly and leaned her head back in the chair. A familiar wave of sorrow rolled outward from her womb, like the ripple of water that radiates away from a sunken stone.

She had tried to fight the emotion earlier on but now gave in to it. It rose in her throat and caused her chin to quiver and ache. She was a good person. She knew how to love and to be loved. Family meant everything to her. So why, when it came to her own unborn child, did she feel nothing but fear? And profound sadness for the absence of any natural maternal instinct?

There could only be one reason, she thought. Ryan instinctively curled up beside her in bed and laid his hand upon her skin, speaking in soft, loving tones to his unborn child— while she never seemed to know what to say.

Shelby pushed herself out of the chair with a heavy sigh and walked over to the desk near the window. Her phone lay upon papers that were strewn across the desktop. No messages. She picked up the phone to text Ryan.

Are you busy?

Never too busy. What's up?

Feeling restless. Please say something to cheer me up.

She smiled when her phone lit up with his quick reply.

Hey, beautiful—let me take you out to dinner.

She happily pushed herself up from the couch and said aloud, "Come on, baby. Looks like we have ourselves a date."

They enjoyed dinner together at one of their favorite restaurants, an intimate, family-owned place that they appreciated as much for its authentic Sicilian cuisine as for its seclusion tucked down below street level.

She had finally been open with him. Funny how it took a small restaurant in the heart of Chicago and a shared plate of simple spaghetti and meatballs for her to stop pretending and instead share her concerns and fears. Once she began talking, the words flowed out easily and she chided herself for not being honest with him earlier. For his part, he acknowledged her fear—he was worried, too, and said it was normal—but also expressed concern that she had been struggling with self-doubt for so long.

"You are going to be an incredible mom; don't you see that?" He adamantly dismissed her fear of turning into her mother. Instead, Shelby would be whatever kind of mother she chose to be. She had to believe it.

Ryan believed in her more than she believed in herself. And his actions, once more, reinforced her certainty that, of the two of them, he would be the far better parent. Their child would be blessed to have Ryan in his life.

After their meal, when Ryan opened the door for her as they left the restaurant, they were confronted by cold air. Shelby felt too good to care. She secured the ends of her scarf into a knot and pulled up her coat collar as she climbed up the stairs and onto the street with her arm threaded through Ryan's. The last time she had been this content was when they were in Zermatt; it was as if they were newlyweds once again instead of expectant parents. She was drunk on her husband's adoration and believed it when he promised that everything would work out. She had faith in him. Everything was bound to get better. It had to.

"I need to swing by my parents' place. My mother has something she needs me to sign, something about a change in the family's trust. It should only take a few minutes and then I'll come straight home, " Ryan said.

"I can come with you."

"I know you well enough to know that you'd be much

happier at home than having to trudge across town only to have to sit and listen to Charlotte talk about family finances."

"Well, she can tend to drone on," Shelby agreed with a laugh.

They walked up to their waiting car with a quick wave to Peter, the driver, through the car window as Ryan opened the door for Shelby.

"It's okay; you take the car," she said. "While we're here, I'm going to run into Saks. I want to pick up a couple of things quickly and then I'll catch a cab home."

"I'll get a cab. Peter can wait for you."

"Really, I feel like being on my own," she insisted. "Besides, if you have to wait for a cab once you wrap things up at your parents' place, who knows how long it will take for you to get a ride back. You keep the car—I'm sure I'll beat you home."

He stepped back onto the sidewalk beside her, wrapping his arm around her shoulders to block out the cold. "What are you shopping for?"

She gave him a sideways glance. "With Christmas right around the corner, do you really think I'm going to tell you all of my secrets?"

"Fair enough," he said, his voice now low as he leaned down to speak into her ear. "You pick up whatever it is you're picking up. And I'll meet you back at the apartment by five. And then I may just give you your gift a few days early."

"Please. I'm a bloated whale."

"You really have no idea, do you?"

"What?"

"You have never been more beautiful." His lips brushed past her ear and kissed her cheek before his hand gently touched the other side of her face and he kissed her lips.

"Someone will see us," she whispered back.

"So let them see," he replied with another kiss that seemed

to melt away the aches, the muscle tugs, the awkward stance, and her concerns. All that was left was the woman who had fallen in love with this man.

Shelby had intended to stop in the store to pick up a gift for Ryan, a garish Christmas sweater that reminded her of her grandfather and was bound to make him laugh, but she picked up a crowd instead.

It started with one woman standing in line beside Shelby at the cashier. The woman's persistent stare was unsettling and impossible to ignore. Shelby tipped her head down to return her wallet to her purse and gave a sideways glance at the woman. In doing so she had opened the window of opportunity a crack, and the woman grabbed hold and barged right in.

"I know you," she said, taking a step closer with an over-eager smile.

"Sorry, I don't think we've met," Shelby replied, turning her attention back to the clerk who was working carefully to wrap the bright-green cardigan adorned with holiday lights that actually came with a battery pack and, once turned on, blinked to the tune of "Let It Snow." It was so gaudy that it was perfect.

"No, I mean I recognize you from something," the woman insisted. "Are you on TV?"

Shelby shook her head politely, willing the salesclerk to apply the tape more swiftly.

"You're not in the movies; I know that," the woman continued, refusing to give up until she conjured a name. "The soaps?"

Shelby offered a polite smile. *Please leave. Please, please leave.*

"Wait—wait! It's coming to me. . . ." The woman set her purchases down on the countertop and began tapping against it with her open hand, the cogs in her brain turning. She was grinning widely as if she were a contestant on a game show and Shelby was the question at hand.

"That's all right; you don't have to put a ribbon on it," Shelby said to the salesclerk with a courteous smile. "I'm in a bit of a rush, so I can finish it up at home."

The clerk looked up from her work at Shelby. "Are you sure, Mrs. Chambers?"

Damn it, Shelby thought. *The credit card.*

"Chambers! Yes, that's it!" the woman burst out. "Of course!"

Try as she might, Shelby still wasn't used to being recognized. In fact, she doubted that she'd ever become accustomed to it. At home in Bayfield, people regularly said hello on the streets. It was common to run into people you knew in town or down by the water. It was a tight-knit community, and being neighborly was part of the lifestyle.

But in Chicago? With absolute strangers? Walking in the city with Ryan, she admired the unassuming manner in which he carried himself. Always friendly, never arrogant, Ryan had an unassuming manner that allowed him privacy but rarely anonymity. "You'll get used to it, Shel," he would say shortly after she moved to Chicago and received glances and outright stares when she walked with him arm in arm. "And by the time you do get used to it, it won't matter anymore."

"What makes you say that?" she asked.

"Because this is all fleeting. I haven't done anything to garner the recognition. It's only a matter of time before this so-called fame will fade away. Face it, Shelby," he teased. "Someday soon I'm going to be that guy who once looked like someone important. You may not want to stick around."

"I wish that time was now," she said. "But seriously, how do you get used to it?"

"Knowing that, for the most part, the attention comes from a good place," he said. "Some people just feel like they know me, or they're familiar with my family. There's never a harm in 'hello.' "

But back at the department store counter, with Shelby standing alone with her purse clutched in one hand, the "hellos" were becoming harmful. One woman became two. They made a fuss to the clerk, which captured the interest of others. Before Shelby was able to take hold of her shopping bag with Ryan's gift inside and quietly make her way out, a small gathering of curious people had surrounded her. They asked questions.

"Where is your husband?"

"How do you like Chicago?"

Like a swallow in a migratory flock, whichever way she turned the group followed.

"You're much prettier in person."

"Would you mind signing this for my son?"

She looked over their shoulders for someone, anyone, who might be able to help. Store security. A familiar face. Anyone.

"Is Will Chambers here today?"

"Can you take a selfie with me?"

"I can't believe it's Shelby Chambers!"

"Excuse me," Shelby said as she kept her head down, placed the shopping bag over her stomach, and she pushed her way through the small but aggressive crowd. She couldn't understand what the appeal was and, more than that, why they continued to push and crowd. Shelby raised her shoulders and held the shopping bag and her purse close. Using her elbows, she pushed through the throng of people. She was nudged roughly from the right and stumbled a bit on a twisted heel, then recovered.

"Excuse me," she said again, louder this time, less courteous. She felt her heart beating rapidly in her chest. She kept her head down, seeing nothing but smooth department store flooring and a collection of boots and shoes. Feet and footprints, and snow clumps melting into small, dirty pools. It was like nothing she had ever experienced during her time in Chicago, and certainly never anything she had seen when she was with her husband.

She had nearly reached the store's street exit and her escape into a homebound cab.

And then, someone's hand reached out from the pushy crowd and touched her pregnant belly. Her baby. *Her baby!* How dare this stranger try to touch her unborn child!

"When are you due?" came the voice of a stranger.

"Stop!" Shelby burst out, stopping in her tracks to address the group. "Back off!" She heard the words but didn't recognize the venom in her voice. "You have no right!"

She turned around in the group with a look that must have been perceived as a challenge. *Don't cross me! Don't you dare hurt my child!* Judging by the looks on their faces, she had succeeded. One by one, people seemed to lose interest and walked away. A few kept taking photographs, but as quickly as the crowd had surrounded her they now dispersed, so that she wondered if she had imagined the whole thing. Gone were the eyes and voices and intrusive hands. She turned once more for the exit and saw her escape. Free and clear.

She set her hand upon the firm curvature in her abdomen and rubbed hard enough for her baby to feel her caress through the thin wall of tissue that separated her from her child's back. "We're going to be okay, little one," she whispered. She held her head high and walked swiftly out of the store and into the cold outdoors with its honking cars, wind whistling between skyscrapers, and the static hum of people's voices on the sidewalk. And in that moment she knew how it felt to instinctively need to protect a child. In that moment, rubbing her child's back, she realized she had loved him all along. What a fool she had been to deny it. To deny *him*.

Shelby was quick to hail a cab and was relieved when one

pulled up to the curb without a wait. She settled into the backseat, smiling, and gave the driver her address. She placed her purse and shopping back beside her and smiled, caressing her stomach and speaking to her unborn child through inner thoughts.

I am so, so sorry. I don't know what I've been thinking all of these months. I think I was just afraid. I wasn't ready to take on the responsibility of being your mother, and there you were—waiting patiently for me. You've been so incredibly patient. I promise you. I will spend the rest of my life making this up to you. I want to give you more love than my mother ever gave me. I am so incredibly sorry, little one.

She stopped moving her hands. Her smile disappeared. It suddenly occurred to her that she hadn't—*No. I'm sure it's nothing,* she thought.

She unzipped her coat and moved her hands underneath the fabric of her sweater, feeling the warm softness of her taut skin. *Come on, sweetheart. Don't be shy. Wake up.*

As the cab continued down the city streets, it began to snow outside. Slow-moving clusters of snow dropped like torn bits of cotton candy, accumulating quickly throughout the city. She heard the rhythmic beat of the cab's windshield wipers, left-right, left-right, ticking off the seconds that passed without feeling anything move within her womb. Not a hungry kick. Or a lingering stretch. Not even a quiver of a foot from a sleeping babe.

Left-right. Left-right. *Swoosh. Swoosh.*

How long had it been? she asked herself, looking down at her middle for a sign. *Dear God, please give me a sign!*

Breakfast? Lunch with Ryan? Had she feel the baby kick while she was leisurely walking through the department store, before the crowd formed?

She looked down at her body, as if it could give her answers. She rubbed his back again, realizing now that he did not push back. He did not wiggle, nudge, or kick. Her mind raced through her day. Reading in the den. Lunching with Ryan. Shopping.

"Oh my God," she said aloud, her eyes opened wide in dread and her lip trembling.

"You say something, miss?" said the driver through the glass partition that separated the front seat from the back.

She felt panic well in her chest like floodwater, moving up into her throat, making her lip tremble. *My God! What kind of mother am I? I can't remember the last time I felt my baby move!*

"The hospital—?" her voice squeaked out quietly.

"What's that, miss?" the driver asked, turning his head back to hear her better through the glass partition between them.

"Please. The hospital. I think it's an emergency." Shelby hoped he wouldn't ask her anything else. She needed him to know where to take her. She had no other recourse than to put her trust in him.

"The hospital?"

"Memorial!" She breathed deeply. *Maybe it's nothing. Maybe he moved at the store and I just didn't notice. I'm sure it's nothing.*

"You change your mind about Lake Shore Drive?"

"Yes," Shelby answered, choking down her fear and trying to maintain her composure. As well as her hope. "Memorial Hospital. Please hurry."

She felt the cab pick up speed and take a sudden left turn at the light, the momentum of which forced her body to lean against the passenger door. Shelby didn't mind; she was grateful for the cabbie's urgency. She righted herself in the backseat and reached for her bag, opened it, and rummaged through its contents until she felt the smooth flatness of her cell phone in her hand. She opened the screen and quickly hit the preset phone number in her contacts list. *Ryan.* With the phone to her ear, she waited for him to pick up while watching the snow continue to fall heavily about the city, noticing how the winter weather had erased most of the color from the surrounding landscape. As the cab sped through the black-and-white city streets, she listened.

Ring.

Ring.

Ring.

CHAPTER 17

LET IT RING

Ryan was sitting in the living room of his parents' pent-house apartment when he heard the faint ring of his phone coming from within his coat, which he had draped casually over a stately upholstered chair in his parents' foyer.

"Oh, just let it ring," his mother said from her seat across from him in the living room. "My God, can we not have ten minutes together without being interrupted? Being with you these days is just like being with your father."

"Just let me check it. It could be Shelby." Ryan rose from his seat and was about to walk past his mother when she reached out her hand to stop him.

"Shelby's a big girl, darling. Can't you call her later?" his mother asked without really asking. She was insisting.

"Mother, she's eight months pregnant," he said, assuming Charlotte would understand, but from the look on her face, clearly she didn't.

"And she has my home phone number. She would call you here if it was an emergency," Charlotte insisted, picking up her wineglass from the end table beside her. "I'm sure it's nothing.

And I'd appreciate it if we could finish our conversation before your father returns home."

Despite his instinct to retrieve his phone, he settled back into his chair. She was right. Their conversation was important to both of them and it would be best to finish it before his father's return.

"All right. But if it rings again, or she calls the apartment—"

"Then by all means, I won't keep you," she assured him, raising the glass to her lips and taking a sip of chilled Chablis. "But really, William, you need to relax. Everything is going to be fine."

"So, back to our conversation," Ryan said, appreciating the unusually intimate talk he had been having with his mother, while also sensing that it was a mistake not to take that phone call.

"I've been very concerned about the way the press has been targeting Shelby," Charlotte said.

"I know. We all have," he agreed.

"Your father and I have talked about it at great length and—"

"And I've told him—I've said to both of you, in fact—that she isn't doing anything to antagonize the press or bring any attention to herself."

"Ryan," Charlotte interrupted, carefully setting down her glass and speaking calmly. "Neither of us blames Shelby. In fact, it's quite the contrary."

"But you've always given us the impression that we need to change our routine, be more open to the press—what has Dad been saying for the past several months? 'Put on a good face, if not for your personal reputation, then for the good of the family business'?"

"Yes. I know."

"Mother. I'm going to continue saying this until I'm blue in the face. Shelby has not done a single thing to incite the press to give her any attention. And whenever she does go out, she's often harassed by a photographer. It's no wonder she wants to stay inside. And I absolutely hate the fact that—hell, that none of us have been able to do anything to stop it."

"I agree."

"I knew this life would be an adjustment for her, but have you seen her lately?"

Charlotte nodded.

"She's a shell of her old self," he said, dropping his head and rubbing the back of his neck. His mother didn't press him for more details. She waited while he took this time, sitting quietly in his childhood home, with his mother's full attention. He rubbed the back of his hand against his eyes, pushing away the emotion. He had to continue to be strong for his wife. He had to find a way to make her life easier. Finally, he looked up at his mother again and told her what he knew she had already suspected. "She barely leaves the apartment anymore. When I leave for work in the morning, she is usually sitting on the couch in the living room. And when I return, it's as if she hadn't moved all day."

"It's difficult. I know." Charlotte stood, picking up her wineglass before moving to sit beside Ryan.

"All day," he muttered again, loud enough that only he could hear.

"You have been incredibly understanding with her. And patient. Protective," Charlotte said with assurance while rubbing his back. It was the kind of attention he had desperately craved while he was growing up, here in this very apartment. "And, quite frankly, you've proven yourself to be a stronger partner than your father ever has been to me."

Ryan turned to look her in the eye, surprised by her candor.

"I'm not here to disparage my husband in any way; he has his strengths as well as his weaknesses, as we all do," she said. "What I'm trying to say is that she is fortunate to have you, William. You will find a way to help her get through this, and I am confident you will be an outstanding father. You make me very proud."

"Thanks. That means a lot."

"Now. About Shelby," she continued, standing back up, glass in hand, and walking to the window to look out upon the snowfall. "We need to find a better way to entice her to get out more, especially in these last several weeks before the baby comes. If she's feeling reclusive now, it's only bound to worsen when she's exhausted with a newborn."

"She actually left the apartment with me today. We had lunch in town, and she wanted to do some shopping," Ryan said. "I saw a lot of the old Shelby in her today. It was great."

"Then why on earth are you here with me? My goodness, you should have run with it. If she was out and about, you should have canceled with me and continued to raise her spirits a little bit. She needs it!"

"But you insisted on—"

"Well, I was wrong. I can be wrong, can't I? Hang on, William. Did you hear something?" She raised her hand to quiet him. "Is that your phone?"

He quickly rose from the couch and rushed to the foyer. His mother set down her glass and followed after him.

As soon as he pulled the phone out of his coat pocket, he saw Shelby's name appear across the backlit screen. "It's Shelby," he said to his mother at the same time his finger slid across the screen to answer the call. "Hey, Shel. How are you? Is everything okay?"

"Mr. Chambers?" came an unfamiliar man's voice from the other end of the line.

"Who's this?"

"My name is Thomas Allen," he said carefully. "I'm a nurse here at Memorial Hospital."

"Wait a minute; I don't understand," Ryan said, standing

but not moving, clutching the phone tightly in his hand. "Why are you calling me with my wife's phone? Where is she?"

His mother moved closer, with tentative steps. "Ryan. What is it?"

He turned away from her, wanting to block out her questions and worried expression as he listened to the nurse.

"We wanted to let you know that your wife has been admitted to this hospital."

"Is it Shelby?" his mother continued to inquire from behind his back. "Is the baby all right?"

"I'm sorry, I couldn't hear you," Ryan said, struggling to keep his voice calm as he covered his other ear to block out his mother's questioning. "What happened?"

"There has been a complication with her pregnancy, Mr. Chambers," the nurse continued. "She said that you're just across town. Do you have someone who can drive you?"

Ryan looked back over his shoulder toward the living room windows, inwardly cursing at the thick snowfall that was coming down swiftly outside, most certainly creating havoc on the city streets below. "What kind of complication?" he said, unable to control the frightened catch in his voice.

"I think it's better if we talk to you in person, once you arrive," the nurse said. "How soon can you be here?"

"Please!" Lashing out in a burst of fear and anger, he lifted the chair beside him and slammed it back down to the ground with a crash on the hardwood flooring. Then he closed his eyes, a quiet prayer running through his mind, and reached out to lay his palm against the wall, bracing himself. Trying to remain calm while inside he was screaming in fear.

The nurse cleared his throat and said, "I am sorry to have to be the one to tell you this, Mr. Chambers, but we have not been able to detect a heartbeat. The sonogram shows that . . . there is no sign of life." Ryan could hear the pain in the voice on the other side of the line, even though he was a stranger to them. *No sign of life.*

"Your wife was already dilated by the time she arrived and has gone into labor naturally. I don't mean to alarm you, Mr. Chambers, but her labor is progressing quickly. You'll want to come as soon as possible."

There was another long pause on the other end.

"Ryan?" his mother asked again, quieter this time, stepping over the legs of the fallen chair and placing her hand gingerly on his shoulder.

Ryan's breaths were shallow. He could barely feel the air move in and out of his lungs. He closed his eyes, shutting out the lavish apartment, the soft light that shone through the nearby windows as the sun fell between the city skyscrapers outside of the adjacent windows, and the intensity of his mother's gaze.

"She's not alone, and we're working to keep her comfortable. I am very sorry for your loss," was the last thing Ryan heard before he mumbled, "Thank you," and clicked off the phone. His arm fell heavily to his side and the phone dropped from his grasp. He barely noticed the sound of it hitting the hardwood flooring.

"Ryan. *Please,*" his mother pleaded. "Tell me what's happening."

"He's gone," Ryan replied.

"I don't understand. Gone?"

"The baby," he said. "Shelby's at the hospital and—"

Ryan's body slumped against the wall.

"And what?" his mother asked, rushing to his side and putting her hands on his shoulders.

"They can't hear his heartbeat."

"Oh, William. I am so, so very sorry." She put her hands on either side of his face and looked him straight in the eye. "You'll know what to do. You're strong."

He looked up with tears welling in his eyes. "I, I need to go; I—"

"I love you, darling. It's going to be all right. Everything's going to be all right." She set the chair back on its legs and guided Ryan to sit before she rushed down the hall and disappeared into the apartment.

Ryan sat, stunned, looking down the hall to the wall of living room windows. The snow was continuing to fall heavily upon the city.

He's gone. God, my God, why did he have to go?

"Lois!" he heard his mother call out to her assistant. "William needs a ride. Please call for a driver. We need to get him to Memorial as soon as possible!"

They can't detect his heartbeat, Ryan thought in disbelief. *He's gone before he ever had a chance to take his first breath.*

CHAPTER 18

SEA GLASS

While delivery nurses worked in Shelby's hospital room to monitor her vitals and prepare the room for labor and delivery, Shelby rested comfortably in an induced sleep, blissfully separated from the reality of what awaited her.

As she slept, Shelby dreamed of walking down a sunlit beach with her son. He wiggled his feet in the fine sand and she did the same, enjoying the way the sand shifted between her toes and tickled the tops of her feet as it piled up and slid away.

He was a beautiful boy with an overgrown mop of hair that matched hers and a dimpled cheek like his father's. Her son extended his arms toward her, proudly revealing a delicate tumble of sea glass that he held in his cupped hands. As she was admiring his tiny handful of blue and green treasures, he closed his hands and reached down to the sand to pick up another piece of sea glass. This one was lavender and he held it up to the sun, smiling proudly. Lavender had been her favorite sea glass when she was a child, too. It was rare and lovely.

Her son laughed in a bubbly hiccup and then, without notice, he dropped the glass fragments into the sand and ran off down the beach in an unbalanced toddle. His arms flapping at his side like wings, as if he could soar up over the waves that rolled along the shoreline. His legs were soft and fleshy and pink from the sun, and the small pads of his feet left delicate impressions in the damp sand as he ran.

Shelby imagined her son would grow up to be the kind of man who never lost his youthful zeal. He would always have a strong heart, be full of laughter, and appreciate the beauty in little things, like footprints and sea glass in the sand.

"You're almost there," she cheered him on toward a destination that was beyond her sight. "I'll be here for you!" she called after him. But he didn't turn back.

Shelby awoke with a start, bolting upright in her bed and taking a desperate breath of air as if she had been drowning. She opened her eyes wide and, instead of seeing the beach, she took in her surroundings and she remembered that she was in the hospital. A pain shot through her abdomen and seared around to her back, causing her to arch, grit her teeth, and fall back onto the bed.

Shelby was in labor.

"You'll be all right, Mrs. Chambers," came the soothing voice of a man who appeared to be preparing something at the foot of Shelby's bed. "My name is Thomas and we're here to help you. You nodded off for just a few minutes. Perfectly normal with the medications you were given. They'll help keep you calm."

"Call me Shelby," she said as the agonizing intensity of another contraction forced her awake.

"I'm Dr. Sorenson. How are you feeling, Shelby?" asked a woman dressed in blue scrubs. Shelby realized she was a physician, although not the OB-GYN who had cared for her throughout her pregnancy.

"Where is Dr. Logan?" Shelby asked breathlessly, her question cut short by another wave of pain that shot through her core.

"You're having contractions, Shelby, and they're coming faster than we had anticipated. Try to breathe through them," said Dr. Sorenson, who then mumbled something inaudible to the nurse. Returning her focus to Shelby, the physician continued, "We called Dr. Logan, but considering how quickly you're progressing, he may not arrive in time. But I'm in his practice group, I've reviewed all of your charts, and he and I are staying in touch. I assure you, we're going to take very good care of you."

And my child, Shelby thought to herself. *She meant to say, "We'll take care of you and your child."* She'd have to correct her later, if only she could catch her breath as another wave of pain rolled over her.

She realized that her body was acting on its own, regardless of how she felt or how she willed herself to move. She vaguely remembered that an epidural had been administered for the pain, but now she realized she could feel everything below her waist.

"I can feel my legs, but I can't move them," she said urgently, trying not to panic. *My God,* she thought, *it didn't take!* The epidural took away her ability to control her body below the waist, rather than the pain, and now her lower limbs were like two heavy sandbags that lay motionless on the birthing bed. Unable to move, she felt every internal twist, every deep pull, and every searing burn within her body. The only blessing she grasped on to was that her son's delivery was relatively swift. As he entered the world, perfect in every way except for a beating heart, she cried out with abandon, "My baby! My baby!"—as if her words of devastation and unconditional love could be heard outside of the cold, sterile hospital room and soar with him into the clouds.

Chapter 19

CALM

The drive from his parents' apartment building to Memorial Hospital felt painstakingly slow as the car drove cautiously through the slick city streets. The snowfall cast a heavy veil upon the city as Ryan looked out of his passenger door window. He knew the streets well and didn't need to read the snow-covered street signs or identify the buildings on each corner to know how far they still had to drive before he could join his wife.

Outwardly, he seemed calm, aside from his legs, which were shaking with nervous energy and eager to burst out of the car and run. *Damn it, move faster!* his thoughts raged as he clenched his teeth and hands. Every muscle felt taut, like a band stretched to its breaking point, ready to snap and strike pain. While Shelby faced unimaginable fear and grief, he was helpless. He wanted desperately to be there. For her, and for their child's bittersweet welcome into the world.

Ryan wanted to scream. Trapped in the back of the car, he wanted to *run*. To shout at every car, bus, taxi, *Get off the roads! Don't you know? Can't you understand? My family needs me and*

I'm stuck in this goddamned traffic! He dropped his head into his hands and sobbed. Feeling helpless and alone, he cried, knowing that he could be missing the moment when his wife and son needed him the most. Ryan was missing it all. *I should never have left her. She needed me and I left her alone.*

"Can't we go any faster?!" he shouted out to the driver, who was watching the road intensely and keeping a firm grip on the steering wheel. Seeing this, Ryan regained his composure, forcing himself not to give in to his emotions, "I'm sorry, Sam. It's not your fault, I know. But seriously, isn't there something you can do to speed this up? Turn on blinkers? I don't care if you run the lights to get there—it's an emergency!" If Ryan was going to be any help to Shelby, he had to resolve to remain calm.

"I'm doing the best I can, sir," said Sam Billings, a lifelong Chicagoan in his late fifties who had been working as Charlotte Chambers's driver for the past several years. "I want to get you there in one piece. We don't need two emergencies tonight." The car picked up speed, its wheels sliding around turns and windshield wipers brushing back and forth against the rough, icy windshield as it made its way through the congested city to Memorial Hospital.

Once Ryan finally arrived in the maternity ward on the fourth floor, he stopped only long enough to hastily inquire about Shelby.

"Your wife is in room one-oh-seven, Mr. Chambers," came the kind voice of a woman at the nurses' station. He barely had time to register her face before he rushed out in the direction of her pointing hand and shouted, "Thanks!" over his shoulder.

The maternity ward was pristinely quiet, except for the distant cry of a woman who he assumed was in the height of labor. The halls were brightly lit and smelled of cleanser and stale air, and something faintly medicinal. The pastel colors and cheerful signage and art on the walls gave the clear indication he was in the right place. His terror made for a stark contrast with his surroundings.

His feet slipped on the shiny white floors as he stopped suddenly at the closed door to room 107. He reached for the door handle, from which a DO NOT DISTURB sign hung, and hesitated for only a moment.

It was actually happening. This was his family's room. He closed his eyes, tried to settle the tormented thoughts in his head, breathed in deeply, and quietly unlatched the door with a *click*.

Her room was dark, except for the dim light that shone softly above her headboard. Ryan walked to the bed, where Shelby lay on her side beneath white cotton blankets. An IV drip slowly administered liquids through a tube that ran under the covers to Shelby's arm. He heard soft *beeps* sounding a slow beat from the vital sign monitor at her bedside.

Ryan walked as quietly as possible to the side of the bed, hoping not to wake her. The moment he saw her beautiful face, looking grief stricken even in sleep, he threw his hand over his mouth to keep his cries inside. He swallowed hard, wiped his eyes, and looked with utter amazement at his wife. Ryan knew she was strong—Shelby had shown that side of herself to him time and time again—and it was one of the things that first drew him to her. He hated himself for not being there in time. He wished so much that she could have leaned on him for strength during the most difficult time in her life. But he hadn't been there. He was late.

He dropped down to his knees and reached his hand out to touch hers. He found it clenched tightly around a corner of the blanket and tucked just under her chin. Her hand was warm to the touch and he was glad, in a way, to have a quiet moment with her to process everything that had happened so that he would have the perfect words to say once she awoke.

But the words didn't come. Only tears and an overwhelming ache that seemed to take over his entire body. It was as if part of his soul had left him and he ached for the emptiness it left behind. His heart was broken.

It was his trembling hand that woke her. Shelby's eyes opened slowly and fluttered as she tried to regain focus in the dimly lit room. "Ryan?"

"Hi, sweetheart," he said gently, now holding her hand in both of his and leaning forward to bow his head down beside hers. "I'm so—" he began to say, but the tears came openly now and he hated himself for not being stronger. He should be comforting her, and here he was, breaking down. "I'm so sorry, Shelby."

"You didn't know," she whispered, her voice breaking from emotion.

"And he didn't . . ." Ryan couldn't say it aloud. He was caught in a nightmare. Saying it out loud made it real.

She shook her head against her pillow and looked intently into his eyes. "I'm sorry," she said in a voice so meek he could barely hear her misplaced apology. "I should have . . ."

Ryan couldn't allow her to take any blame. He interrupted her with tender kisses on her trembling lips. Kisses that said he loved her. He was there for her. He was as devastated as she was. They would survive this. They *had* to survive, for the sake of their son, who would always be a part of their lives. They were a family.

There was a gentle rap on the door, followed by a click of the latch. A light in the entry area behind the room's privacy curtain turned on. The curtain was pulled back just enough for Ryan to see a nurse, dressed in pink scrubs and white shoes that looked as soft and padded as marshmallows. "Excuse me, Mr. Chambers. But we saw that you arrived and thought, if you and Mrs. Chambers are interested, now might be a good time to see your son."

Ryan looked into Shelby's glistening eyes. She wiped away her tears, tightened her lips together, and showed a brave face. She gave a nod.

"Yes, thank you," he told the nurse.

"I'm Megan," said the nurse. "I have been with your wife all night." It was obvious to Ryan that it had been a difficult night for Megan as well; he could see her eyes were puffy and her face looked drawn. He wondered how long she would stay, or if she was working well past the end of her shift.

Megan whispered something to another person who had been waiting behind the curtain. She gently pulled away the drape, like a curtain that revealed a star to an adoring crowd. Another woman, also dressed in nurse's scrubs, walked into their room with her head cast down. She looked young, barely out of school. She pushed a bassinet that contained a woven Moses basket, carefully lifted it up, and gave it to Ryan. Without saying a word, Ryan could see in her expression that she considered his child precious. When he looked down at his son's face, Ryan saw that he *was* precious.

But more than that, in that first moment, Ryan fell in love with his son's past, present, and future—for the baby's life was all of that in a single day.

Ryan heard Shelby's voice catch as she attempted to utter her thanks for the nurses' care. Then to Ryan, Shelby whispered, "I'm scared."

"I know. I am, too," Ryan reassured her. "But we'll be all right."

Ryan moved gingerly as he carried the basket that held his son's fragile body to Shelby's bedside. He hardly heard Megan's words as she described how the nurses had made a ceramic impression of her and Ryan's son's hands and feet, how the yellow receiving blanket had been crocheted by volunteers, how they had taken the liberty to dress Ryan and Shelby's son in a gown that had been gifted to the maternity ward.

As the nurse spoke, Ryan held Shelby's hand and looked down at his son's perfect face. His small, round nose. A dimpled chin. Wisps of dark hair. Curled lashes forming a soft crescent on his closed lids. And pouting lips, which were perfectly shaped, but instead of being warm and berry pink, his were cold and lavender in color.

Megan's voice came in and out of Ryan's awareness. He caught bits and pieces of what she was saying. He knew her instructions were important, but they slipped out of his comprehension like flour through a sieve. Only a few pieces of information remained.

"Be careful; his skin is tissue paper thin . . . grief counselor will stop by in the morning . . . resources . . . Shelby, you were incredibly brave . . . umbilical cord . . . unpreventable . . . arrangements later . . ." Megan then lifted the still baby wrapped in the crocheted blanket and held him out to Ryan. "Would you like to hold him?"

Ryan nodded. There were no words.

"Please take as long as you need," Megan said gently before passing the baby to Ryan and leaving the room to offer them privacy.

Ryan held his son in his arms and drew him tenderly to his chest. He then bent down and kissed his cool lips. In that smallest gesture, the briefest moment, Ryan's fear mercifully disappeared. Every heart-wrenching emotion was replaced with pride. Adoration. And an unconditional love that was so powerful it took his breath away.

When he looked up at Shelby, he saw nothing but absolute love in her eyes when she caressed the baby's cheek and whispered, "My beautiful, beautiful boy."

CHAPTER 20

SHADOWS

Shelby didn't remember falling asleep. She didn't remember waking, either. Minutes dragged into hours as she passed in between nightmares and reality, and she didn't know which was harder to bear.

The room was dark and eerily still. A light fixture near the doorway gave off just enough illumination so that she could make out the pastel patterns on the walls. They were meant to soothe new mothers and their babies but only made her feel that she didn't belong there. Her baby was gone and she could hardly call herself a mother. Shelby had never felt so disconnected to her surroundings.

She was desperate for home.

Aside from the silent heart monitor beside her, and the IV drip that was connected by a lead and needle inserted into the top of her left hand, there wasn't much else in the room. No baby monitors, lactation pamphlets, or bouquets of congratulatory flowers. Her son's weight, height, and name were not written boldly on the whiteboard near the closet. Instead, its blank white space caught the faint light in the room and glowed in the shadows. There wasn't a bassinet by her bedside. It was just her and her dear husband.

She knew he was exhausted from the emotional trauma of the day before. He was asleep on the couch with his arm tucked beneath his head and a white hospital blanket lay draped over the length of his body, which was too long to fit comfortably on the compact piece of furniture. Shelby noticed he was wearing the same clothes from the day before and that his feet, in black socks, peeked out beneath the end of the blanket. Ryan's jacket was still thrown carelessly over a chair, where he had discarded it the evening before, and his shoes had been cast off next to the couch.

Shelby heard Ryan's breathing falter, perhaps from a dream. She whispered his name, but he didn't wake. The pained expression on his sleeping face broke her heart.

Shelby checked the overhead clock on the wall across from where she lay. Four o'clock. The evening nurse had finished her shift a short while ago, after administering pain medication through Shelby's IV and setting a cotton ball that had been dabbed in a lavender-scented oil beside her pillow. She had closed her eyes and breathed in the calming fragrance, imagining herself far away from this place. The nurse had replaced Shelby's top blanket with a warm one, set her hand compassionately upon Shelby's shoulder, and assured her that she and Ryan would be left alone to rest for the next several hours.

"Before you go, would you mind turning off this machine?" Shelby had asked with a weak voice, nodding toward the wires that were taped to her chest and which tethered her to a heart and blood pressure monitor. "I'm having a hard time sleeping with it, and really—considering everything—do I even need it?"

Shelby was surprised that the nurse took pity on her and agreed to turn off the machine. "Just while you're sleeping.

We'll have to check your vitals again first thing in the morning," the on call nurse had said with understanding. "Now try to get some rest. I'll be sure no one else comes into your room tonight, unless you need us." The nurse offered a comforting smile and then left the room while closing the door quietly behind her.

As the medication made its way through her veins, Shelby felt its warming relief travel throughout her body. She gingerly pushed herself to a seated position, and even with the medication, she felt an electric bolt of pain shoot through her abdomen. She carefully pulled the blankets off and moved her legs over the edge of the bed. Biting her lip to bear the pain, she pushed off of the bed and felt a rip inside where a child had been growing and thriving just twenty-four hours ago.

One day. Her entire life had been altered in a single day.

The day before, when everyone thought she was sleeping, Shelby had overheard Dr. Logan speaking with Ryan in hushed tones behind the privacy curtain.

"I have spoken in great length with Dr. Allister, who delivered your son, and we've gone through the pathology results and post-delivery examination notes," she overheard him tell Ryan. "Your wife was already in labor by the time she arrived at the hospital. She may have been unaware of the early contractions, which isn't unusual for a first-time mother. After her rapid delivery, her uterus did not contract as it should have. We needed to do a procedure to stop the bleeding and now she is being given a medication that will continue to help speed the healing process."

"But she'll be all right, won't she?"

"I have to be honest with you, Mr. Chambers," Dr. Logan said carefully. "Your wife lost a significant amount of blood. Ordinarily, she'd be able to go home after a stillborn delivery.

But under the circumstances, we'd like to keep her under observation and examine her again in the morning. It will take some time for her body and uterus to heal."

"What does that mean, exactly?" Ryan asked in a hushed voice.

"It's too early to tell. We're hopeful that with some rest and care she will recover fully. However, there is a slight chance, should her internal injuries not heal properly, that it will be difficult—or, worst-case scenario, impossible—for her to carry another pregnancy at all."

Shelby couldn't understand Ryan's reply, as it was muffled, but just the tone of his voice filled her with despair. It didn't matter. Shelby didn't need to know his exact words, for the message was clear. Ryan was devastated. Her husband might never become a father, and for this only she was to blame.

She had spent so much of her pregnancy focused on her ability to be the kind of mother that her son deserved, that she had lost her focus on him. By worrying that she would be a parent like her own mother, she wound up being far worse. Just like her mother, Shelby had put her own needs before her family's. But Shelby's negligence far eclipsed that of her mother. Shelby's failure had resulted in her son's death, and for that she wouldn't expect Ryan to ever forgive her. Particularly when she knew she would never be able to forgive herself.

Standing beside her bed in a loose hospital gown and a flimsy robe, slightly hunched over from the pain, Shelby considered the narrow, clear tubing that tethered her to the intravenous drip. She gently removed the flesh-colored adhesive tape on the top of her left hand, exposing the blood-filled end of the IV tubing and the needle that was secured in her vein. At the prospect of what had to be done, she felt a wave of nausea roll through her stomach. Shelby knew what she wanted to do and knew she had to act quickly. Gritting her teeth and fighting back her tears, Shelby swiftly pulled the needle out of her vein and let it drop onto the bed. At the sight of blood rushing out of her hand, it only took her a moment of thought before she used her good hand to free the cotton tie from her robe and wrap it multiple times around her left hand to stop the bleeding.

Then, walking with great care with her hand pressed over her abdomen, she slowly made her way to the closet to retrieve the maternity dress she had been wearing when she arrived at the hospital with the taxi driver. She recalled how kind he had been to make sure she was safe with a nurse before he left, refusing payment for the ride. She grabbed a few more personal items and then entered the bathroom, closing the door quietly behind her. As soon as she turned on the light, she winced against the brightness. Once her eyes adjusted, she looked into the mirror and stared at the unrecognizable woman reflected back at her. Sallow skin surrounding tired eyes that were rimmed red from tears and shadowed with dark circles. *So that is what it looks like,* she thought bitterly to herself. *Failed motherhood.*

She turned away from the mirror and sucked in her breath at the pain caused by taking off her hospital gown and replacing it with her maternity dress.

A single day, her voice repeated in her mind as she splashed cold water on her face and smoothed out her hair before pulling it back in a binder she found in her purse. Her husband's heart broken. The light of a baby's life blown out in a breath. No one to fault but herself. *All in a single day.*

She set her purse on the bathroom sink and took out what she didn't need—her cell phone, a hairbrush, travel-sized hand lotion, and a pair of sunglasses. She replaced them with the personal care items for post-delivery that her nurses had left for her on a shelf in the bathroom.

Shelby turned the bathroom light off before opening the

door without a sound and then made her way painstakingly back to the closet, wincing from the pain. She pushed her bare feet into her winter boots and slipped on her coat. She noticed the shopping bag on the floor of the closet, which contained the gift she had purchased for Ryan. Regretting that Christmas wasn't going to be as she had imagined, she left the bag for Ryan to discover after she was gone.

Shelby returned to her bedside table, where she scribbled a note to Ryan on the back of a pamphlet on parental grief. When she was done she pocketed a small bottle of prescribed pain relievers. As she withdrew her hand from her coat pocket, her set of apartment keys caught on a button on her sleeve and fell to the ground with the tinny *clank* of metal on tile flooring.

She looked down to retrieve the keys but realized that they had slid somewhere in the darkness and, even if she saw them, it would have been too much effort and pain to bend down to pick them up. *I don't need them anyway,* she thought.

Before she left, Shelby took one last look at her beautiful husband. With tears in her eyes, and trembling lips, she mouthed, "I love you," before making her way through the darkened room, past the privacy curtain, and then to the door.

Just as she reached for the door handle, she remembered the hospital identification bracelet that was still on her wrist. She pushed up her coat sleeve and pulled the bracelet off with her teeth, letting it drop to the floor. At the same time, she heard the sound of Ryan's phone vibrating from its place in his coat pocket. She froze and listened. The phone buzzed a few more times and then nothing. When she didn't hear him stir or the sound of his footsteps, Shelby let out her breath. Grateful that Ryan continued to lie sleeping, she snuck out into the dim maternity ward hallway with one last thing on her mind. She was wrong in thinking that she didn't have a parenting role model—she had her grandmother. And right now, Shelby needed her desperately.

CHAPTER 21

SEVEN HOURS

When Shelby burst out of the hospital's front doors, the
bitterly cold wind felt like a deserved slap in the face.
But it didn't deter her. She felt like a maimed animal, in pain
and now set free, skittering into the darkness.

Beneath the circular glow of a streetlight, just beyond the
well-lit entrance, Shelby saw a white taxicab sitting idle with
its exhaust billowing into the winter air. She pressed her abdomen to stifle some of the pain she was feeling and made her
way across the fresh snow that was accumulating on the sidewalk in front of the hospital.

When she knocked her gloved hand on the taxi's passenger
door window, she startled the driver, who was clearly preoccu-
pied with checking his phone. The electric window rolled
down—along with a fluff of snow that had collected along the
base of the window. It opened just enough for Shelby to lean
toward the car and ask for a ride.

"Where you headed?" asked the driver, a heavyset man with
dark eyes, ruddy complexion, and a black knit cap pulled down
to his ears.

"Can we discuss it on the way? It's freezing out here and I'm in a hurry."

"Hop in."

The window rolled back up and Shelby opened the back passenger door and carefully eased herself into the backseat, gritting her teeth as a bolt of searing pain shot through her middle and ran up her back.

"Your timing was perfect," the driver said as he pulled away from the curb. "I just dropped off someone for their shift. The guy's car didn't start, so he needed a lift. If it hadn't been for that fare, you woulda had to call for a pickup. The hospital doesn't let us park here."

"My lucky day." Shelby closed her eyes and leaned her head back against the seat.

"So, what's the address?"

"Hmm?"

"The address. Where do you need to go?"

"Bayfield."

"Bayfield? Is that a street . . . an apartment building . . . ?"

She kept her eyes closed without answering. The pine tree–shaped air freshener hanging from the rearview mirror was ineffective in masking the scent of cheap coffee and stale cigarettes that permeated the cab.

"Never mind. I'll punch it in my GPS here, now that we're coming to a light." She felt the vehicle slow down to a stop, the motion of which made her body ache. She winced against the pain, knowing she deserved it. "You okay back there?"

She heard the wipers move back and forth across the windshield. They were too slow to syncopate with the rhythm of her racing heart. *Just go,* she thought. *Drive.*

"There's a Bayfield Court in Tinley Park," he said as Shelby felt the car accelerate again. "That's a little over an hour from here. Is that where you live?"

"I just need to make it to Bayfield," she said, hearing a slight slur in her voice. She felt light-headed, just for a moment. *The pain relievers must be hitting now.* She forced her eyes open. *Just stay awake long enough to get out of the city.*

"Can you just drive north?" she asked.

"North? But the GPS says Bayfield Court is south of here."

"Not Bayfield Court," she said, trying to sound confident but failing to carry it off. "We're driving to Bayfield the town."

"Bayfield?!" She saw his look of surprise reflected in the rearview mirror. "Jesus, lady—that's what? Five or six hours from here?"

The heater kicked in with a burst of warm air that streamed out of the vent and warmed the backseat. Shelby removed her gloves and laid them carefully across her lap. The bathrobe tie was still wrapped around her left hand. She was relieved to see that the bleeding had stopped and the blood hadn't soaked through the fabric. Reaching down, Shelby ran her fingers over the leather seat cushion before settling on a rough crack in the leather and feeling a tuft of foam just below the surface.

"I think it's more like seven," she said casually. It wasn't a perfect plan, but it was her only plan. Seven hours and she would be home, where she would have the privacy and support she needed to sort through the shattered pieces of her imperfect life.

"Seven!" The car suddenly veered off of the main road and pulled into a deserted gas station. The driver stopped the cab and turned around in his seat to face her. "Sorry, lady, but there's no way I'm driving all the way to Lake Superior tonight. Now, I'm happy to take you to the bus station, or even the airport to get you up to Duluth. But Bayfield? That's off the grid for me."

"I have money. I can pay you."

"It's crazy. It would cost a fortune—not to mention, I'd

have to spend the night there before driving all the way back to Chicago."

She took hold of her purse, set it on her lap, and began rummaging through it until she pulled a platinum credit card out of her wallet. It was a card she rarely ever used, with a limit that she knew far exceeded anything she would ever buy, but Ryan had insisted on her having it.

She handed it through the divider between the front and backseats until the driver took it from her fingers. He looked down at the card and then back to her.

"Chambers?"

She nodded, noticing his permit mounted on the partition between them:

EMANUEL ELVIN PRATT—CITY OF CHICAGO, ILLINOIS.

Shelby caught him staring at her, squinting in the faintly lit cab while trying to make out her face. "You're one of those newscasters, aren't you? Wait, no. That's not it," he said, slightly tilting his head to the side. "I got it. You married that Chambers guy?"

She looked the cabbie in the eye. "Believe me, Emanuel. Whatever it costs to get me there, I can afford to make it worth your time."

He studied her a moment longer. "Including lodging for the night?"

"Yes. Now, can we go? We'll make better time if we keep driving while it's still dark—before the morning traffic picks up." She was fighting off sleep now, waiting for him to agree to her plan so she could rest during the drive north. *Seven hours and I'll be home.*

The man settled back in his seat and shifted the car out of Park. "You can call me Manny," he said as the taxicab pulled out of the gas station and began its long drive north.

CHAPTER 22

EMPTY BEDS

Ryan woke with heavy eyes, a stiff back, and the returning awareness that he was in the hospital. He squinted against a narrow beam of light that filtered in from a broken bend in the closed venetian blinds. He turned away from the light and sat up, stretching out the ache in his back and being careful not to wake Shelby. In addition to having to face the deep sadness of what had happened, she would also be recovering from the physical pain and injury she had endured during childbirth. She had much more to overcome than he did.

Aside from the morning light breaking through the slits in the closed blinds, the room was dark and still. Ryan walked around the end of Shelby's bed, being careful not to wake her. He stopped to rub the sleep from his eyes and then looked at the pillows and rumpled blankets that lay atop his wife. As his eyes focused and adjusted to the dim light, he realized that the bedding was not covering her at all. The bed was empty.

He turned to the closed bathroom door. "Shelby? Everything okay?"

As Ryan walked toward the bathroom he stepped on something sharp. The pain of it caused him to jerk back his foot. He bent down to pick up Shelby's keys. Turning them over in his hand, he called out to her, "Shel?" He moved to the door and knocked, but still there was no reply. Ryan tried the handle and was a bit surprised when the door opened easily.

He rushed back to flip on the light switch beside her empty bed and, standing alone in the bright room, Ryan realized the open closet door revealed empty hangers. Her boots, purse, everything. Gone.

In a panic, he pulled the cord next to the light switch to alert the on-call nurses before rushing about the room to find something, anything, that would explain his wife's sudden disappearance.

He was about to put on his shoes, thinking he would probably find her walking the halls of the hospital, when he discovered a hastily scrawled note.

> *R—*
> *I didn't want to wake you. You looked so peaceful,*
> *and I don't even know how to face you right now. I*
> *know I'm being a coward. I've failed you both and to*
> *stay is more than I can bear. I know you'll make the*
> *best decisions for our son today. I trust you. And I'm so*
> *sorry. Maybe someday you will be able to forgive me. I*
> *will always love you both.*
> *—S*

"No!" Ryan shouted, throwing the keys across the room in a moment of panic. Fear. Disbelief.

"Mr. Chambers?"

He wasn't sure that he actually heard someone speak, as his thoughts were ablaze in disbelief, already trying to sort through his next steps. His wife? Their baby? What was he supposed to do?

"Is this a bad time?" the woman's voice asked again. He turned toward the room's entrance, where a gentle-faced nurse stood, holding a Moses basket in her arms. He could see that a blue blanket was carefully tucked around its precious contents.

"Mr. Chambers, I thought you and your wife would like to spend some quiet time with your son."

"She's gone!" *Hold it together,* Ryan demanded of himself as he rushed around the room gathering his things. He needed to find her. They would greet their child together as parents do. She couldn't have gone far.

"I know this is a difficult time, Mr. Chambers—"

"No—my wife—I think she left the hospital," he said quickly while slipping on his shoes. "Call Security!"

It took what little strength he had at that moment to pass the basket without touching his son and looking at his newborn face, but Ryan needed Shelby beside him. The life of one loved one had already been stolen from Ryan. He wasn't about to lose two.

Hours had passed and Ryan felt utterly helpless. There were apologies and talks of a security breach, surveillance tapes, and police bulletins. For reasons he couldn't fathom—and might never understand—his wife had left him alone in the hospital to face a mountain of emotions. The grief over the death of their child was unbearable. Compounding it with an overwhelming fear for Shelby's safety left Ryan emotionally drained.

He passed the time sitting alone in the corner of her hospital room, rocking in a chair meant for a nursing mother rather than a distraught father. His son was in Ryan's arms, still and swaddled in a blue blanket, held close to his heart. He looked in his son's perfect face and rocked, back and forth, oblivious of how much time was passing by. Ryan imagined that each click of the rocking chair was another day of life, a moment, a year—time that he and his son wouldn't have. He

didn't want to look away, for this would be their lifetime together. This was all they had.

People came in and out of the room. Ryan could hear rapid
padding of feet that rushed down the corridor, only to stop
while the person gained composure before entering Ryan's
room. The room that had a sign with a butterfly tied to the doorknob. The sign that let the staff know that a child had not sur-
vived. No flowers would be delivered. There was no need for a
lactation consultation. No warm baths with gentle bubbles and
nervous laughs of two parents who had no idea how they
would manage on their own, once they took their baby home.

Instead, each visitor entered quietly, respectfully. They spoke
with concern in their voices and compassion in their eyes.

"Grief will come in waves," said the woman in the navy-
blue dress with the sign of the cross on her lapel.

"We spotted her on our surveillance cameras. She appeared
distraught when she left the hospital at three o'clock this
morning," said a hospital official whose every word and action
was an effort to avoid liability.

"The nurses would like to create a plaster print of your
son's hands and feet. Something to take home," said the head
nurse with the teddy bear print smock.

Ryan's parents had come and gone, giving their deep con-
dolences and offering to speak with authorities to help find
Shelby.

Ryan had spoken with Ginny, who of course wanted desperately to travel to Chicago. Ryan explained that the police
were still looking for the taxicab that Shelby had left in, but
that it was an unmarked cab and its license plate numbers were
illegible due to the accumulated snow. Before they ended their
call, Ginny asked, "What have you named him?"

Ryan was ashamed to admit that he and Shelby had yet to
name their son.

"We haven't," he said quietly, looking out the frosted window, wondering where she could be. Hoping she was safe. "I guess I was waiting for them to find Shelby, so we could do it together."

"I remember talking to her on the phone, a few months ago. Anyway, she told me that you two had already settled on a name, dear," Ginny said. "She seemed delighted. I recall that she wanted it to be a surprise, but said it was the perfect name."

"It was," he remembered, looking at his son once more and smiling for the first time in what felt like an eternity.

"So, in a way, you did name him together. During a happier time."

He thought back to that day. It was in October—one of those days when the foliage transformed into a stunning display of color, the air was fresh and cool, and the sun seemed to warm you from the inside, like a steaming cup of honey-sweetened tea. They were walking across a footbridge that crossed the Chicago River when they paused to lean on the iron railing and look down at a few kayakers gliding across the calm water and passing beneath where they stood.

"I think I've come up with the perfect name for this baby," Shelby announced, looking up at Ryan with a smile that brightened her entire face.

"Is that so?" he asked, wrapping his arm around her shoulders and holding her close. "Tell me. What is this perfect name?"

"Try to guess."

"Norton."

"No."

"Newton. Norman. Nelson."

"Not even close." She laughed. "Come on. It's an obvious name."

"Not William, I hope," he groaned. "I don't think the world needs *another* William Chambers."

"Not William," she said, shaking her head. "Now think about it. If you could be named anything other than your given name, what would you want to be called?"

It only took a minute before he was nodding in agreement. "It's perfect."

"It is, isn't it?"

Early in their relationship, Ryan had told Shelby that at times, particularly when he traveled, he used an alias. There were many, but his favorite was one he came up with at a very young age. When he was a child, Ryan had been captivated by the story of a boy named Charlie Bucket who discovered a rare golden ticket tucked within a foil-wrapped Willy Wonka chocolate bar. Ryan wasn't as interested in the ending of the story, when Charlie's good behavior led to good fortune for his family—it was the beginning that intrigued him most. He had always thought it would be wonderful to be tucked away in a tiny room, covered protectively in warm blankets, surrounded by parents and grandparents who loved him unconditionally.

"Charlie," he said, liking the name immediately.

"Charles William Chambers," she said, hearing the sound of it bounce off the waves and follow the kayakers under the bridge.

"What about Charlie Meyers Chambers?"

By the end of Ryan's call with Ginny, she had reluctantly agreed to stay in Bayfield, as they both knew it was likely Shelby would try to reach her there. The distress in Ginny's voice broke his heart when she said good-bye. Ginny knew more than anyone how dire the situation was. Shelby's actions were so out of character. She had her faults, like anyone else, but one thing they knew and loved about Shelby was that she would never abandon her family.

★   ★   ★

Finally, after the papers were signed, the blessings were given, and all of the necessary arrangements were settled, it was Ryan's turn to say good-bye.

Evening had fallen and the hospital room was dark again when he carried Charlie to the bed where the basket had been placed. Ryan lowered his face to Charlie's. "I love you," he said aloud. This time, the tears came freely and fell upon his son's cool complexion. Ryan kissed him again—his cheeks, forehead, nose—trying to use every sense he had to capture Charlie's face to memory. Already terrified that he would forget.

He set his son tenderly into the basket and took great care in tucking the blanket around his body, so that Charlie would be snug and safe and out of harm's way. He ran his hands over the blanket, smoothing out each little crease. If this was the only thing he was to do for his son, he would do it perfectly.

"Good-bye, my sweet baby boy," Ryan finally said when the nurse returned to the room. "I will always love you."

Ryan carried the memory of his last kiss on his son's lips as he walked alone down the brightly lit corridor. He had declined an escort, as he could no longer bear the looks of the staff. Those who knew his story offered sympathetic smiles or cast down their eyes. He couldn't help but wonder if, in some way, they were secretly glad to see him leave. The maternity floor was a special wing of the hospital—a place where miracles happen daily and are the cause for celebration and where cries of pain usually end with tears of joy.

He was a few steps from the ward's exit when one of the double-wide doors was pushed open. A child, no more than four, raced toward Ryan and in his haste ran right into his legs. Ryan instinctively put out his hands to prevent the child from falling down. When the boy looked up, Ryan felt weak. The sparkle in his eyes, the blush in his full cheeks, the shine of the boy's hair. It intensified the reality of Ryan's loss. Standing in front of the child in the brightly lit hallway, his eyes brimming with tears, Ryan felt emotionally exposed.

He cleared his throat and quickly wiped his eyes with the back of his hand. "I'm sorry," he said as the boy stared up at him.

"It's okay," the boy said, shrugging his shoulders. "Don't cry."

"Simon!" a man's voice called out as the door opened again. "Simon, wait for me now."

Ryan heard a giggle and then the sound of small shoes scuttling away from him, continuing toward the maternity rooms.

Ryan shoved his hands into his coat pockets as the man approached. "Sorry about that," he offered, pausing briefly to greet Ryan but keeping his eye on the child. "He's a bit excited tonight. You know, new baby and all that."

"No, it's fine," Ryan said. "He's fine."

"Hard to imagine that little guy is now a big brother," the man said with a broad smile and a shake of his head. "To twin sisters no less!"

Ryan forced a smile. "Congratulations."

"Is your wife also . . ."

"We had a son," Ryan said without pause. *We had a son,* he repeated in his own head, enjoying the sound of it while also feeling the pain sweep over him again.

"Then congratulations to you, too. But watch out; they can grow up to be a handful," the proud father said with a laugh as he continued past Ryan.

Ryan turned to leave, but his steps fell short. Instead, he slumped into the wall to steady himself, not knowing if he had the strength to find his wife.

CHAPTER 23

BUMP IN THE ROAD

When Shelby's eyes fluttered open, she realized she was lying down in the backseat of a moving car, but in that initial moment she couldn't remember why. She could no longer see the bright flashes of highway lights and passing headlights reflected in the car windows. In fact, the only light in the car now was the faint green glow from the front dashboard. Wherever they were now, it was coal black and devoid of even a trace of moonlight.

The car hit a bump in the road, causing her head to bounce on the cracked leather seating. It was enough of a jolt to bring it all back to mind. The baby, Ryan, the hospital.

"Where are we?" she called out over the sound of the radio before closing her eyes again. It was easier to keep her eyes closed and her body curled up on the seat.

"What's that?" a man's voice replied from the front seat. Through the radio static, she could make out a Bee Gees song, though she couldn't remember the chorus.

What was his name again? Shelby wondered, but the answer didn't come.

"Where are we?" she repeated.

"You've been asleep for a while, lady. We're just outside of Fond du Lac."

When Shelby opened her eyes again, the road seemed rougher than it had earlier. As her mind cleared, she couldn't think of a place along the drive where he would have veered off of the highway and onto a rural road. Shelby lifted her head up to get a better view but fell back onto the seat. The pain was too great.

She felt the car pull quickly to the right, bump along some rough spots on the road, and then come to a stop. *Why are we stopping?*

"What are you doing?" she asked, but the driver didn't reply. Instead, she heard the sound of his door opening and felt a bitterly cold stream of air enter the car. She pulled her coat closer around her body and forced herself, once again, to sit up. A sharp pinch shot through her side, causing her to gasp and grab it. Her entire body ached, as if she had been bruised internally and externally. She fumbled in her coat pocket until she found the prescription bottle she was looking for. As she removed the safety cap and shook out one pill into the palm of her bandaged hand, she looked out of the steamed windows, trying to find the driver.

The cold air continued to filter in through his open door. Something wasn't right. *What is he doing?*

"Sir?" she called out, fainter this time, as she felt light-headed again. The pain intensified, Shelby placed the pill on her tongue and forced herself to swallow it down a dry throat. *Did he say his name is Danny?* If she hadn't been so exhausted, her protective instincts would have kicked in. She didn't know where she was, parked in the dark on the side of the road on a snowy winter night with a complete stranger. She blinked her eyes to stay awake, but it was too much.

★ ★ ★

The sound of the back door opening and the feel of the cold night air woke her again with a start. The driver, a big man with thick hands, was reaching for her body in the backseat. Panic set in like an alarm and without thinking she pulled her leg up and quickly gave a kick to his groin.

"Jesus Christ, lady, what the hell?" he shouted, falling to on his knee to the floor of the car.

"Don't you dare touch me," she hissed, ready to strike again with her other boot despite the pain it caused her.

He quickly raised his hands to calm her down. "Listen. No one wants to hurt you. You need help. I'm only here to help."

"Get me to Bayfield. Please. That's all the help I need."

"I just pulled over to take a leak. When I came back to the cab, you didn't look so good."

"Let's go." *Just get back behind the wheel and drive. We have to be getting closer.*

"You're very pale."

"I'm fine."

"Were you a patient at that hospital? Is that why you were in such a hurry to leave in the middle of the night?"

"Please." Then, remembering his name, she added, "Manny."

He placed his hands on the backseat, pushed himself up from the floor, and stood at the open passenger door.

He looked down at his hands and, this time, it was Manny's complexion that went pale. "My God. Ms. Chambers, you're bleeding!"

She struggled to keep her head up and her eyes open. *If only I could disappear.*

The last thing she remembered was the feeling of Manny's hands reaching for her, and him calling out her name.

Before everything went black.

CHAPTER 24

FOUND

O nce Ryan left the hospital after Shelby's disappearance, his parents joined him at his apartment to offer their support. They hadn't been there long before the police called.

"Mr. Chambers, this is Lieutenant Ochoa from the Fond du Lac police department. I'm pleased to tell you that we have located your wife," she informed him over the phone, using a voice that offered a reassuring balance of professionalism and empathy. "She was admitted to Regency Community Hospital here in Eau Claire."

"Fond du Lac? I don't understand. How on earth did she get all the way there?"

"An officer on the scene is gathering that information as we speak. What I can tell you now is that she was brought into the emergency room by a man named Emanuel Pratt. Do you know him?"

"Never heard of him," Ryan said, his mind immediately flashing to the worst-case scenario. "My God, she wasn't—"

"At this time, we don't believe she has been assaulted or harmed in any way," the lieutenant assured him. "It appears your wife hired Pratt as her driver and once they arrived in the area he realized she was in very poor condition. Physicians are examining her, but it appears she is suffering from complications that have resulted from her recent delivery."

"What is it, William?" his father asked. Ryan hadn't noticed that his parents were now standing at his side, watching his face intently and waiting for news.

He covered the mouthpiece on the phone and whispered, "She's back at the hospital."

"Well, let's go!" William Senior said with urgency, motioning to Charlotte to grab her purse and coat.

"Not here, Dad. She's in Fond du Lac."

Charlotte dropped her purse back on the kitchen counter and William Senior's expression went from concern to disbelief. Neither one of them said a word, but they didn't need to. Ryan knew. Something inside of his wife had snapped and it terrified him.

After Ryan ended the call with Lieutenant Ochoa, he set down his phone, placed both hands on the kitchen counter, and leaned in with his head down. *How did we get here? How on earth could this have happened?* He was trying to process it, to think through his next steps, when his father interrupted his thoughts.

"I know you're hurting right now, Ryan, and I don't mean to sound insensitive," his father said with some reluctance, "but we have to consider what the media is going to say about all of this. I mean, a young mother racing out of the hospital in the middle of the night? Abandoning you and leaving you—leaving you alone to grieve and take care of everything on your own after the death of your child?"

"I know, Dad."

"You know this will become fodder for the press," his father added.

"No one should have to go through this alone. It's terrible

enough that we lost little Charlie. But Eau Claire? Think of what people are going to say," Ryan's mother said tearfully, taking a tissue out of her purse to dry her eyes.

"We need a plan," William Sr. said.

"William, this isn't the time or place to talk about the public ramifications of Shelby's actions," his mother said, placing her hand on her husband's forearm. "We need to take care of family first."

"You're being naïve, Charlotte, if you don't think this is going to come out quickly. Ryan needs to go to Shelby, make sure she's well, and we need to come up with a logical explanation for all of this. Make a public statement before someone from the hospital, or that cabdriver, starts talking. We need to nip this in the bud."

"I don't really give a damn about what people say," Ryan said, raising his head and looking directly at his father. "Right now, all I can think of is Shelby. I need you to help me here so I can go take care of my wife." And with that, he left his parents alone in the kitchen while he quickly gathered a few belongings in an overnight bag and hurried out of the apartment.

CHAPTER 25

TRUTHS

When Shelby opened her eyes, she found herself back in the hospital, tethered once more to an IV drip and a beeping heart rate monitor. Once her eyes adjusted to the darkness in the room, she realized she was somewhere new. Gone were the floral prints, pastel colors, and gliding rocking chairs intended for nursing mothers in the Chicago hospital. Instead, this room was simple and uncluttered, devoid of anything maternal and warm.

At least that's what she thought, until she heard the sound of a body shifting in a chair. She turned to see the person sitting in the shadowed corner of the room and simply said, "It's you."

"Go ahead. Say it." Shelby believed that, this time, she deserved whatever harsh words her mother had to offer.

"What do you expect me to say?" Jackie Meyers replied flatly.

"I can imagine there are any number of accusations you can throw my way," Shelby said. "Why don't you just get it over with? Tell me again how much of a disappointment I am and then leave. You're so good at it, Mother."

Jackie said nothing. Instead, she stood up and pushed the chair across the floor until it was at Shelby's bedside. "How are you feeling?" Jackie asked, taking her seat again. "Are you in pain?"

"Where am I?"

"We're in Eau Claire. But the better question is, *why* are you here instead of Chicago, where you belong?"

"Is Gran here?" Shelby asked, sitting up abruptly and then buckling over in pain. She cried out and then said with urgency, "I need to see her."

"No. She thought it best that I come."

"Why?" Shelby asked, her eyebrows pinched together as she fought off the piercing pain in her abdomen. "I don't understand why you would come instead of her."

"I know you're in bad shape, Shelby, but Jesus. You don't have to be so rude."

Shelby shook her head and sighed.

"I was nearby," Jackie said. "Chad has a sister who lives in Sheboygan. We just happened to be there, visiting for a few days. Kind of a holiday thing. Mother called me because she knew I could get to you faster."

Chad. Wonderful, Shelby thought, not ready to give her mother credit for coming to her aid. She needed her grandmother desperately. She would know what to do. She would know how to fix everything that Shelby had ruined.

"So really, how are you?" Jackie asked again, softer this time.

Looking into her mother's eyes, Shelby wished now more than ever that she felt comfortable enough to hold her mother and cry—to share all of her fears, failures, and grief. Instead, she turned her head away and closed her eyes tightly, fighting away the tears.

When Shelby didn't answer, her mother asked, "Do you realize what has happened? Are you aware of your actions?"

"I'm tired," Shelby said with a weak voice. "I'd like to be alone, if you don't mind."

There was another pause as Jackie continued to stare at Shelby and Shelby avoided her gaze.

"Does Ryan know where you are?"

Shelby tried to roll onto her side, away from her mother, but pain ripped through her middle and forced her onto her back once again.

"We should call him," Jackie stated, appearing to be taking charge, which was a rare sight. "Where's your phone?"

Shelby laid her arm over her eyes. *What have I done?*

Jackie stood up from her chair and took it upon herself to go through the few belongings Shelby had hanging up in the hospital room closet until she returned to the bed with Shelby's phone in hand.

"You're nearly out of battery, but you have more than a dozen phone calls and even more texts. All from your husband," Jackie said. "We'll need to charge this and use another phone to call him."

Shelby nodded, feeling her chin tremble and that familiar dull ache in her jaw. She fought to hold back her tears. There were so many tears. Her mother must have noticed, because Shelby heard the sound of a phone being placed on a nearby table and then felt her mother's hand upon her shoulder. Although Jackie's touch was uncharacteristically gentle and her voice and words appeared sincere, Shelby was reluctant to open up to her own mother. While their relationship had improved greatly over the past two years, there was still too much pain below the surface.

"We don't have to call him just yet. The police contacted him shortly after you arrived. In fact, he was the one who called your grandmother. He knows you're safe," Jackie said. "You scared all of us, you know, Ryan most of all."

Shelby nodded. Nothing she could say could make up for her actions.

Jackie walked back around the bed and sat down in the chair. "Seeing you here in the hospital really takes me back. You know, to the time when you were born."

Shelby burrowed her head into her pillow and pulled the blanket over her shoulders, not interested in hearing once again how she was an unwanted baby. "I'm going to go back to sleep."

Jackie ignored Shelby and kept talking. "I don't think I ever told you about my pregnancy with you, did I?" Jackie paused before continuing, clearing her throat and adjusting in her chair.

"Too many times," said Shelby.

"Actually, no. I'm sure I haven't."

"It's okay, Mom. You can tell Gran that you've come to see me. You've been very helpful," Shelby said from behind the covers. "I'm just fine being on my own for a while."

"I know," Jackie replied. "In fact, I know exactly how you feel. When you were born, I thought my life had come to an end. My guess is that you're feeling that, too."

Shelby turned her head abruptly, wanting to sit up and face her mother but instead having to lie still and wince against the pain. "You do *not* know how I'm feeling. You couldn't possibly," she said, incensed at the comparison. "I am nothing like you."

"Which is harder to deal with—the grief? Or the guilt?"

Shelby stared straight ahead, the tears welling up, her bottom lip aching from holding back a cry. Yes, she felt guilt. Heavy, heartbreaking. And yes, like her mother said, Shelby thought her life had come to an end. There was no way to undo the damage she had done.

Jackie reached for Shelby's hand, and this time, whether

because she was broken and exhausted or because she needed her mother's comfort—even if it was insincere or fleeting—Shelby didn't pull away.

"I was much younger than you. A kid, really—only nineteen. But you knew that," Jackie started. "But, unlike you, I had no clear idea of my future. Hell, let's be honest, I'm still a fly-by-night woman. I've never really made a plan for my life, just kinda took it one day at a time, go with the flow, you know what I mean.

"It was fall and I was so happy to be back on campus. California was a dream compared to northern Wisconsin. At least that's what I thought back then. I had wanted to get as far away from my parents and the farm as I could. I know that you loved growing up there, but I saw our home as absolute isolation. Not an oasis, like you do. I felt trapped on the orchard and I never wanted to have to go back and work the family land. I was the type of teenager who lived for fashion, celebrity magazines, the latest movies, and Casey Kasem's *American Top Forty* on the radio every weekend. California was a dream. I thought it represented everything that was beautiful and glitzy—and it was the total opposite of my life in a small Wisconsin town."

Jackie dropped Shelby's hand and stood up once more. "It's too dark in here, don't you think?" She walked to the window and opened the blinds. The morning sun filtered into the room and Shelby had to squint her eyes at the bright assault.

"When I was in high school, I used to know a guy named Stewart; he went by Stuckey, although I'm not sure why," Jackie continued. "He ran with a group of guys, not the best kids in the area, and I suppose you could say he was their leader. They used to cut school, drink beer out in their cars after school; they were disrespectful to teachers in school—I'm sure you know the type."

Jackie walked across the room to pour a glass of water with

the pitcher that a nurse had left for them. "Water?" she offered Shelby.

She nodded and accepted the glass. Jackie helped to prop her up comfortably on the pillows while she continued to share her story. "You have to understand that this was a time in my life when I wasn't making the best decisions. The more your grandparents told me to stay away from Stuckey and his group, the more I was drawn to them. I was bored up on the farm, I felt isolated, and I was desperate for adventure. Excitement. I thought Stuckey was wild and bold and there was something intriguing about him. I was fascinated by him, and I was also completely naïve about how much trouble they were capable of getting into."

"This guy was your boyfriend at the time?"

"Of sorts. He went with a couple of girls during our senior year of high school. I was one of them. I didn't have the best judgment—or self-esteem. It wasn't the high school experience I had always thought I'd have."

"Why are you telling me all of this? What does that guy have to do with Chad?" Shelby asked as she set down her glass on the bedside stand.

"I'm getting to it," Jackie said. "Chad ran in Stuckey's crowd, too. But he was different. While the other guys were getting into trouble, Chad was always the one who held back. He tried to encourage the group to ease up and he always seemed uncomfortable, but those were the boys he had grown up with. They were his friends, or so he thought."

"Now I understand why Gran and Grandpa told me repeatedly how important it is to choose good friends. Sorry, but they used you as an example of what *not* to do," Shelby said.

"I know. I'm glad they did. I've regretted those choices all of my life," Jackie said. "You see, I developed a terrible reputation simply through my association with Stuckey. Even though I was a pretty good kid on the inside, I'm sure I looked like trouble on the outside. Rumors started, most of them lies. People thought I was promiscuous and I didn't fight it. By the time I turned eighteen, most people were ready to see me leave, including my own parents. I was too young to see myself differently."

"So you left."

"I did. By some miracle I managed to get into college in California, and I couldn't wait to go. I thought I'd be able to make a clean break. Start over again, you know? New people, clean slate. Once I graduated from college, I knew I wouldn't ever go back home."

"What happened with Chad?"

"I was home over summer break from college when I met up with Stuckey again. He never left Bayfield, and he never went to college. Stuckey ended up working for his father, doing odds and ends around town. Mostly construction work, handyman projects, that sort of thing. I was lonely. No one was calling the house; no one around town really wanted to see me. So when Stuckey asked me to join him and the guys as a party down at the beach, I agreed.

"I don't want to get into the details, but I will tell you that I drank too much and one thing led to another. Stuckey was getting too rough with me. I wanted to leave, but he wouldn't allow it. He took me to his car. It was one of the worst nights of my life."

"I'm so sorry," Shelby said, realizing that her conception was worse than she had ever imagined. No wonder her mother never wanted her to know about her father.

"Afterward, he bragged about it to his friends and I never met up with him again," Jackie said. "When I found out I was pregnant at nineteen, I let people think whatever they wanted. It was a different time back then, and Bayfield was and still is a small town where everyone seems to know everyone else's business. No one would have believed it if I told them I was raped."

"You didn't even tell Gran?"

Jackie shook her head.

Seeing the sadness in her mother's eyes, as difficult as it was to hear Jackie's story, Shelby was grateful to finally have a better understanding of her mother's actions. "So when I was born and you wanted to give me up—"

"At the time, I wasn't thinking about you," Jackie said. She smoothed out the blanket on Shelby's bed. "I was only thinking about myself. I didn't want to be connected to that time in my life. Fortunately, your grandparents had a better sense of things than I did."

"And that's when I came to live with them."

"Yes. I was running away from the constant ridicule and judgment I thought I would receive. So I stayed as far away as I could. I wanted a fresh start for myself and for you, and parents who would love you without judgment. When Mom and Dad insisted on taking you in, I agreed. I made that decision partially out of fear that I'd only mess things up more—but, to be honest, I hoped that one day you would become the source of pride for them that I never was. I held on to that hope for all of those years."

"I still don't understand, then, why Chad would come to our wedding and insist that he's my father. When, clearly, he isn't," Shelby said. "That part of the story still doesn't make sense."

"Chad always knew the truth of what happened between me and Stuckey. He was there that night, at the beach party. He knew what was happening, but he didn't do anything to help me. I found out later that he had carried that guilt with him all of his life." Jackie pointed to the four flower arrangements that were placed on a cabinet near the window. "Those are all from him, you know."

"Really?"

"He thought you must have gone through hell and back.

When you woke up this morning, he wanted to make sure you had something beautiful to look at."

Shelby felt her emotions welling up inside again, this time being triggered by a man she hardly knew and whom she had considered an absolute embarrassment. Until now. *I've been so wrong about so many things,* she thought with remorse.

"After his marriage fell apart a few years ago, he was unhappy where he was and felt he needed a fresh start. So he decided to move back home. That was the same month as your wedding. When he heard about the wedding through one of his mother's friends, he told me that he had a hunch that I would be there."

Jackie continued, saying Chad had never forgotten about her. He took a chance that he could find her and apologize, to free himself of that guilt. That opportunity came when he discovered her leaving the groom's dinner in downtown Bayfield on the night before the wedding. They ended up talking well into the night. Jackie fell apart when Chad told her that he knew who she really was and he hoped that girl would eventually find the courage to return home.

Wanting to protect Shelby from the truth, even though it was a reckless thing to do, he blurted out that he was her father. Jackie was shocked but didn't correct him. Jackie admitted that it was poor judgment on her part. Needless to say, soon afterward news of that announcement went out, and once it hit the media they agreed that more harm would be done if they retracted the statement.

"The truth is, as crazy as this seems, through all of this I've actually fallen in love with him," Jackie said.

"After everything our family has gone through, no. It doesn't sound crazy."

"He feels the same way about me."

Of all of the things that had been consuming Shelby's thoughts over the past year, the least of her worries had been her mother. And that coincided directly with the day that Chad Covington reentered her mother's life. If Shelby was being honest, she would have to admit that her mother seemed uncharacteristically grounded. Responsible, even.

"I came back to Bayfield reluctantly," Jackie admitted. "But now, I can honestly say that I feel good. Maybe more comfortable than ever."

"Because I'm gone," Shelby couldn't help but say.

"You're never gone, Shelby. Your presence is everywhere in that house, as it should be," her mother said. "I'm comfortable there because, for the first time in a very long time, it feels like home."

Shelby let that sink in for a moment, the idea of home. It was ironic that now her mother was the one who felt settled on the family property, while Shelby was the one who felt unsettled. And detached.

"So, let me ask you again, Shelby. How are you feeling?"

CHAPTER 26

OLD FRIEND

Ryan was there when Shelby was released from the hospital. He was unable to hold back his surprise when he found Jackie at his wife's bedside and then learned that Chad had freshened Shelby's room with yellow roses and had held vigil in the hospital's family waiting room until Jackie was ready to leave. A nurse told Ryan that Chad even requested that Shelby's bed linens be replaced regularly with fresh, warm blankets to help keep her feeling safe and secure.

Ryan and Shelby hadn't seen much of Jackie and Chad since the wedding, and even though he was emotionally and physically exhausted, Ryan could clearly see that his first impression of Chad didn't hold. The same was true for Jackie, who Ginny had said had taken on a great deal of responsibility on the farm. But until now, Ryan hadn't seen the transformation firsthand. If Shelby weren't in such a pained state, he knew she would notice it, too.

He thanked Jackie and Chad before they left, closed the door to Shelby's hospital room, and walked slowly to her bedside. He was grateful to find her asleep. It gave him time to take in the enormity of what they were facing together. He couldn't fathom how they would come out of this—not even a year into their marriage and already facing a hardship that could tear them apart.

Coming to Shelby's side in Wisconsin meant leaving his son. . . . *Oh, God,* Ryan thought, pushing his hands onto his eyes to fight off another wave of agonizing grief. *No no no.* His son's body would be safe until they could retrieve his cremated remains.

Ryan wiped away his tears and quietly pulled a chair up to the bed. He wanted to reach out and touch her, to kiss and comfort her. But instead, he studied the features of her face while she slept. She looked so peaceful. He couldn't imagine what images filled her dreams. Her skin was flushed and warm. Soft. Long lashes twitched slightly against her closed lids. He followed the curve of her cheekbone with his eyes and settled on her lips. Lips he had kissed so many times. Lips that had shaped her laughter, her wit, her visions for their future.

What would she possibly say now?

He was lost in thought, bent over in the chair with his elbows resting on his knees and his chin in his hands, when she spoke.

"Ryan," she whispered.

He opened his eyes and leaned toward her.

"I don't . . . I'm not sure what to say." She was struggling to express herself when her words were overwhelmed by shallow, quick breaths. "I'm so sorry." Her eyes were swollen and the soft skin beneath her lashes was a violet gray.

"Shh," he softly hushed, feeling his own eyes well up in tears again. He didn't know when the grief would end and he could think clearly again. Every word, every recollection of these past days, was a stab to the heart. The long drive north had been almost more than he could bear and he now felt the heavy weight of fatigue on his body. He took her hand in his and pulled his chair closer. "I know. We don't have to talk about it now."

"I do," she sobbed. "I have to tell you."

"Later."

"Did you see him?" she struggled to ask. "Did you see how beautiful he was?"

"He was perfect," Ryan said, bowing down his head and wiping tears with the back of his hand. "And I gave him the name we talked about."

"Charlie."

Ryan nodded and dropped his head upon her chest. She stroked his hair and kissed the top of his head. "I don't know why I left like that," she sobbed. "I'll never forgive myself."

"No. I'm the one who's sorry. I am so sorry you had to go through it alone."

In the privacy of her hospital room, they clung to each other and mourned together until they were too exhausted to keep their eyes open.

Once Shelby was released from the Wisconsin hospital, Ryan helped her to the car and together they completed the drive north that Shelby had begun in the Chicago cab. They were going home.

Unlike the day before, Shelby was now unusually quiet and withdrawn. During the drive, Ryan found himself being careful with his words, concerned for her fragile state and not wanting to trigger another wave of grief. She had been through too much already. As much as he wanted to help her through it, he felt inadequate. Outwardly he tried to be strong, while inside he knew he was failing her. The truth was, Ryan had no idea how to pull Shelby out of her despair.

"We're just about there," he said as they rounded County Road J and reached the juncture in the road that was marked with haphazard arrows nailed to a wooden post, each pointing the way to one of the many orchard and berry farms on the Bayfield bluffs that overlooked Lake Superior. Rather than going to the cottage he had purchased before their wedding, Ryan knew she would want to see her grandmother first. At the signpost, Ryan turned onto the gravel road and continued the final mile in their journey home.

"Ginny is going to be so happy to see you. She's been worried." He turned to offer Shelby a comforting smile, but she didn't look at him or reply. She continued to lean on the passenger door, with her eyes fixed on the barren trees that stood row upon row in the snow-covered orchards.

He slowed down the car as he approached the familiar sign to their property, a barn-red sign with white trim and wording. Ryan then proceeded down the driveway, hearing the icy shell of the packed snow crack beneath the weight of their car until he reached the farmhouse.

The car had barely stopped when Shelby's hand was already pulling on the door handle and she had stepped out, making her way to her childhood home. Ryan unbuckled his seat belt and looked up just in time to see Ginny race out of the house without having put a jacket or boots on and throw her arms around her granddaughter. They clung to each other for some time, out in the cold, oblivious to anyone else. He didn't need to hear what Ginny said to Shelby. Ginny's warm embrace of his wife and kissing away the tears conveyed more than words could say.

Shelby's instincts had been right. Ginny would give her the mothering she needed to guide her through the grief.

After Ginny waved to Ryan in the car and the two women retreated back into the warmth of the Meyers home, he took some time before gathering what little he and Shelby had brought with them—nothing more than his overnight bag, her purse, and a few items the hospital sent with Shelby to aid in her recovery. He stepped out of the car and stretched out his legs. The cold air felt good after their long car ride. He took his time outside, walking down the driveway a short ways, peering into the barn where they had celebrated their marriage. Ryan wanted to give Shelby time with her grandmother, but he also needed time to himself.

When he finally entered the home, the reception he received took him completely off guard.

"Oh, Ryan, dear." He couldn't help but notice that Ginny was the only one to greet him.

"It's good to see you," he said, and meant it.

"You must be exhausted. What can I get you? I have a fresh pot of coffee on in the kitchen. And I think there's still a fourth of a pie in the fridge—apple. Your favorite."

"Thanks. Maybe later," he replied, looking over her shoulder and into the dining room, where his wife was in the arms of another man. Ryan's back stiffened and Ginny pulled back. She followed his glare into the other room.

"Oh, um," she said, realizing at the same time Ryan did the awkwardness of the situation.

"Is that John?"

"Yes. He's been—well, he's been waiting here for Shelby to arrive. I mean, for the two of you to arrive, of course," Ginny said, unintentionally making an awkward situation worse. "They've known each other for a long time. You know how it is . . ." she said, her voice trailing off.

Ryan did know how it was. It was quite clear. Judging from the way John held Shelby, and the hushed voices in which they spoke, he was someone she could confide in. During the most difficult moment of her life—of her and Ryan's married life—she had risked her own health in order to rush to Bayfield to be with John.

While she physically had left Ryan that night at the Chicago hospital, the emotional abandonment was a much greater pain to bear.

★ ★ ★

Although Ryan was a part of the Meyers family, he felt like an outsider. The connection between his wife and John was indisputable. They had a history and a friendship that had lasted nearly a lifetime. Ryan was her husband, but in this moment, although he didn't understand it, she needed Ginny and John more than him.

Shelby and John were seated next to each other on the sofa in the living room when Ryan walked up behind them and set his hands gently upon her shoulders. "Shel, it's been a long day," he said. "We should get going—settle in at our place. We can come back first thing in the morning."

She first looked at John, which felt like an affront, before turning to address Ryan over her shoulder.

"Actually, I really would rather stay here."

He refused to believe she wanted to continue her conversations with John, rather than be alone with her own husband. Ryan looked at the way John was nodding in Shelby's direction, giving her a compassionate smile that Ryan saw as a betrayal. "We haven't been alone since—"

She shifted in her seat to face him but turned back immediately with a pained expression. She wrapped her arms around her middle.

"Are you all right?" John asked, instinctively placing his arm around her shoulders.

"Come on, John, seriously. I'd like a moment with my wife—alone."

John kept his eyes on Shelby before moving.

"It's okay, John. Thanks," Shelby assured him, pushing herself up from the couch and out of his embrace. She walked around the couch and took Ryan's hand, leading him to the front door. "I'm going to tell John to go. You know he's harmless. He's just trying to take care of us."

"Us? He isn't here to take care of *us.*"

"I can tell that you're getting upset, and I assure you, there's no reason for it."

"I don't want to talk about this now—not while the others can hear us. You have to know that after everything we've gone through—and everything we need to talk about, but you've said you're not ready—your old boyfriend is the least of my concerns."

"He was never my boyfriend."

Ryan wasn't going to push it. He recognized the look on John's face, the expression he had whenever Shelby was near, but this wasn't the time to let idle jealousy get in the way of something much bigger. She had left Ryan—and Charlie—without offering a reason why.

"I really want to sleep in my old bed tonight. I haven't really slept at all over these past few days. I need it," she said.

"And I want to be beside you," he said, glancing briefly over his shoulder, noticing that John was still within earshot. Ryan wouldn't allow himself to feel this resentment toward John. He wasn't worth it. Shelby set her hands on Ryan's chest and leaned toward him to lightly kiss his lips, but it held none of the warmth of her kisses as they stood on the sidewalk after a romantic lunch together—just before he took the car to visit his mother's apartment and Shelby walked off toward her favorite store. *How can this be happening?* he thought. Everything that he had been looking forward to and counting on had disappeared in an instant. He wouldn't let any of it stand in the way of his love for her—not John, the truth about Olen's accident, the media fallout, and especially not the distinct possibility that they may have lost their chance at parenthood. He would do everything he could to recover what they once had.

Taking care not to cause her any pain, Ryan tenderly put his arms around her, pulling her in close, and pressed his lips against her forehead. After his kiss, she dropped her head into his chest and sighed. "I need you, Shelby. I love you. And I can't do this alone."

"I know," she whispered. "We'll talk tomorrow. I promise."

A few weeks later, Shelby was still sleeping alone at the farmhouse. To help pass the time and occupy his mind with something other than his broken family, Ryan had picked up his camera and started taking long walks around the property. On this day, Ryan was sitting at the dining room table, editing photographs on his computer as snow fell lightly outside of the kitchen window. He couldn't help but lament how much could happen in such a short amount of time to two people who loved each other.

It didn't seem that long ago that he was in this same place, finishing the edits to his *Family Trees* series, a bachelor in seclusion, unsure if he was prepared to alter his life in order to be with the woman he had grown to love. While he had worked in the cottage she had been helping her grandparents in the orchard. It was just a few years ago. Even though he had been wrought with indecision and torn between his obligations and his heart, the decisions he faced then paled in comparison to what he and Shelby were dealing with now.

She should be with him—they both knew that—but Shelby said she wasn't ready, that she needed time. In his understanding of her needs, he neglected his own. As she dealt with her grief over Charlie's death, safe in her childhood home, Ryan felt isolated and removed. He buried his grief in the cottage, shoveling the snow off the drive, making minor repairs, washing the floors again and again. And when he wasn't moving, he was here, at his computer. Delving back into his photography that had given him so much pleasure in the past. It was a beautiful distraction. But now, looking at the images that lit up his screen, he knew he had been fooling himself. These were not the type of photographs that he was used to taking—the ones that nearly leapt off the paper and told stories in single shots—these were linear images of nature that were as cold as January and devoid of human interest. These were images of the solitude he felt. He had been fooling himself.

Ryan pushed his chair away from the table and stood up. He needed some air. He grabbed his coat and winter gear, shoved his feet into a rugged pair of Sorels that sat beside the door, and then ventured into the cold outdoors. After securing the door behind him, Ryan walked down the shoveled path that led to his car and then, in a spontaneous decision, decided to leave the path and trudge through the deep snow around the back of the house.

How could he expect Shelby to face her fears if he couldn't do the same? It was time that he reconciled his feelings about Olen's accident and was truthful with Shelby about it if they were going to share an honest life together.

He needed to touch the ice. Feel the frozen lake beneath his feet. Look out on to Lake Superior as if he could look into Olen's face and apologize.

But then, he stopped in his tracks. He couldn't do it. Physically, he was too afraid to take another step.

CHAPTER 27

TAKING THE FALL

Ryan was waiting for Jackie when she arrived at Spill the Beans coffee shop on Main Street. It was nine o'clock on a bitterly cold morning and there were only two other patrons sitting at the counter near the window, reading the paper. He knew they'd be able to speak in private.

Ever since he learned of Shelby's desperate trip from the Chicago hospital, he knew she would be a media target. Ryan's parents knew it, too, and had acted swiftly to diffuse the situation as best they could while he drove to Fond du Lac to be with her. He feared that any mention of her as an unfit mother or emotionally distraught and careless would make it virtually impossible for him to ever convince Shelby that living in Chicago was right for her. She had been so patient, so resilient. He feared a reputation like that would be too much for her to overcome.

Fortunately, there hadn't been much news coming out of Chicago about Shelby and the baby—and thus far, no one had enough facts to put the story together. The hospitals weren't releasing information, and neither was his family. He didn't know what had happened to the cabdriver who was kind enough to take Shelby to the nearest hospital, but Ryan had a hunch his father had something to do with it.

There was only one other person who would ever consider sharing their story with the media. She had done it before. And right now, he needed to speak with her.

Jackie made eye contact with Ryan as she stood in the entrance of the café, stomping the snow off of her boots and unzipping her parka. She nodded in the direction of the barista. Jackie proceeded to place her coffee order, grabbing a raspberry scone while she waited, and then walked across the shop to join Ryan.

"Hey," she said simply, placing her coffee mug and plate down on the table.

"Morning."

The legs of the chair she grabbed scraped loudly against the wood flooring. "You aren't hungry?" she asked as she sat down, noticing his coffee cup, which was lukewarm and nearly empty.

"I ate breakfast earlier," he said. "How's Shelby this morning?"

"Not sure. She was still in her room when I left."

Neither one of them needed to say anything more. He imagined Jackie felt as inept at pulling Shelby through her grief as he did.

He reached into the inside pocket of his winter coat and withdrew a rolled-up glossy magazine. Ryan then flattened it out and pushed it across the table to Jackie.

"What's this?" she asked while chewing a mouthful of her breakfast pastry.

He tapped on the masthead. *Signature.* A national weekly magazine that had been interested in covering his life with Shelby since the beginning of their relationship.

Jackie swallowed hard and wiped the crumbs from her mouth with the back of her manicured hand.

"I assume you were expecting this to come out?" he asked.

She looked up at him and opened her mouth to speak but then thought better of it. Instead, she picked up the magazine and flipped through it until she reached the article that Ryan wanted her to read.

BABY BLUES

*Tragic and bizarre end to
Shelby Chambers's pregnancy*

by Avery Martin, Senior Writer

What should have been a happy moment for newlyweds Shelby and William Chambers Jr.—the birth of their first child—turned tragic at Memorial Hospital in Chicago, Ill. Less than 48 hours after Shelby delivered a stillborn son, the events at the hospital turned bizarre with her disappearance in the middle of the night and a search that led police more than 150 miles north of Chicago to Fond du Lac, Wis.

While Memorial Hospital is not being accused of any wrongdoing as it relates to her disappearance, a spokesperson for the hospital said that they are carefully reviewing security procedures to ensure that this type of incident is not repeated in the future.

Chambers Jr. met Shelby (Meyers) Chambers in Bayfield, Wis., during a kayaking trip with friends. At the time, Shelby worked at Meyers Orchard, the apple farm that her family continues to own and manage. The couple were married in June of last year at a private ceremony on the Meyers property. Once they returned to Chambers's hometown of Chicago, they became the focus of public interest. However, Shelby Chambers showed an aversion toward the Chambers family's public lifestyle and media accounts claimed the bride was developing a reputation for being austere and icy.

"We are pleased to report that our daughter-in-law is safe and resting comfortably. She has been through a tremendously difficult time, both over the course of the past several months and, of course, with the devastation that occurred during her delivery," wrote Chambers Media CEO William Chambers Sr. and his wife, Charlotte, in a joint statement that was issued the day after Shelby's disappearance. "She has been unfairly portrayed in the media. This young woman has shown nothing but genuine affection for our son and this family, and has tried to embrace the Chicago community with the trusting and generous values that were instilled in her by her grandparents, Olen and Ginny Meyers. We can only hope that the town returns that warmth and welcomes her back to Chicago, whenever Shelby decides she is ready to return."

While there was some initial speculation that Shelby Chambers was dealing with emotional distress or that her marriage to Ryan Chambers was beginning to crack under pressure, those rumors were put to rest when her own mother, Jacqueline (Jackie) Meyers, contacted *Signature* magazine with an exclusive account.

"My daughter would never willingly abandon Ryan, no matter what the circumstances, and particularly not during a tragic time such as this. I take full responsibility for her disappearance. If anyone is to blame, it is me," Jackie Meyers says.

According to Jackie Meyers, she and her daughter had been estranged until recent years. "I wasn't there for her during childhood, so I decided that if she would have me, I was damn well ready to make amends and be there for her and my grandchild now." Meyers became increasingly protective over the unwanted attention her daughter received over the past year and knew that it was becoming a growing cause of stress during her pregnancy.

"As soon as I found out she had lost the baby, all I could think about was removing her from the spotlight and bringing her home to recover, where she belongs. I was the one who gave her the idea that she would be safer at home. I was the one who arranged for her transportation north. I was using poor judgment and taking advantage of my daughter's fragile state. I put her in danger, and I hurt both her and Ryan because of my selfish need to be the one to take care of her."

Earlier this year, Jackie Meyers made news after Chad Covington of Ashland, Wis. arrived unannounced at Ryan and Shelby's wedding, claiming to be her biological father. No one from either side of their families has spoken publicly about Covington's claim, which has not yet been confirmed or denied.

Charlotte and William Chambers Sr. have requested privacy for their son and daughter-in-law during this time of bereavement.

"You took the fall for her." Ryan looked at Jackie and saw her expression turn from concern to warmth as easily as a cloud breaks in the sky to reveal the sun.

"I didn't do anything that you or anyone else wouldn't have done."

"But it was you," he said, astounded by this woman whose transformation was as baffling as it was beautiful. "Why?"

"It's simple," she said. "I had to protect my daughter."

"But after all of these years. After everything you put her through. I don't understand—"

"That's just it. I've put her through too much. It's time that I stood up for her," Jackie said, taking hold of her coffee mug and turning it in her hand. "I'm not an idiot. I read magazines like *Signature;* I know how these stories come out. It would have been devastating to her. I mean, we can keep the news from her now, but she'd read it eventually. Or your future children would."

I can only hope we'll have more children, Ryan thought. Before releasing Shelby from the hospital, the doctors said that there was still a chance for a healthy pregnancy. As long as she took care of herself, rested, and recovered.

"But what gave you the idea to—"

"To lie?" Jackie said, finishing his sentence. "Because I knew it was so close to the truth—to what I used to be capable of doing in my past—that it would be believable. I would much rather have people continue to think of me as the bad mother than *ever* put that label on my child."

"I'm afraid that's what she thinks of herself."

Jackie took a sip of her coffee, considering what Ryan had said. "I think she misinterpreted fear. Fear of failure. Fear of history repeating itself. But in time, I believe she'll see herself in the same light that you do—that her entire family does. You just have to encourage her to open her eyes to see it for herself."

Jackie closed the magazine and pushed it back across the table to Ryan.

"And this?" he said, picking up the publication and rolling it back into a tight scroll.

"She doesn't need to know."

CHAPTER 28

COLD HANDS, WARM HEARTS

Just over a month had passed and Ryan felt as though he and Shelby had weathered the most difficult period of their grief. Now the waves of sorrow came less frequently and, when they did, he didn't feel as though he were drowning. He and Shelby were finding some normalcy in their days again. She was helping Ginny and Jackie with the house and farm, and she began journaling. Not just a few passages here and there, but writing regularly. Sometimes sitting in her room and writing for hours on end, lost in thought.

That's where Shelby was when Ryan, anxious for something to do, enticed Ginny to join him on a walk.

"I'm not sure what else I can do, Ginny," he told her as they strolled leisurely down a snow-packed path that ran between rows of dormant apple trees.

Ginny looked upward at the sun, which was struggling to come out from behind an endless parade of slow-moving gray clouds. "It's going to take time," she said. "You've been incredibly patient. Really. No couple should have to go through what you two are dealing with, and I love you for how supportive you've been to her. But you have to keep being patient."

"But what else can I do? How do we pull her back from this?"

"We can't," she said, stopping to turn toward him. "Look up at the sky. What do you see?"

"It's cloudy."

"And?"

"It's February in Wisconsin. It's cold and gray."

"Are the clouds going to stay here permanently?"

"No, of course not," he said. They continued down the path as Ginny continued to make her point—a bit drawn out for Ryan's patience. He was tired of waiting. He needed solutions.

"You were saying . . . ?" she nudged, wanting to make a point.

"The clouds will move on, eventually."

"Exactly."

"Ginny, you know I adore you, but what are you trying to tell me?"

"Clouds are only temporary. Some float by quietly; others billow up angrily and thunder and strike. No matter how they affect any given day, they are constantly moving and changing. The only thing that you can count on is the sun. It will be there until the end of time. We may not be able to see it, particularly during times like this when the sadness that you and Shelby are feeling is like a long period of dark skies, but the sun is just beyond those clouds."

He nodded, understanding what she was trying to say in her own unique way.

"The Shelby that you fell in love with—and the girl I raised—is still there. Her personality is going to shine again,

Ryan. You can count on it, just as you can count on the sun. You just have to remain patient."

"Let's hope you're right."

"Of course I'm right," she said with an air of seriousness, and then, with a laugh, added, "I'm *always* right."

It felt good to be outside. It's one of the things he appreciated most about his wife's hometown—even when the land was frozen and the lake entombed in ice, the air still had the same healing qualities and freshness of the warmest days of summer and the crispness of autumn. It cleared his head and made him feel alive.

After a while, it was Ginny who spoke again.

"And you? How are you doing today?"

It was an interesting way to phrase the question, he thought, for each day was unique. It was a process for him, missing someone he'd never met and giving up a lifetime of dreams he had unwittingly mapped out for his son. Ryan couldn't look her in the eye. "Alone."

"Yes," Ginny said, nodding. She knew. "I think it's time that she gets out of the house."

"I've tried. She won't go."

"Well, maybe this time you don't ask. You just do," she said. "And I know just where you should take her."

Ginny proceeded to tell Ryan about an annual event that would be held the following evening, which was Valentine's Day. The "Cold Hands, Warm Heart" event was held annually in the old recreation center down by the marina, where residents gathered to hear the local choir lead a love song singalong, which had always amused her husband, Olen. People of all ages carried lanterns, candles, and flashlights as they walked, skied, or snowshoed along a snow-cleared path on the ice just offshore. The one-mile ice path would be marked with frozen luminarias that glowed with candlelight.

"There's a group of men in town who make them every year, using five-gallon pickle buckets," Ginny explained. "They've been using the same old buckets for the past twenty years."

"Let me guess. Olen was one of the guys?"

"Damn right he was," she said with a laugh. "He lived for these types of things. Helped make the long winter a bit more interesting. That and sauna gatherings at the Browns' house, up on Fire Tower Hill. Those always ended with shots of Jameson, naked leaps into the snow, and something catching fire."

Just when you think you know someone, Ryan thought, smiling.

"Fire department had to come up to the house one year. My God, that was a year to remember."

"I'm afraid to ask, but what caught fire?"

She put her hand on his back and said, "You'd never believe me if I told you."

Ryan enjoyed her optimism as much as her storytelling. It felt good to laugh again, and he wished Shelby were there to enjoy it, too.

"After the walk, we gather at a community bonfire. There's a cauldron of hot chili, plenty of beverages, cocoa for the kids—and then they light off fireworks right off of the frozen lake. The display is nearly as big as the one on the Fourth of July," Ginny said, clearly proud of her community and its traditions. "Shelby had always loved attending it with her grandfather and me. I have a feeling that, if you bring her down tomorrow night, she'll come around. It's worked for us in the past."

Ryan and Shelby arrived at the Bayfield Lakeside Pavilion just in time for the ceremony to begin. He held Shelby's hand and led her to two open seats near the back, very close, he noticed, to a long table filled with home-baked cookies and dessert bars spread out on plastic trays, a pair of tall coffee dispensers, and a tower of Styrofoam cups. After two more families walked in with their children, a pair of volunteers shut the doors and dimmed the lights. He held Shelby's hand, hopeful that he would feel a reconnection.

The room quieted when a middle-aged man wearing a bright-red dress coat and pink bow tie stepped in front of the risers, which were positioned next to an upright piano at the front of the room. Ginny had mentioned that Hugh Greenberg served twice a year as the community choir leader and was also the purveyor of one of the town's bed-and-breakfasts—which explained the coupon for the "Cupid weekend special" at the Bow & Stern printed on the back of the program in Ryan's hand.

"Welcome, everyone. Here we are again, celebrating Valentine's with our neighbors and friends. A pretty good night, I'd say. If you'll remember, we had a dickens of a cold snap last year—what was the official temp that night, Olsen?" he asked a portly man in the front row.

"Nineteen below windchill!" the man shouted back for all to hear. A collective groan made its way through the room. When Ryan looked toward the sound of the voice, he noticed Ginny near the aisle with Jackie and Chad. They had arrived earlier to help position the luminarias on the lake.

"Well, we're blessed tonight with a downright *balmy* twenty-nine degrees!"

As the audience cheered, Ryan gave Shelby's hand a squeeze and detected a slight upturn at the side of her mouth. It was a start, he thought, as he noticed how beautiful she looked in something as simple as a heavy parka, jeans, and boots, her hair falling loosely around her shoulders.

The room was decorated with strands of overhead white holiday lights, Valentine hearts that spun slowly from the ends of fishing lines tied to the rafters, and a vase of red roses on the top of the choir's upright piano. The decorations had a quaint, childlike charm that was just right.

"And now, let's get things started with Elvis's 'Can't Help Falling in Love,' with a solo by Julia Baker. Roger Peters will accompany on the piano."

The space was infused with the warm scent of coffee, burning candles, and sugar cookies. Nearly a hundred people sat shoulder to shoulder in neat rows of folding chairs, some holding song lyrics photocopied on pink paper, singing along as the choir harmonized the Elvis love song. Looking around, Ryan doubted he had ever seen so many flannel shirts, knit hats, and Scandinavian sweaters in one place.

At the conclusion of the sixth song of the evening, a special trio was introduced. The pianist pushed away from the piano and went behind the risers to retrieve his accordion. Meanwhile, Boots, the grocer, left his spot in the bass section to join a third man who waited on one of two stools that were set before the microphone. As Boots made his way to the front, Ryan was surprised to see him carrying a set of bongo drums under one arm and a band saw in his other hand.

"And wasn't that a lovely rendition of 'What's Love Got to Do with It'?" Hugh said to the crowd, with merriment that was reminiscent of Lawrence Welk. "And now, a quick announcement. Sally O'Dell just informed me that she's ready to make her last trek of the night across the ice to Madeline Island. If anyone is hoping to catch a ride in her van, now's the time."

Ryan then watched with amusement as a thin, balding man with a down vest and red bowler hat made his way off the risers, gave a little wave, and scooted out the side door behind the piano.

"Looks like we lost one of our baritones to Sally," the director joked. "And now, with our trio ready for their instrumental solos on the accordion, bongo, and saw, it looks like everyone is in place to begin our final song of the night—Ray Charles's 'I Can't Stop Loving You.' " He gave three taps of his baton to the side of his music stand, waved his arms, and the choir began.

Just as the audience joined in to sing the chorus, Shelby's hand pulled away from Ryan's. She stood without a word and nudged her way down the row of seated people, and walked toward the back of the room. He was about to follow when everyone stood up, swaying arm in arm with neighbors while rounding out the song.

"Thank you, thank you, everyone," came the director's voice through the corner-mounted speakers. "Another wonderful night—and a beautiful job by our talented community choir." When the room burst into applause, the man who had been seated to Ryan's left extended his arm for a handshake. "Good to see you and your wife here. You two headed down to the ice?"

"We're planning on it," he replied, looking over the heads of others to keep his eye on Shelby. She wasn't by the coffee table. Or the refreshments. In no time, people were zipping up their coats, pulling hats low over their ears, and helping children with their mittens. He could see the volunteers near the door, already handing out candles and lanterns as people began a procession down to the ice.

"Sorry, excuse me," he said to the man beside him, pushing politely past. He rushed to the door, pulling on his hat and gloves, but a crowd had already formed and the doorway was blocked. He strained his neck, looking everywhere for Shelby as he moved with the crowd in a slow shuffle toward the door. He considered pushing his way back out of the throng and exiting at the door by the piano, in the front of the hall, but he realized it was blocked by choir members who were packing sound equipment and dismantling pieces of the choir risers.

Let's go! his voice shouted within his head. Although he

was in Shelby's hometown and he knew she would be safe, a part of him felt the same desperation from the moment in the hospital when he had discovered that she was missing. It had happened once. Could she possibly do it again?

When he finally made his way through the crowd and to the open doorway, a volunteer handed him a lantern with a lit candle within and directed him to follow the crowd down to the shore.

"Do you know Shelby Chambers?" he asked. When faced with the woman's puzzled face, he corrected, "I mean, Shelby Meyers?"

"Oh, Shelby—yes, of course. She must be down at the starting line by now," the woman said with a smile, pointing down the street toward the frozen lake. "After the ice walk, just leave the lantern at the warming tent at the end of the night, before you leave."

With the lantern in hand, Ryan wove quickly through people who were walking from the recreation center to the shoreline. He hurried past them, looking into their faces, searching for her in the moonlit evening.

When he arrived at the waterfront, he walked directly to the roaring bonfire and warming tent that had been set up for the chili cookout. He thought she might be waiting for him there. The fire illuminated the faces of men, women, and children as they strapped on their cross-country skis and mounted snowshoes on their boots. More skis were plunged into the deep snow around the fire, like a picket fence that had no rails. His eyes darted from person to person, searching in vain for his wife.

The appeal of the event was easy to see. There was the novelty of skiing at night, under star and moonlit skies, the way lit by iced luminarias that gleamed like jewels in the dark. Shortly after the skiers shushed off onto the illuminated path, the snowshoers were strapping on their equipment and the walkers were making their way to the shore. She was nowhere to be seen.

Then, just before he turned back to the pavilion, he caught sight of a flicker of light off in the distance—on the ice. It was moving away from town; its glimmer was fading.

He knew in an instant that it was Shelby.

CHAPTER 29

SNOW ANGEL

Shelby wasn't sure what compelled her to stand up and leave the concert, except for a longing to search for answers. She needed a sign, a signal, anything to grasp on to and pull herself out of this hole of sorrow in which she felt trapped.

Perhaps it was because her grandfather had often preferred Lake Superior over the church as his personal haven and sacred place—or perhaps she knew that, out here, she would finally be alone.

She could hear the faint sound of laughter bounce across the ice. Looking over her shoulder, she saw people and stars of amber lights collect along the shore. She knew that Ryan's light would be among them and hoped he would understand. While she knew she had been selfish with her time and wasn't giving him the love he deserved, she was so heavily burdened by the weight of her guilt and the feelings of failure that until she found the strength to pull herself out of it she knew she wouldn't be able to be the kind of life partner that he deserved.

The lantern she held in her hand cast an amber halo of

light as she walked into the darkness, but she didn't need it to find her way. Hundreds of visitors had trekked to the ice caves during the day, making it easy for her to follow their well-padded path in the snow. The full moon was partially veiled by feathered clouds, but when its light shone through it cast the frozen lake in a heavenly lavender blue. Although she was alone in the cold, she felt safe.

Walking across the ice was akin to walking on sacred ground. The lake's history and majesty was far greater than any challenge she could face in life, and here she prayed she would find the answers. Lake Superior had been called many things—Kitchi-gummi, Le Lac Supérieur—and been admired by generations. The lake had witnessed more loss of life and far greater heartache than anything Shelby would face.

She was far enough away from town now that the only sounds she could hear were the quiet crunch her boots made with each step across the snow and the moans as the ice shifted and settled beneath her. *Keep moving,* she imagined the lake would say. *Olen is here. Jeff, too. Even your son's spirit is here on the lake. You're home.*

"She is your lake," Shelby's grandfather had told her since childhood, especially during the times they sat together on the water's edge, keeping warm in the winter by sharing a thermos of hot cider. "You can count on her being cold. And beautiful. And great. But most of all, you can count on her to always be here for you." Shelby remembered the way he would lean in and kiss the tip of her chilled nose. "Just like your gran and me."

Only he hadn't been with Shelby for the past few years. *Maybe he's here tonight,* she hoped as she continued to forge into the dark.

Snowflakes began to fall soundlessly and broke into her thoughts. They started slow, settling on her nose and getting caught in her lashes and quickly melting away. She hadn't walked more than another hundred feet before the light snow transformed into flakes that resembled the downy fluff of white goose feathers. They cascaded lazily downward from the evening sky and settled on the ice like a blanket being laid across a bed. She found it comforting. If it continued into the night, she knew that two inches would quickly accumulate to eight or nine. After their walk along the ice luminarias and the chili potluck, Bayfield's residents would return home, being careful while driving on the slick roads. She watched as moonlight gleamed through the mainland trees and cast shadows onto the pristine snow gathering from its shore.

Shelby could see the ice caves in the near distance now, while she imagined young children slipping into warm baths and then footed pajamas, getting ready for bed. Women like her grandmother would be wearing thick bathrobes and cozy socks while reading books in their favorite chairs or leaning into their husband's embrace while watching the evening news. Young lovers would use slippery roads and poor driving conditions as the perfect excuse to stay a little longer and crawl into bed.

Rather than loud traffic, demanding schedules, intrusive news reporters, and insurmountable expectations, the simplicity of these imagined moments made Shelby happy. A collection of quiet, compassionate family moments was what made life meaningful.

After walking nearly two miles, Shelby finally reached the ice caves that had formed along the brownstone cliffs that rose up from the lake. The first few cave entrances were too narrow, so she continued down until she reached a cavernous opening. In the moonlight, the jagged rock wall appeared like a frozen face of Poseidon, water cascades suspended in a frozen state with icicles of varying lengths and thicknesses clinging to and hanging from the surface. The cave entrance was an open mouth on the icy, bearded face.

Shelby walked closer and felt the upper crust of the ice crumble under each weighted step, as if she were breaking through a burnt-sugar layer on a French custard. She paused, noticing how snow was accumulating beside the cave entrance, where the curvature in the rock caught the breeze, spun the snow upward, and then let it settle into a low, smooth drift. Without thinking, she stepped off of the trail and walked toward it. Then, Shelby turned her back to the pillow of snow, extended her arms to her sides, closed her eyes, and let herself fall back. The landing was soft and the snow puffed up into the air and fell back down around her head. In synchronicity, her arms and legs moved back and forth like wipers on a car, pushing the snow up around her. She looked up at the sky and let the snow fall onto her lips and eyelashes. A sudden gust blew across the sinewy treetops that stood along the cliff's summit. In the faint evening light, she watched as a plume of fine snow whirled into the air and then fell down around her.

Shelby took care when getting up, wanting to leave her impression in the snow. She looked down at the impression and, satisfied, walked toward the rocks and disappeared into the gaping, dark mouth of the cave.

The snow angel guarded the entrance until the snowfall filled in its angular skirt and rounded wings. Before long, it would be blanketed in snow, never to be seen again.

CHAPTER 30

TRUTH IS KEY

A s soon as he realized Shelby was out on the ice alone, Ryan's instincts kicked in and he took off running.

There wasn't time to tell Ginny or anyone else what was happening because Ryan feared that by the time he found anyone to help he would have lost sight of Shelby's light. He had been living with the belief that he had already caused one tragedy on the ice, and he would rather die himself than stand by while another person he loved fell victim to this lake.

When he reached the shoreline, the place where a crackling of fine ice skirted around exposed rocks in the shallows and broke easily underfoot, he felt a moment of panic. Out of breath, his heart racing, he bent over and put his hands on his knees. *Breathe!* He tried to steady his nerves, push images of breaking ice and waves of dark, icy water out of his head. He raised his head and looked out at the tiny light of her lantern, twinkling like a single star in the sky. Fading with each minute that he wasted in fear.

He stood up, felt inside his jacket to make sure the key he

always carried with him was secure in a deep pocket, took a deep breath, and saw the cloud of his exhalation dissipate into the night air. He charged forward.

When Olen and Ryan went out on the ice that day, a few winters ago, they did so in a caravan of snowmobiles with roughly twenty other anglers. The forecast had been for a cold but otherwise bright winter day. No one had expected that a storm would blow across the lake as fast as a freight train and turn a day of bonding into a day of devastation.

He remembered how Olen had chastised him for not having the proper gear and insisted that Ryan borrow his coveralls, thermal fishing gear, and wool hat and face mask. Thinking back on that day, Ryan could almost smell the stench of stale sweat and old fish oil that clung to the clothes.

Once they had finished loading the snowmobile with gear, they took off in a roaring caravan of anglers racing off down the tree-marked ice road. One by one, the other snowmobiles veered off to find their perfect fishing holes until only Olen and Ryan continued racing across the hazy morning ice.

That morning Ginny had warned them of the possibility of a storm, but Olen had been certain that the weather would hold long enough for a full day on the lake. To this day, Ryan still couldn't believe how quickly the conditions had changed from tranquil, gray, overcast skies to a torrent of snow with barely a warning.

Their fishing spot had been windblown and devoid of snow. Although it was immensely thick, the ice had also been extraordinarily clear, a phenomenon unique to Lake Superior. Ryan recalled how the sun shone down through the ice and illuminated the seventy-five-foot depths of frigid water that moved below them.

The men caught some lake trout and a few herring that day. Not great, but a strong enough showing for Ginny and Shelby, who waited for them back at the farmhouse, and certainly enough for a shore dinner. "You earned your supper, rookie," Olen had said to Ryan, along with a hefty whack on his back.

Everything about that day had changed in an instant. The skies turned sinister and a storm crossed over the expanse of Lake Superior's frozen surface so quickly that once the two men noticed it they barely had enough time to pack up their equipment back on the sled before they were engulfed in a torrent of snow and wind. And then, to make a bad situation worse, the ice started to break apart. The waves were building quickly and surely, creating powerful movement beneath the ice. Section by section, the underwater force was shattering the serene, glass-like surface that Ryan had admired all morning.

When Ryan had told the story about his final moment with Olen on the ice, he held back key details. He let the Meyers family believe that, just when Olen was about to start the snowmobile engine—which would have given him and Ryan enough time to race ahead of the storm before the ice broke around them and make it safely back to shore—Olen had noticed some gear lying on the ice some fifteen feet away. Then, Ryan said, Olen left him by the snowmobile while he went to retrieve it. Before Olen had time to return, they were separated by a break in the ice. The men tried to reconnect, but the conditions on the lake deteriorated too quickly for that to happen.

Now, as Ryan trudged across the ice in search of Shelby, the truth of what had happened that day was forefront in his mind.

After the other snowmobilers took off to find their own

respective fishing areas spots, Olen had chosen to go out a little bit farther toward Basswood Island. When he finally turned off of the ice road, Ryan assumed they had reached the spot where Olen intended to fish, but instead Olen asked him if he'd ever driven a snowmobile.

Olen had put the vehicle in Park and left the ignition running before calling out to Ryan over his shoulder, "You've never driven one of these sleds! You want to give it a shot?"

"That's all right, Olen, maybe another time," Ryan had said. "I don't know enough about this lake—where the ice is thick enough to ride."

"Hogwash," Olen had replied, moving off of the snowmobile to allow Ryan to move up to the front and take hold of the handlebars. "Now's as good of a time as any! This ice is as solid as asphalt on a city highway. Come on, what do you have to lose?"

"If you're sure—"

"Key's in the ignition, throttle and hand brakes, just like a motorcycle—it will come to you easily," Olen had said as the men switched places.

Ryan had gone a bit heavy with the throttle at first, causing the sled to jerk at the start. But it did come easily to him and Olen motioned with his hand for Ryan to go off of the designated road and onto the untouched snow.

"How does it feel?" Olen had shouted from behind.

"Amazing!"

Once they reached their destination, Ryan had slowed the vehicle to a stop and set the brakes. He had helped Olen unload their gear and was about to walk it over to the spot where they would set up for the day when Olen said, "Don't forget the ignition key. I'm putting you in charge of getting us home in time for dinner tonight."

"Got it." Ryan went back to the sled and removed the key. He held it briefly in his hand, finding it amusing that Olen had attached the key to a neon-orange rabbit's foot key chain, before slipping it into the pocket of his coveralls.

Hours later, when the storm hit and they were racing to pack up the snowmobile, Olen didn't make that last-minute decision to retrieve forgotten gear that had been left on the ice, as Ryan had claimed.

Once everything was secure, the two men actually climbed aboard the snowmobile with Olen in the driver's position. The wind howled and whipped snow around their bodies as if the weather were toying with them—challenging them to get off of the ice in time—pushing their bodies like a shove from the bully on a playground. *Go!* the wind demanded. *Get off the lake!*

Olen's gloved hand had fumbled around the ignition, looking in vain for the key. Then, at the same moment, the men remembered that Ryan had been the last to drive. Olen shouted over his shoulder, "Hand me the key!" just as Ryan was reaching for his pocket.

It had felt flat to the touch.

It must have dropped in deeper, he remembered thinking. Then he had gotten off of the sled again, removing his glove and shoving his hand all the way down into the pocket until he reached the seam. It was empty.

Ryan had removed his other glove, holding the pair clenched between his knees, while he frantically checked the other side pocket and then both chest pockets. Nothing.

"Ryan, the key!" Olen had cried.

Ryan returned empty handed. He looked at Olen, wide-eyed and furious with himself. "It's gone."

"What?!" Olen had jumped off of the snowmobile and

begun feeling his own clothes, checking for the noticeable bulge of the key. "Think!" he demanded. "Where could it be?"

Ryan's eyes had gone to the ice, its glassy surface now swirling with windswept snow that was already beginning to form drifts around their feet.

Olen's eyes followed. "Shit! You don't think it dropped out of your pocket, do you?!"

Ryan had been too furious with himself to look Olen in the eye. He knew he had to find the key. An orange rabbit's foot in the snow. He had begun kicking up the snow around him and feeling with his boots for the key. But every time he pushed away the snow, the wind just quickly covered the spot again, leaving him unsure of where he had searched.

"You check here—I'm going back to our ice hole. Maybe it fell out of your pocket while we were fishing," Olen had said without panic and without blame. He had been level-headed and determined as he trudged across the ice alone in search of the key.

A short while into their futile search, their time ran out. A series of loud cracks shot into the air like rifle fire and then they watched helplessly as the lake surface split open. Icy waves splashed over a rapidly expanding area of frozen shards and fractures.

It had all happened so quickly. As the storm's rage intensified and visibility lessened, the two men found themselves stranded and separated on ice fragments that were no bigger than eight feet across—frozen life rafts on an unforgiving lake.

In the end, while fear and remorse coursed through Ryan's body, he had listened to Olen's final words. "Watch over my family," Olen had said loudly over the sound of the wind, but without a hint of anger or fear.

It was in that moment that Ryan realized, perhaps too late, that he had fallen in love with Shelby. No matter what happened on the lake that day, he was compelled to proclaim his feelings to Olen and, more important, to himself.

"I'm in love with Shelby!" he had yelled across to the older man who was barely visible as he lay limp and cold on the broken ice. "I love her!"

Ryan was unsure if he heard Olen reply, as the sound was weak and overpowered by the wind. He lifted his head, hoping to hear it again. "Make her happy," came Olen's frail but assured voice. Ryan vowed to himself that, if given the chance, he would try. He would give his heart to the incredible woman who was waiting for him onshore, the woman whose love and infectious joy made his life richer than he had ever imagined it could be.

Just as Ryan set his head back down on the ice, fatigue taking over his body, he saw it. He had blinked a few times, trying to clear the hoary frost that had formed on his brows and eyelashes. Then his eyes focused on a shallow crevice in the ice that was just within reach of his outstretched hand.

Inside of it, caught on a slight ridge of white snow, was the orange rabbit's foot.

Shelby had never known the full extent of what happened on the ice that day, just as she never knew Ryan had removed the key from the rabbit's foot and kept it hidden in the deepest corner of his pocket whenever he ventured out on the water. He carried the key with him during their time sailing out of the Chicago marina on Lake Michigan. He had it the day he proposed, while boating on a windless day, and during the video shoots and film debuts for Olen's memorial fund. He had it with him even now, on the evening he had hoped would end with a walk with Shelby along a path of luminarias that glowed along the shore.

His heart raced as he continued walking across the frozen surface of the lake as snow fell around them and isolation set in. He kept his eyes fixed on the glimmer of light that came from Shelby's lantern, shining like a beacon in the snowfall. It reminded him of the lights of the rescue vehicles he had set his eyes on, back on the ice, telling Olen that soon they would be rescued.

This time, Ryan wouldn't fail.

CHAPTER 31

CHANDELIERS

Shelby brushed the snow off of her parka as she entered the dark cave. She held out her lantern as she walked, marveling at the way the light illuminated the glassy stalactites of ice that hung from the ceiling like chandeliers. Then, slowly turning in a circle, she watched the spectacle of light and shadow dance across the frozen walls. Looking up, she knew the highest peaks in the cave ceiling reached upward of thirty or forty feet, although it was too dark to see. The ceiling was covered with shimmering icicles, the magnitude of which took her breath away. Smaller archways and caverns in the rock were laced with ice particles that resembled a galaxy of frosted stars, seemed to soften the rock, and added to the enchanted quality of the space.

Coming here at night was reckless, Shelby knew, but she had been drawn to it. It didn't make sense logically; it was simply a yearning to be in a sacred place on the lake where she could try to sort through everything that had happened and try desperately to find a way out of her despair.

She sat down on the ice with her body facing the cave entrance. Her grandfather would have likened it to a cathedral on the lake. Although he never would have allowed her to come out alone and in the dark, he would have agreed that it felt like a spiritual journey. For the first time in a great while, Shelby felt at peace as she sat beneath the ice crystals and chandeliers, watching the snow fall against the ice-blue backdrop of Lake Superior.

"Shelby?"

The figure of a man appeared at the cave's entrance. She recognized his voice immediately and wasn't entirely surprised.

"Are you in here?" he asked again when she didn't answer.

"Yes. Here."

Ryan's face was illuminated by the lantern he carried and, as he approached, his features—and concern—became clearer. "Shelby, are you all right?" he asked, rushing to her side.

"You didn't have to come."

"I don't understand—what are you doing here?" He raised his light to look around the cave, shaking his head in disbelief. He was visibly shaken, almost staggering around the cave to take in the scene, before turning his light toward her.

"I'm sorry."

"You should be sorry—coming out here in the dark? On your own? Do you even realize how crazy this is?" he said loudly, visibly shaken. He was pacing now, stopping to look at her, shaking his head. "Just think if something had happened to you!" He stopped moving and raised his free hand to rub the back of his neck. His posture slumped, and when he spoke again his voice was distinctly quieter. "What were you thinking?"

It broke her heart to know that she had been the cause of such sadness.

"Please tell me why you would put your life at risk just to break away from me, because—because I just don't know what more I can do to keep you. . . ." Ryan's voice trailed off, and then his head dropped and he slowly lowered himself to sit on the ice.

Part of her wanted to run out of the entrance to the cave, past the massive icicles that clung to the brownstone arches. Keep on running out onto the ice. Run until she couldn't go any farther. *Just. Run.*

"I don't know what else to do, Shel. Tell me what you want me to do." His voice broke with emotion. He wasn't accusing or making demands. He looked as broken as she felt.

Shelby fixed her eyes on the lake. The snow had stopped falling outside of the cave's opening, and judging from the way the lake's surface had changed from indigo to lavender, she guessed that the moon had reappeared from behind the clouds. She couldn't imagine a place more private than this. If she was ever going to confide in her husband, now was the time. *Everything is my fault. My college boyfriend, Jeff—sailing off on Lake Superior right after we had had argued. My grandfather—taking Ryan out on the ice as a favor to me. And now our sweet baby boy, who never had a chance at life. I bring nothing good to the men I love. I'm the only one to blame. Ryan deserves better.*

"Ryan, I—" she began, looking up at him.

"It's all my fault." His admission took her off guard.

"No, it wasn't at all," she said, thinking he was referring to Charlie. "I was the one who wasn't paying attention to the baby's movements. You had no way to know—neither of us could. The doctors said it was an accident. You got there as fast as you could; you—"

"Shel, I'm talking about Olen." Ryan moved closer and sat down on an exposed rock beside her.

"I thought this was about the baby," she said, turning to face Ryan. *He can't possibly know that I'm feeling connected to Grandpa tonight, too.* "What do you mean?"

He removed one glove and unzipped his parka, hesitating

for a moment before reaching inside. When he withdrew his hand, Shelby saw that he was holding on to a key.

"This was your grandfather's." He held it out for her. She removed her glove long enough to hold the key, turn it in her hand, and return it to him.

"What is it for?"

Ryan returned it safely into his jacket. Then, sheltered from the rest of the world in a frozen hideaway, he told her everything.

CHAPTER 32

MOTHER MOON

Shelby had once heard that the true test of a relationship is seeing how two people can navigate through the storms that rise up over the course of their lives. She and Ryan had been through physical storms on Lake Superior, familial storms that ripped apart relationships and took time and patience to rebuild, and, of course, the emotional storm of losing a child. Ultimately, they found a way to survive.

"We're going to get hurt; we'll feel lost from time to time," Ryan told her during that night they shared in the ice caves. "But through it all, you have to promise me that you'll come to me first. I will always be here for you."

"And I'll do the same for you, no matter what happens."

He had opened his arms to her, and she welcomed his embrace, for there wasn't another place she'd rather be.

"So, where do we go from here?"

"Home?"

"Chicago or Bayfield?"

"Maybe a better balance of the two."

"I couldn't agree more."

Even when she stumbled Ryan had been there for her. Strong and faithful, often more sure of their marriage than she had been, Ryan was her anchor in the sand. He kept her from getting lost in the storm. True to the promise he had made to her grandfather on the ice, Ryan kept her safe and secure.

Life in Chicago fell into a more livable rhythm than the highs and lows they experienced during their first year of marriage. Shortly after learning the truth about Chad Covington, Ryan communicated the story with Chambers Media's publicity director, and it took less than a week to douse the media flames that surrounded Ryan and Shelby. She never knew how much she would appreciate being old news and how, when the cameras were finally turned onto someone else it would allow her to actually fall in love with Ryan's hometown and to slowly begin to feel it was her home, too.

On this weekend, they returned to Bayfield for their second anniversary and were staying in their cottage. The guilt and fear they both felt that night in the ice cave had since melted away with the ice and snow, but the memory of what they had shared would always remain.

"What do you say, Beautiful?" Ryan asked from behind, wrapping his arms around her waist and nuzzling her neck in a way that sent delicious chills down her spine.

"But we need to get going, or we'll be late. . . ." Shelby closed her eyes and raised her hand to lay her palm on his cheek.

"I'm not sure what *you're* thinking of, but I was talking about heading down to the park," he said with a playful kiss her behind her ear.

Blushing, she recovered. "Of course. I knew that."

"Mmm," he murmured, lowering his hands down her body and stirring her desire.

"You're teasing me again."

"I wouldn't dare."

She tipped her head back and turned in his arms until she found his lips; then she kissed him fully on the mouth. *Who cares if we're late?* she thought. *No one will notice. They'll start without us.*

"We need to go," Ryan said again.

"I know," she whispered, pressing her body against his. Her hands found their way beneath his shirt and she kissed him again.

"Your family," he reminded Shelby, kissing her back.

He was right. Shelby was sure her grandmother had worked hard all day. And Nic was planning to meet them there with Hank, as well as Shelby's mother, Chad, and others. Even John would be joining them with his new fiancée—it had taken a lot to convince Shelby's husband that she and John were never more than friends, but finally Ryan had accepted it as the truth.

Shelby reluctantly pulled away from Ryan, smiling and placing her hands out to create space between them. "You're absolutely right. We need to go. This—sadly—will have to wait."

"That's fine with me." Ryan seemed to regain his composure much faster than Shelby had. "I was just testing you."

"What?"

"Just checking to make sure your pregnancy hasn't affected your libido."

"And you expect me to believe that."

"Come on, Shel. Like you said, we're going to be late if we don't head out right now. People are expecting us."

When Ginny had offered to host a small anniversary celebration for family and friends, it was Ryan who suggested that they take it down to Memorial Park, near the marina where he and Shelby had shared their first date. It was a lazy summer evening complete with picnic blankets, beer, sandwiches, and Ginny's pies to share. Shelby and Ryan could have afforded to travel for their anniversary or host a lavish affair, but the truth was that Shelby couldn't imagine anywhere she'd rather be. And, much to her delight, neither could Ryan.

After the meal, everyone sprawled out on the lawn to pass around pieces of Ginny's pies and to enjoy the last of the day's sunlight. Ryan was lying on his side next to Shelby, with his head propped up on his elbow.

"Great day?"

"The best."

"I have one more thing to show you," he said with a boyish grin.

"What is it?"

He scrambled to his feet and extended his hand to help Shelby up from the lawn. "Follow me," he said simply.

Ryan continued to hold her hand as he led her toward the shoreline, close to the spot where they had skipped rocks and talked well into the evening, just getting to know each other. Before they reached the water, Ryan stopped at a park bench that had wood slats and scrolled iron armrests.

"Let's sit down for a minute, Shel."

She looked up at him with puzzled brows but followed his lead and sat on the bench.

"What do you think?"

"About what?" she said with a slight laugh, unsure of what he had planned.

Instead of elaborating, Ryan gave the bench seat a few taps with his open hands.

"What—this bench?" She touched the wooden seat, new and varnished a lovely cherry color, and then ran her hands along the armrests. Taking a closer look at the well-crafted armrests, Shelby realized that the swirling design depicted tree branches that twisted and braided together until they circled around a single apple in the arm support. "Ryan, did you do this?"

He stood up from the bench and offered both of his hands, leading her to the back of the bench. There, written on a small bronze plate, were the words:

In this place, hold tight to those you love, and remember those who will never be forgotten.

When she turned to Ryan, she was speechless. Emotion had taken hold of her voice and all she could do was kiss him with trembling lips. "Thank you" simply wasn't enough to show appreciation for someone who demonstrated, time and time again, that he knew her so intimately well.

They sat down again, his arm wrapped securely around her shoulders, and she leaned into him. A breeze blew in off of the water and lifted the stray hair off of her face. The ferry was making its way to the marina, where she could see a line of cars waiting for their turn to cross Chequamegon Bay to Madeline Island. Farther out on the lake, they watched as a cluster of half a dozen sailboats caught the last of the day's winds before twilight set in. Their sails were full and bright against the steelblue Lake Superior waters. She heard the call of a gull in the distance and children laughing as they raced through the grass behind her and Ryan.

She was home.

"Should we head back to the group?" Ryan asked after they had spent some time enjoying the quiet.

"You go back," she said as they rose from the bench. "I feel like walking down to the water for a minute. I won't be long."

"Do you want company?"

"I love you, but no. Please. You go ahead."

He placed his hands on either side of her face and tenderly kissed her on the forehead. "Don't be long."

Once he walked away, Shelby stepped out of her sandals and made her way down to the rocky shoreline. She carefully climbed over the boulders and round stones until she reached the water's edge. Timid, lazy waves rolled in over the smaller stones in the shallows. She heard the stones rattle as they tumbled in the cool water. Just as she reached her foot out and stepped in, Shelby felt something move deep within her body. With one foot in the lake and the other on the rocks, she paused to lay her hand protectively over her abdomen. The feeling inside was slight—no more than a butterfly flutter or the gentle pop of champagne bubbles.

Her baby's first kick.

Shelby looked out upon the lake and smiled. In her imagination, she pictured a girl. She had full cheeks and wide, brown eyes and walked in a wobbly cadence on two beautifully rounded toddler's legs. The child would peek out from behind a tree in the orchard and then try to grab the fruit that hung heavily off of low-lying branches, just out of her reach. Shelby pictured herself running up behind her daughter and snatching her up in her arms. She would swing her around in a slow circle, the orchard a whirling blur around them, and Shelby would breathe in her daughter's heavenly scent.

Standing at the lake's edge, Shelby reached down and picked up a smooth rock, flat and thin and perfect for skipping. She drew back her arm and then cast the rock across the water with a snap of her wrist. It bounced six times before sinking into the water.

"That one's for you, Charlie," she said aloud to the lake, hoping her son could hear her voice.

She was looking down at her submerged feet, hoping to find another good rock, when another vision came to mind. This time, it was a memory of an old woman named Bernice whom Shelby had met in a quiet bar in Tamarack while on assignment with Ryan. She spotted another rock, this one a bit thicker and darker than the first. She rubbed her thumb over its smooth edge and recalled how Bernice had brought up the subject of babies.

"Bernice, I don't have a baby at home," Shelby had said at the time, back before she was aware she had been pregnant.

"Just because he isn't in your arms doesn't mean he isn't here."

Shelby recalled how the quirky woman had gone on to share a poem by Louisa May Alcott. " 'As the tranquil evening moon looks / On that restless sea, / So a mother's gentle face, / Little child, is watching thee,' " Bernice had recited.

"That's lovely, but I'm not sure what that has to do with—"

"Those words were written over a century ago, and yet, on this day, they are perfect for you."

"I don't understand."

"You are drawn to the lake like a child to her mother. Your Mother Moon is always there for you. She shines down upon you on Lake Superior's waters. She takes care of those you love, while you live your life grieving. While you live your life afraid."

Shelby had been taken aback by the woman's assertion. "I'm not afraid."

"She will be there when your first child is born," Bernie continued. "When you need her, she'll be waiting for you at the lake. When you need answers, go to her."

Shelby threw the second stone into the water, but it caught a wave and fell into the water quickly with a *plunk*. She turned away from the water and watched as Ryan helped Chad load up an orange cooler. Ryan looked up just then and offered her a smile and a wave. Everything was going to be all right. *We're going to make it,* she told herself, and she believed it.

Shelby resumed her search for the perfect rock. As she took a step deeper into the water, she felt something wide and smooth underfoot. This time, instead of a skipper, it was a piece of lavender sea glass partially hidden in the sand. Blue and green sea glass was common, and brown even more so. Lavender was a rare find, and to discover it was a joy. She picked it up and turned it back and forth in her hands, feeling how smooth its frosted surface had become after spending years in Lake Superior, tumbling in the sand. Lifting it up to the sunlight, she marveled at its color. It was perfect. In fact, she was certain it was the loveliest piece of sea glass she had ever seen. For that reason, she wanted to give it back to the people whom she had loved and lost and whose memories she associated with this Great Lake.

Shelby kissed the glass lightly before flinging it out onto the water, watching as it skipped several times before disappearing back into the lake. She watched as delicate ripples circled away from the splash and caught sparkles of sunlight as they traveled back to her.

Then, feeling her baby's butterfly flutter a second time, Shelby knew. Instinctively, she just knew. A girl.

Their daughter would never take the place of Charlie, but she would benefit from the lesson he had taught Shelby during his brief existence. Being Charlie's mother showed Shelby just what a gift it is to love a child, in life and in spirit. Shelby was confident that she would love her second child unconditionally. She would take her here, to the lake, and sit on the park bench on a snowy morning with warm mittens and a thermos of cocoa. She would teach her daughter about the history of Lake Superior and offer assurance that it would always be there for her—just as Shelby's grandfather had promised her when she was young.

On the day of their baby's birth, she and Ryan would hold their baby close to their hearts. Together, they would name her Lily, kiss her sweet lips, and welcome her into to the world.

ACKNOWLEDGMENTS

Writing my second novel on the heels of the first would not have been possible without the incredible support of family, friends, and colleagues.

There simply aren't enough words to express my love and gratitude to my husband, David. Thank you for reading, listening, advising, and holding down the fort on those days when I couldn't break away from my writing. And most importantly, thank you for believing in me. It's time to celebrate!

Big hugs to our children, Logan, Ethan, and Kate, who are sources of endless joy in my life. I couldn't be more proud of you, particularly as you branch out and explore your unique interests and talents. Love you to the moon and back!

Thank you to my parents, Lars and Mary Carlson, whose love and simple words "I'm proud of you" fill me with as much confidence now as it did when I was a child. Also, an additional thanks to my mom, who set aside time to preview this novel while writing her own nonfiction book on the history of Bayfield, Wisconsin. I'm proud of you, too!

Heartfelt thanks to my talented literary agent, Joëlle Delbourgo, for your advice, encouragement, and belief in me—even when I decided late in the writing process that Shelby and Ryan's story needed to go in an entirely different direction. Cheers!

A million thanks to Martin Biro, who I knew from day one would be the perfect editor for me. Your patience, enthusiasm, and guidance were tremendously helpful as I wrote my second novel.

Thank you to Karen Auerbach, Vida Engstrand, Paula Reedy, Lauren Jernigan, Kristine Mills, and the rest of the talented team at Kensington Publishing for everything you have done behind the scenes to help launch my first two novels.

To Egmont LYX in Germany for your enthusiasm to take this small-town story to an international audience, *danke schön.*

Sincere thanks to my extended family; my wonderful circle of friends; to authors Laura Sobiech, Lindsey Palmer, and Kristina Riggle for your kind words of support in advance of my first two novels; Amy Kelly, M.D., for reviewing the hospital scenes for accuracy—and for so much more; and Anne Greenwood Brown, Beth Djalali, Heather Anastasiu, Jacqueline West, Li Boyd, Lauren Peck, and David Nunez, for your feedback at the start of this novel.

And finally, thanks to *you,* the reader. I hope that you enjoyed reading the continuation of Ryan and Shelby's story as much as I enjoyed imagining it.

Best wishes,

Kerstin

BRANCHING OUT

Kerstin March

About This Guide

The suggested questions are included
to enhance your group's reading
of Kerstin March's
Branching Out and *Family Trees.*

DISCUSSION QUESTIONS

1. In *Family Trees* and *Branching Out,* Shelby Meyers experienced how it felt to live in a bubble. First, she grew up in a small Midwestern town, where it often felt that everyone in the community knew her family's business. Then, in *Branching Out,* she married into a notable family who captured the public's attention. What are the similarities and differences of both situations? Which lifestyle was she better suited to handle? What about Ryan? Or Jackie? How did they fail or succeed at living in these environments?

2. One of the themes the author explores is people embracing their place within a family tree while also finding the courage to branch out on their own. We often hear it described in comments such as, "The apple doesn't fall far from the tree." Considering your own family, do you believe we grow up to become like our parents, even if our life choices are greatly different from theirs? If you have children or grandchildren, can you see characteristics of yourself in them? Do you hope they'll carry on your physical or personality traits? How do our parents and family history shape us?

3. Which is a stronger influence in our lives: the environment in which we are raised, or the people who raise us? What is the significance of the titles *Family Trees* and *Branching Out* in terms of discovering who we are?

4. After the loss of Shelby's grandfather, Olen Meyers, and later their stillborn child, Shelby and Ryan respond and cope in different ways. Do you feel that the experiences drew the couple closer together or pulled them apart? How do you think those experiences will

impact their roles as mother and father to their second child? Has the loss of a loved one in your life ever had a profound impact on your relationship with someone in your family—either strengthening that relationship or causing a rift between you?

5. How does Shelby's unexpected pregnancy early on in their marriage affect her relationship with Ryan? When you realized that Shelby was feeling detached from her pregnancy, did you find her less sympathetic? Was her detachment realistic and understandable, or was she succumbing to fear? Do you think, as a society, we expect mothers to instinctively have nurturing qualities? Do we have the same expectations for fathers?

6. One of the central themes in this novel is motherhood—as seen in Shelby's relationship with Ginny and Jackie and then in her own responsibilities of mothering her unborn child. During her first pregnancy, she was fearful of hurting her son emotionally—as Jackie had hurt Shelby. Why do you think she was more concerned about the effect Jackie had had on her life than Ginny and Olen's love and support? If you were Shelby, would you have forgiven Jackie and tried to repair the mother-daughter relationship? Do you think Jackie always loved Shelby?

7. When Shelby left the Chicago hospital in the middle of the night, she was desperate to return to her hometown to be with her grandmother. When Shelby was admitted to a second hospital during her journey home, were you surprised that it was Jackie—not Ginny—who came to her aid? Was Jackie the best person to take care of Shelby at that time? Why or why not?

8. While Shelby traveled to small Wisconsin towns on a film assignment with Ryan, she met an intriguing older woman named Bernice. What was the significance of this scene? At the end of the novel, when Shelby stood on the lakeshore and thought back to Bernice, do you believe she felt a sense of comfort from their brief encounter? Was Bernice a sort of soothsayer, or was Shelby simply reading too much into their conversation? Was Bernice even real?

9. Ryan and Shelby both had to grapple with forgiving the ones they loved. Do you think Shelby should have forgiven Jackie? How about Ginny? Should Ryan have forgiven Shelby for abandoning him and their stillborn child at the hospital? How about Ryan: Should he have been forgiven for not doing more to help Shelby during her transition into life in the spotlight, particularly during an emotionally difficult pregnancy? Or for his actions on the lake with Olen? What about Shelby's feeling of responsibility and guilt over her unborn child's death? Is forgiveness an act of love? Can we ever really forgive—and forget? Or is it healthier to forgive and remember? Are there some things that can never be forgiven?

10. There are many references to home in both novels. When you think of home, what comes to mind? A place of residence from your past, or where you live today? A city or community? A place in nature where you feel most at peace, similar to how Shelby and her grandfather felt about Lake Superior? Or can home be anywhere, as long as you are with people you care about?